Terror On

BLACK OAK RIDGE

*A novel from the top-secret days of the
Manhattan Project*

Daniel S. Zulli

W A J
BOOK PRESS

WAJ-BOOK PRESS

Terror on Black Oak Ridge: A novel from the top-secret days of the Manhattan Project

Daniel S. Zulli

Cover design by JD Smith Design

If you would like to reproduce any part of this book, please seek permission first by contacting us at

editor@wajbookpress.com

Published in the U.S.A by WAJ-Book Press, San Antonio, Texas.

Paperback Version: ISBN 978-0-9904990-7-7

Kindle Version: ISBN 978-0-9904990-6-0

Library of Congress Control Number: 2018958383

For information about special discounts for bulk purchases, or speaking opportunities, please contact us at

editor@wajbookpress.com.

The views expressed in this book are solely those of the author.

All photographs by Ed Westcott (courtesy of his family and public domain), except Norris Dam (courtesy of the Tennessee Valley Authority); map of Oak Ridge (public domain, Wikipedia article: Clinton Engineering Works); and Harry Truman (courtesy of the Harry S. Truman Library).

Dedication

This book is humbly dedicated to Mr. Ed Westcott, the hard-working and intrepid photographer of the Clinton Engineering Works Project in Oak Ridge. Not only are his outstanding pictures fascinating in and of themselves, but without them we wouldn't have any record of Oak Ridge, the most incredible and singular military/scientific/social project in the history of the United States. An Oak Ridge can never happen again, and Mr. Westcott's pictures captured for future generations the story of this only-once work. For an Oak Ridge native, his pictures are invaluable and have helped me find my place in history. For a writer, they have provided the visual clues necessary to weave a tale based on fact. Historians and fans of Oak Ridge are forever in Ed Westcott's debt.

And if that weren't enough, Ed worked with my father at the Atomic Energy Commission and was my sponsor at my confirmation when I attended St. Mary's Catholic School in Oak Ridge. How I wish I could have talked to Ed when I lived there and heard his stories of being the only person allowed to chronicle this top-secret city, the City Behind a Fence!

.
.
.
.
.
.
.
.

Daniel S. Zulli

Acknowledgements

First and foremost to God, who allowed me to be born in the coolest place in America. Six weeks earlier, I would have been born in Salina, Kansas, as Dad was still in the Air Force at Smoky Hill Air Force Base. God also let me attend Dallas Theological Seminary, in Dallas, Texas, which has given me a proper biblical understanding of His moving throughout the ages past as well as the future. Lastly, God has given me the love of reading and writing as well as this crazy thought for a book in my head.

Second, I have to give a shout out to not only my two main editors (D'Ann and Monica) but also to the others along the way (like my friends at Gemini Ink) who looked my work over and gave me tremendous hints, tips, advice and critiques that have forced me to find the better choice of words or to leave otherwise great scenes on the cutting room floor because they didn't help the story.

Third, to the men and women who came to Oak Ridge to be a part of this incredible work called the Clinton Engineering Project. They left their homes to come to a place that didn't exist and endured mud, dirt, shortages of every kind and worked in top-secret conditions to heroically do the job they were called to do. They raised families, lived and thrived and gave me a complete city in which to spend my first 11 years. The pioneer spirit was definitely evident in them. To the founders of Oak Ridge, I say, Thank You.

Lastly, to not only the founder of the Internet, but to all who uploaded the countless articles and material (like the hit songs of 1944), which made my research such a snap right right at my fingertips. In conjunction with this, I'd like to thank Steves Jobs and Wozniak, my heroes who invented the wonderful computer that I first got while in seminary and the machines that revolutionized everything I've written since then. For those who have never used a manual typewriter, you'll never truly appreciate what a life-saver and joy wrap-around texts, cut-and-paste, right justified margins, italics, different fonts, and backspace/delete are. From my first Mac Plus with MacWrite to my current MacBook Pro with Pages, the pleasure has been all mine. How did anyone ever write anything prior to the Internet and without a computer and word-processor? I have no clue and can't remember anyway. But it's great now. Thanks, Steves.

Daniel S. Zulli

Introduction

In October 1942, the area called Black Oak Ridge, Tennessee, was a conglomeration of four rural farming communities. By the end of World War II, in the summer of 1945, it was a full-fledged industrial/military/civilian town of 75,000 people. The K-25 uranium-separating plant was the largest building in the world.

Yet - it didn't officially exist!

Oak Ridge - and the Manhattan Project - was so top-secret that when Harry Truman was vice president of the United States, even he didn't know of its existence. He didn't learn of it until April 1945, when he became president.

Beating Adolph Hitler in producing an atomic weapon was the number one priority of World War II. President Franklin Roosevelt commissioned General Leslie Groves to lead that which became known as the Manhattan Project. Oak Ridge was one of three sites chosen. Its job was to enrich the uranium-235 that would fuel the bomb. It was called the Clinton Engineering Works in order to say "officially" that something was going on there.

But no one in Oak Ridge even knew what they were working on, only some unnamed "gadget."

Germany surrendered in May 1945, not having successfully producing an atomic bomb. But Japan refused to surrender, forcing the U.S. to take extreme measures to avoid an all-out invasion of the Land of the Rising Sun. Thus, we used the "gadget" on Japan, bringing her to the battleship Missouri to surrender and ending the war.

Oak Ridge moved from military to civilian control. The Manhattan Project became the Atomic Energy Commission, and Oak Ridge became an official town in Tennessee in 1959.

My father worked at AEC, having left the Air Force in March to come to Oak Ridge, where I was born in June. I spent my first 11 years there and in the surrounding towns of Norris, Oliver Springs and Coalfield. I was born in the hospital built for the health care of the CEW workers. I swam in the same swimming pool the workers and families did. I watched movies in the same theater and shopped at the same stores they did. When I lived there during the height of the Cold

Daniel S. Zulli

War, Oak Ridge was Russia's first strike on America, as it was the hub of America's nuclear capabilities.

Sadly, the legacy of Oak Ridge and its place in history is, in my opinion, being lost. While Los Alamos (where the bomb was actually built) is much more recognizable to many people, Oak Ridge is not. When most people think of the atomic bomb, they think of Los Alamos, New Mexico. In fact, the recent television show, Manhattan (2014-2016), was set there. Outside of historians and war buffs, few people know the role Oak Ridge played in ending World War II.

I proudly call Oak Ridge, Tennessee, the most fascinating and singularly incredible military/scientific/social project ever to happen in U.S. history. What those people accomplished in just three short years was incredible and could never happen again.

I have chosen the town of my birth for the setting for my novel, as it's the perfect backdrop for a suspense thriller. We know there were Russians spies there (enabling them to produce their own atomic bomb in 1949). Although Terror On Black Oak Ridge is a work of fiction, by putting historical people and places in the novel, as well as using Ed Westcott's wonderful photos, my goal is to transport the reader back to those top-secret days when everything was going into Oak Ridge, but nothing was coming out (as the expression went), and weave a tale that is a good way to spend one's time.

I hope you like it.

7

Chapter 1-Upheaval

Dale Hargrowe was not pleased. At all.

Everything had been going so well. He had just graduated from the Massachusetts Institute of Technology with his Ph.D in the new field of nuclear physics this past June of 1944.

In August, he had been asked to stay on with MIT in charming Cambridge to teach first-year students as well as to continue assisting Dr. Ronald Tupper, the department chair, in research. Dr. Hargrowe had a bright future. It was going even better than had he planned it. Most importantly, he was in perfect control of his life. Despite America being involved in a world war on two fronts, Dale was doing well. Life was going well.

Until now.

Dr. Tupper's secretary, Miss Gloria Blanchard, had summoned Dale to the office. That by itself seemed strange to Dale. Miss Blanchard had never done this before. Further, Dr. Tupper's door routinely stayed open. Dale had been there many times before and no conversation had been deemed personal enough to make the white-haired physics professor have a closed meeting.

When Miss Blanchard secured the door behind him as he entered, however, it signaled to Dale this conversation was not going to be a normal one.

This was when Dale Hargrowe's neat and orderly world changed forever. This was when he became not pleased.

Dale suddenly sat upright.

"Are you serious?" he challenged his friend and mentor, when he heard the news.

"I know, Dale," Dr. Tupper said, his head nodding in understanding. "I'm not happy with losing you to the war, either. We were very much looking forward to you staying with us and working here. But when these men from the war department came with an urgent need for someone with your skills, I had no choice but to recommend you."

Dale had no counter-argument. He had been immune from the war effort ever since he had been classified 4-F due to a knee injury from when he tried out for football his freshman year of college at Amherst. Then, being a full-time college and post-graduate student allowed him to continue his life unaffected by the war.

But, he also knew, if big-time baseball stars like Ted Williams and Johnny Pesky of the Red Sox and Joe DiMaggio of the Yankees had their careers interrupted by the war, then why should he be protected?

Still, Dale was not happy at having his personal and professional plans interrupted. Surely the war could be won without him. Surely there was someone else in all of America who could fill this bill. His life had been going just the way he wanted, right on schedule, just as it always had been. Surely there wasn't a need for fate to step in and mix up the works now. Surely.

Dale drummed his fingers on his thighs. "I guess there's no way out, is there?" he asked in a surrendered tone.

"I'm afraid not, son," Dr. Tupper softly said.

"So, what is it I'm supposed to do?"

"I don't know that. Even if I did, I wouldn't be able to tell you. If I could hazard a guess, I'd say your dissertation on fission has something to do with it."

More finger drumming. "Where am I supposed to do whatever it is I'm supposed to do?"

"Miss Blanchard has your travel details. The public name is called the Clinton Engineering Works Project, near Knoxville, Tennessee. Beyond that, I don't know."

Dale was having a difficult time imagining what could be so important in the lower part of the Appalachians. He could imagine New York, Chicago, Washington D.C., or somewhere in California, but not some place in the Smoky Mountains. Tapping out imaginary tunes on his legs did not produce any answers.

"What could be so doggone important to the war down there?" he said, thinking aloud.

Dr. Tupper raised his right hand and looked at Dale through his rimless, round glasses. While Dr. Tupper often spoke with a good-natured twinkle in his eye, this time he did not. Whatever this was, it was serious. "Dale, my first piece of advice is to keep your thoughts and opinions to yourself. I don't know much of anything about this, but by putting two-and-two together, I have some theories. Regardless, I do know that from this point on, it would serve you well to merely salute smartly and carry on without undue noise."

Dale exhaled, acquiescing to the inevitable. "When do I leave?"

Dr. Tupper turned his chair around and faced the window behind him.

"Tomorrow morning," he said in an almost inaudible tone.

Dale just about sprang out of his chair.

"*Tomorrow morning?*" he roared. "Are you serious? You can't be serious!"

Dr. Tupper turned back around to look at his protégé. "You are to pack clothing for all the seasons in one trunk, as well as any comfort items, like books and papers and such."

"But what about all my personal affairs? This doesn't give me any time at all!"

"We'll have someone take care of everything for you. Look, son, we do not like this anymore than you do. But the war is our top priority and demands all our best efforts. I know you'll do a great job down there."

Dale sat stunned and speechless, a thousand images of the war effort flooding his mind. Everyone was doing their part to win this war. Americans were rationing sugar, metal, rubber—materials needed for use on the front lines. Enthusiastic boys and girls collected every available scrap of these items in their neighborhoods and brought them to local collection points. Victory gardens were grown. No effort was too small and no person too important to not contribute to winning this terrible war. Still, he did not like this demand on him. It messed up everything.

Silently, Dale stood and reached across Dr. Tupper's desk to shake his hand. As he turned to exit the door, Dr. Tupper softly said, "God be with you, son."

Feeling utterly numb, he opened Dr. Tupper's door and walked out of the office, head down. He did not break stride as Miss Blanchard placed an envelope with travel details in his hand. He felt as if a bailiff was handing him his jail sentence.

As Dale strode out in the warm August sun, he thought of Dr. Tupper's last words to him: "God be with you, son."

God? Dale never thought about God. To him, God was a nice story for people who needed something to believe in. Dale's very nominal church upbringing did not leave an impression, other than bland messages from ministers who did not seem to believe it themselves.

Dale was a scientist, raised and educated in the world of Darwinian theory. Man was the highest evolved animal, not descendants of Adam and Eve. Dale dealt with empirical evidence, like fossil records and vestigial organs, not to mention cold equations and test-tube results. God was a nice crutch for those who needed something to lean on. He did not.

If God did in fact exist, Dale thought, He must be playing a cruel joke on him.

Dale had never ever talked to God, other than recite the few prayers he was forced to memorize as a youth. But now, he had something to get off his chest.

He looked up to the sky, pointed a finger upward and declared, "I'll go, but just for the record, I am *not* pleased!"

Daniel S. Zulli

Chapter 2-Arrival

By the time the train stopped in Knoxville, Tennessee, at 7:28 Wednesday morning, Dr. Dale Hargrowe had been traveling slightly less than 26 hours.

It felt like 26 weeks.

He had been awake for the better part of 30 hours. And he still was not entirely sure why he was here. He knew he did not want to be.

He had begun his journey from Massachusetts on Tuesday, reporting to the train station at the Dorchester Extension at 7:30 a.m., and leaving for Boston at 8:15. From there, the train rumbled through Springfield, Hartford, New York City, Philadelphia, Baltimore, D.C., Richmond, Charlotte, then finally wound its way through the southern tip of the Smoky Mountains toward Knoxville.

The rail cars had been packed - mostly fresh-faced G.I.s - forcing Dale to sit upright in the coach car, nodding off but not really sleeping. He had left deep sleep in his comfortable bed back at his Cambridge apartment.

As the train finally halted at the Southern Railway Station on West Depot Avenue in Knoxville, Dale decided that being in eastern Tennessee in August was not good. The air was hot and thick; bugs chirped and hummed as the new day broke. While it had been warm back in Cambridge, the nearby ocean had generated enough of a cooling breeze to make life palatable. Knoxville had no ocean breeze, and Dale's clothes stuck to his skin. He could not wait until his next shower and change of clothes.

Dale got up and arched his back. He shook and wiggled his limbs to restore their full function. If he would have had to run for his life, he would lose.

This is nuts, he thought. He should still be in historic Cambridge, getting ready to begin his first year of teaching at MIT, enjoying his life. Even though the Red Sox were mired in fourth place in the American League, a .500 team, Dale had plans to see a couple of games at Fenway before the season ended. Dale had lots of plans which did not include being in hot and humid Tennessee.

As he detrained, the black porters began unloading the various trunks and luggage of the passengers who were making Knoxville their destination. It was a large stack.

He passed a portable stand where the Red Cross was passing out fresh coffee and donuts, the aromas of both filling the air. G.I.s flocked to it like bees to a flower. After gathering his trunk, Dale looked up. A sign read, "Clinton Engineering Works Inside." This was where he was supposed to report once he arrived, according to Miss Blanchard's

Daniel S. Zulli

instructions. Lugging his trunk behind him, he entered this section of the train depot.

Dale felt like he was inside some armed forces recruiting station. Uniformed Army personnel were processing anxious-looking men as if they were reporting for basic training. There were a variety of desks and stations with signs above them, hanging from the ceiling tiles: "Construction." "Food Services." "Truck Drivers." "Secretarial Pool." "Laborers." And then the one to which he was to report: "Engineers." Soldiers moved about with clipboards, directing this fresh batch of "recruits" in a systematic fashion, with low tones and blunt looks. An Army private told everyone to leave their trunks over in one corner of the room.

A 4 x 8-foot sign with bold red letters dominated the room:

Security Starts Here!

Below these stark words was another line:

You will be told only what you need to know.

Dale's mind reeled. Even though he knew he had not been drafted, no civilian job he had ever applied for in his past ever felt like this.

This was different. There was no idle conversation. No smiles and handshaking. No questions asked or answered. Talk was short, to-the-point and business-like. Eyes were hidden underneath military caps. This was not the place for forging relationships.

Dale entered the line for engineers. There were two others before him, standing behind a taped line on the floor several feet in front of a somber Army sergeant's desk. They were not to cross it until the three-striper barked, "Next!" Dale approached him when it was his turn.

"Name?" the sergeant asked, not even looking up from his stack of paperwork.

"'Dale Hargrowe,'" he answered. "That's H-A-R-G-R—"

"I can spell," Sergeant "Somber" growled. "Dale Hargrowe," he confirmed. "I.D." That was not a request, but an order.

Dale fumbled around in his back pocket and produced his MIT employee badge and his Massachusetts driver's license.

Sergeant Somber looked at them both, looked up at Dale, looked down to his paperwork, checked it off and made an entry next to his name. He handed the documents back, along with a badge labeled CEW 7-39XR, and pointed for him to proceed to the staging area where the other engineers had been directed to wait.

13

Dale dutifully obeyed. He apparently was the last one expected, at least for this round. He desperately wanted to talk to these other men and ask them where they were from, what form of engineering they did. Was it chemical, structural, biological, or nuclear like Dale? He wondered what their jobs would be at the Clinton Engineering Works.

But since this was not the place for questions, Dale could only speculate on the answers.

"Get your IDs out again as well as the badge just handed to you," bellowed a short, stocky man with round glasses, wearing a gray civilian suit. He had come out of a room adjacent to the desk occupied by Sergeant Somber, who had given the man in the gray suit the list of the three waiting engineers. The man walked past the three engineers and ordered them, "Follow me to the bus."

Outside, he directed, "When I call your name, show me your IDs and badge. Then enter the bus only when I have cleared you."

He went down the list alphabetically: "Alders!" He checked Alders's credentials against the list Sergeant Somber had produced, then he jerked a no-nonsense thumb toward the door of the bus.

"Gilchrist." A jerk of the thumb. "Hargrowe."

That made three. Once they were all on the bus, a porter opened the back door and started loading the luggage and trunks. The bus was full of road-weary men and women who had journeyed to Knoxville. Dale had to assume they were as clueless as he was about what they were getting into. They all looked that way.

Dale plunked down behind the driver of the bus, a black man of about 50, immaculately dressed in his official bus driver's uniform, with official bus driver's cap jauntily tilted to the right side.

"Y'all just sit back and relax now, folks!" he cheerfully announced, closing the door with a swing of his arm on the lever. "I'll have you at your destination in no time flat. Yes, sir! I'll have you right there, or my name isn't Ernest Eugene Cummings."

Then, to no one else in particular, Ernest Eugene Cummings, bus driver, went on his own little soliloquy. "I wanted to be called 'E.E. Cummings,' but that there fancy poet fellow already took that name. My folks used to call me 'Ernie' growing up, but I never did like 'Ernie,' or even 'Gene.' Hated *that*. My sister was a 'Jean,' short for 'Jeanette,' so I couldn't be 'Gene,' too. So, I had all my friends just call me, 'E.' I like the sound of that: 'E.' Yes, sir!"

Dale grinned slightly, despite his need for sleep. Food would not hurt either. But to hear some semblance of joy in the otherwise nervous-system shattering experience of the last two days was quite a relief.

He leaned forward and addressed the driver. "Say, Mr. E., how long of a bus ride will this be?"

"Oh, about 43 minutes even, boss. You're in luck: they just fixed that bridge by the river after last week's rain. If they hadn't, it would take over an hour with the detour. But it should be 43 minutes. I've done this just a few times." He chuckled and glanced at his passengers in the rear-view mirror. "Y'all look as tired as everyone else I've brought in!"

"I sure am," Dale said. "It was a long train ride down. Any good places to eat where we're going?"

"Y'all be dropped off at a housing office where they'll give you your room assignment, and right there next to it is this little trailer that's a cafeteria where you can get some grub."

Dale raised his voice a little, his tiredness and hunger making him feel slightly exasperated. "Where exactly are we going?"

Mr. E. dropped his voice lower than his normal conversation level. "To a place that doesn't even exist," he said, glancing again in the rear-view mirror to see if anyone was watching his lips move. "Listen, boss, take some advice from old Mr. E. It's not good to say things too loud around here. And don't ask too many questions. It ain't good for you. But it wasn't all that long ago, where I'm taking you was just a couple of old run-down, raggedy farms with nothin' but a few families who could barely put shoes on their kids' feet. But now, it's all built up to a real town. The saying is that everything comes in but nothing comes out. So, do yourself a favor and keep your eyes open, keep your mouth shut, and keep to yourself. I don't know no more than that."

With that, Mr. E. once again raised his voice to speak to all of the bus occupants. "We'll be there sooner than you think, folks! You just sit back and relax and leave all the worrying about things to your friend, Mr. E. I'll take you right to where you need to go. Yes, sir!"

The bus took them southwest on U.S. 75, then northwest up Highway 62, crossing the Clinch River. Mr. E. was right - 43 minutes to the dot.

Despite being tired, Dale kept alert during the ride, looking around. He wanted to know more of what he was getting into, this world of hush-hush down in eastern Tennessee. For the life of him, he could not see how these rural backwoods could have any role in winning the war. Or his part in it.

As they approached a gate a starched military policeman with sidearm waved the bus over to a side lane, to the right of passenger cars. Dale's eyes at once went to the sign above the gate:

MILITARY AREA
WEAPONS - AMMUNITION - EXPLOSIVES
CAMERAS - FIELDGLASSES - LIQUORS
TELESCOPES - RADIO TRANSMITTERS
PROHIBITED
ALL VEHICLES & PASSENGERS
SUBJECT TO SEARCH

Mr. E. dutifully pulled over and opened the door. The MP bounded up the steps. "Produce one form of picture ID as well as the badge issued to you at the in-processing center in Knoxville."

After the guard checked the passengers' credentials to his satisfaction, he stepped off the bus. "Proceed. Stay out of trouble, now, E.!"

"Aw, you know me, Private Howard," Mr. E. hollered back, with a grin. "I never get in any kind of trouble. At least that's what I tell me wife! Haw! Haw! Yes, sir!"

He glanced at the rearview mirror again. "We're almost there, folks! Next stop, your quarters assignments."

If the other bus occupants were as worn out as he was, Dale knew they all needed the same thing: a room, a shower, a bed, some food. Hopefully, the rest of the necessary steps to carry out these things would not take long.

A few twists and turns later, Earnest Eugene Cummings pulled up and parked in front of a small hut-like shack marked, HOUSING.

"This is it, folks - your new home! Y'all go on inside now and I'll unload your bags and have them sitting right out here in front. Don't worry, they'll be safe. Just go on in and the man will give you your room assignments. Welcome to Tennessee! Yes, sir!"

Dale was the first off and led the way into the housing shack. When he glanced around, he was stunned. He had never seen anything like this before: In the middle of rural eastern Tennessee was what

16

looked like a combination of an Army post and regular town. There were both barracks structures and civilian buildings. There were military vehicles and civilian cars. There were soldiers as well as civilian men and women with their kids moving about.

And there was construction, on a scale unlike anything he had seen in the northeast. Bulldozers moved earth, graters smoothed everything in sight, trucks hauled every type of material to and fro, men scurried around at a frantic pace. And *dirt*. Dust, dirt and fumes permeated the air, filling the nostrils, choking the lungs and stinging the eyes.

Inside the Housing hut, there were two desks, one for the main person who looked like he was in charge, the other for a secretary/assistant. When the man in charge gave the new recruits the card with their house and room assignment, he handed the duplicate to the young lady, who filed them in her multiple cabinets.

"Name and your badge, please," the man at the desk said.

"Dale Hargrowe." He then produced his CEW 7-39XR badge. The other two engineers followed suit.

"All the engineers have your rooms on Outer Drive." The man handed the house and room cards to his assistant. She stamped them, gave them to each engineer and filed the duplicate in the card catalog box next to her desk. She then issued one key to each new occupant.

"A transit will be by here in about 20 minutes to take you to your rooms," the Housing man said. "Just sit tight until he comes."

Chapter 3-Meeting

Dale remembered he was hungry.

"Excuse me," he said to the Housing official. "Our bus driver said there was a place close by where we could get a bite to eat. Do we have time before our ride gets here?" Fingers and toes were crossed. He was famished.

The man pointed to the left rear position behind him. The other engineers stayed in the Housing office while Dale went out the door and to the left. It was just nothing more than a big trailer, but the sign above it said, "Kaye's Kafé," and that was good enough for him.

There were a few people hunched over coffee and some snacks which looked like a combination of pastries and sandwiches. Some were military, some civilian. Cigarette smoke rose up in curls and wisps, joining together to form a solid cloud at the ceiling. *Don't Sit Under the Apple Tree* by the Andrew Sisters came from the small table radio in the corner of the diner.

Dale didn't know if the lady at the counter was Kaye or not, but from her he ordered a ham sandwich, no mayo, with lettuce and tomato, and a glass of milk.

Taking his culinary goods, Dale ambled over to an empty table to take care of 50% of his needs; the other 50% - sleep - would come shortly.

Dale passed two young ladies enjoying malts and small talk. Giggles laced their dialog as they seemed to be taking a break from whatever it was they did in this strange, new environment. One girl looked fresh out of high school, a cute strawberry blonde with holdover freckles from her childhood. Her starched dress had her company's name imprinted on the left breast pocket.

The other girl was a bit older, mid 20s. She was slim, wearing no makeup to speak of but having a natural kind of beauty. Her chestnut brown hair cascaded down a little below her shoulders. Her fresh complexion highlighted sparkling blue eyes. She was a wonderful example of femininity despite wearing simple slacks and a blouse.

"Well!" the brunette said, taking in Dale's rumpled and bloodshot look. "Look what the cat just dragged in!"

Dale responded, "Not just dragged in, but threw up with his last hairball." The girls giggled.

"Got a name, Mr. Tall, Dark and Wrinkled?" the strawberry blonde asked in a charming southern accent.

"Dale Hargrowe, lately of Cambridge, Massachusetts, but now, apparently, from here, wherever this is."

18

Daniel S. Zulli

"Shouldn't that be, 'Dale *Hairball,*' if the cat threw you up?" the brunette said, sending the girls into another episode of giggling.

Dale rolled his eyes. "Swell. I travel 1,500 miles in two days and who do I run into but Abbott and Costello? I really liked you in *Buck Privates.*"

The girls' giggles morphed into a paroxysm of laughter.

"And from whom do I have the pleasure of being so mercilessly teased?" Dale sat down at the table next to them.

"I'm Trudy McIntyre, but everyone calls me 'Trudy Mac,'" the strawberry blonde said first. "Everyone is a 'Mac' in my family. My daddy is Bertie Mac, Momma is Tessie Mac, and my three brothers are Billy Mac, Bobby Mac and Barry Mac. I'm from a little town near Chattanooga, called Jasper."

"So, the boys got the 'B's' and the girls got the 'T's,' right?"

"Say, he's a sharp one, Brenda!" Trudy Mac jabbed.

The brunette set down her malt. "I'm Brenda Andrews, from Cincinnati by way of Covington, Kentucky, right across the river."

Dale bowed his head. "Good to meet you, ladies. I haven't been abused by such lovely company in ages. How long have you two been here?"

"We've been here since the beginning," Trudy Mac said.

"How long ago was that?"

"They started building this place up in March of '43," the southern girl said. "We both got here about the same time and even had to live in a tent until our girls' dorm was built."

"And, we've been roommates ever since," Brenda added.

"Well, if Hope and Crosby retire, I think you two might have a future in Hollywood." Dale bit into his sandwich.

One of the other engineers - Gilchrist - stuck his head into Kaye's Kafé. "Bus's here. Got to go!"

Dale grinned. "Glad I could help make your day go better, ladies. Let's do it again some time!" He found this friendly exchange refreshing.

Rising, Dale grabbed his ham sandwich off the plate and the glass of milk and followed Gilchrist out the door to the bus, ready for the last stop of a very long journey.

The two young women watched Dale leave for the bus.

"He's cute," Trudy Mac said, "even if he does look like death warmed over."

"I agree," Brenda mused. "I wouldn't mind seeing him again when he doesn't look like he's been on a three-day bender."

It did not seem possible, but the two young ladies laughed even harder.

19

The woman at the counter - it was probably Kaye - looked out at the girls and said, "Say, did that fella just walk out of here with my glass?"

The bus pulled up to a small, pre-fabricated "cemesto" house on Outer Drive. This was a lovely setting, with the houses amid pine trees, topped with blue skies.

Looking at his housing card, Dale found his address. Going in, he saw it was a neat, two-bedroom number. His name was taped onto the door to his room, while "O'Neil" was taped onto the other room.

Just as he was hauling his trunk inside the home, a man entered.

"You must be the new guy," he said. "I'm Bob O'Neil, the old-timer in this joint."

Bob O'Neil was about 35 and spoke with a thick New York accent.

"Dale Hargrowe," Dale announced. "Just got in, as you can see. From MIT in Cambridge."

"Sox fan?" Bob asked. "I can live with that. Just as long as you're not a New York Giants fan. Then we'd have problems."

"Like baseball, I take it?"

"Are you kidding? I'd denounce my own grandmother before I left the Brooklyn Dodgers," he said with a chuckle.

"Someone else live here before me? What happened to him?" Dale asked.

"He blabbed. Shot his mouth off once too often. They shipped him out so fast I never saw him leave. Gone. Let this be your first lesson here: don't talk."

The house was sparsely furnished with basic chairs and table. Dale's room had a small night stand, lamp, bureau, basic bed frame. It had a new mattress, fresh out of its plastic wrapper. Linens were laying in a neat pile on the bed. Dale knew that while this was not as comfortable as his old apartment, this was better than what most seemed to be getting at this site. He was too tired to complain anyway.

Dale flopped down on the bed, sighing loudly after a long and arduous trip.

Before he left the land of the conscious, Dale rummaged through his trunk, pulled out some stationary and jotted a quick note to Dr. Tupper:

Dr. Tupper,
    Made it safely to the secret location outside Knoxville. This is a strange place. It looks like a combination Army post and regular town. I wonder how this place fits into winning the war, or how I'm supposed to help. I imagine I'll start work tomorrow.

When you pack up my apartment, please give my few living plants to Miss Blanchard, with my compliments. I Hope she succeeds in finding a husband someday soon. I bet she's a real catch.

Take care. Hope to see you when this is over, hopefully soon.

Regards, your friend,
Dale

The final version of the letter, however, looked different when it finally arrived.

Dr. Tupper,
    Made it safely

I imagine I'll start work tomorrow.

When you pack up my apartment, please give my few living plants to Miss Blanchard, with my compliments. I Hope she succeeds in finding a husband someday soon. I bet she's a real catch.

Take care. Hope to see you ▮▮▮▮▮▮▮▮ hopefully soon.

Regards, your friend,
Dale

Chapter 4-Inquisition

O'Neil banged on Dale's door.

"Up and at 'em, Dale!" he bellowed in his Brooklyn accent. "Transit will be here in 10 minutes!"

Dale awoke into what felt like a world-class hangover. The connections that ran from his ear canals to his brain to his limbs seemed to be absent. Assembling all the pieces from the day before to the immediate present took a Herculean effort.

O'Neil could not hear any movement in Dale's bedroom.

"Better get moving, buddy!"

Somehow, someway, Dale's autonomic nervous system kicked in, despite all its individual parts not working. He threw the covers off himself, sat upright, planted his feet on the bare floor, then headed to the shower. Full comprehension would have to follow.

Soap, hot water and clean clothes made Dale Hargrowe able to rejoin the living. He was ready in nine minutes and was standing outside in front of their house when the transit truck showed up.

"I guess you know where to take me," he said to the driver.

The morning was crisp and clean for an August day. Dale could see and hear the day shift's activities all around him. Buses and cars moved people to and from places. They had their routines down. He was the new guy who did not know which end was up.

The recent rain had left enough water in the ruts and divots to cause an occasional *splash* as they drove. When they hit a dry spot, dust drifted into the truck's open windows. Dale saw the vast construction that was going on, the cause of all the dust.

As the transit truck wound its way into the heart of this strange town, Dale saw another warning sign, like the one he saw at the train terminal:

WHAT YOU SEE HERE
WHAT YOU DO HERE
WHAT YOU HEAR HERE
WHEN YOU LEAVE HERE
LET IT STAY HERE

The message was received, loud and clear. He did not want to be the next one kicked out of his room.

The truck pulled up to a dark green, two-story building that read "ADMINISTRATION 2" above the main entrance. It looked like an Army barracks. An all-business-looking woman stood outside. When Dale opened his door, she directed him indoors. The rooms were numbered 1 through 7 on the right side of the first floor and 2 through 8 on the left side. Outside each room, file folders were visible in a holder by the door.

Dale was expected. He found his folder on door #3 and entered.

"Have a seat, sir," the young secretary directed him to the chair against the wall. "Would you like some coffee? You look like you could use some."

"That would be great," Dale replied.

"Black? Cream and sugar?"

"As black as you can get it. Yesterday's coffee would work too."

As soon as Dale got the cup of ebony gold in his hand, a man from the inner office stepped out. "Dr. Dale Hargrowe," he said, calling the newly-awarded Ph.D from MIT into his office.

He waved Dale to the chair in front of his desk. If Sergeant Somber from the train station was serious, this new man - Howard Lohorn, from his name plate - made him look like a vaudeville comedian.

Mr. Lohorn pulled out the papers from the folder on his desk. He looked down at them on top of the glasses perched precariously on the front of his nose.

"Dale Franklin Hargrowe," he began in a monotone. "28. Born in Bristol, Connecticut. Parents David and Deborah..." he paused, glancing up above his glasses. "The letter 'D' must run in the family," he said in an unfunny attempt at humor.

He continued his flat reading of Dale's file. "Moved to Baltimore when you were 12. Graduated from Heritage High School in 1934, number 2 in your class. Attended the University of Massachusetts in Amherst on an academic scholarship in Chemistry. Wanted to play football as well, but hurt your knee your freshman year, rendering you 4F for the draft.

"Graduated top of your class with a scholarship to MIT for your post-graduate work. Completed both your Master's and Doctorate in six years. Was about to start teaching this year while working on more research in the field of nuclear fission as it relates to the production of energy."

Mr. Lohorn solemnly concluded the dossier reading of Dale's life and took off his glasses. "Now you're here. Dr. Hargrowe, you will be here until the war is over or until you are dismissed, should that happen before the war ends. Whatever plans you had are now on hold. You belong to us. The plant in which you are to be working has not been built yet. It will be soon. As of now you are to work in the Y-12 trailer.

"But this effort needs your expertise. That is why you got the nice house you did. Some of us weren't so lucky," he said, with a touch of resentment in his voice.

"From this moment on, Dr. Hargrowe," Mr. Lohorn's voice became even more melodramatic, "you will talk to no one about your job except your immediate supervisor, whose name you'll learn later. No one is your friend. *You* are no one's friend. You are suspicious of everyone, as they are of you. You will not inquire from other workers what they are doing, for they will not know any more than you will know of yours. You will be told everything you need to know, nothing more, nothing less. Therefore, if you don't know something, do not ask.

"Your work here will be your number one priority. If you have to work 24 hours a day, seven days a week, you will. As I said, you will be here until the war is over. Do you 100% hear and understand what I have just briefed, Dr. Hargrowe?"

Dale felt as if he had just been interrogated by the F.B.I. "Yes, sir, I do." Mr. Lohorn silently slid with his left hand a sheet of paper toward Dale and held out a pen with his right. This was the non-disclosure agreement that would be used against him at his trial if he violated any of the spelled-out tenets. Dale signed, "Dale F. Hargrowe," and dated below it.

"Now, then, do you have any questions for me, Dr. Hargrowe?"

The flippant side of Dale wanted to break the mood and ask, "When will the golf course be built?" but he wisely refrained.

"Well, I have two, actually, in no particular order," Dale said, being just told to not ask any questions. He wasn't sure if this were a test or not, but slowly concluded that stoic, no-nonsense Mr. Lohorn's inviting him to ask a question was legitimate.

"The first is," Dale continued, "what about my pay?"

"You will be paid, minus your housing, approximately $78.35 every two weeks. It may not be as much as you would make in the private sector, but you will have many of your needs already met, and most of the prices on items you normally get are low. And the second?"

"Yes, sir. Where am I? I mean, I know I'm near Knoxville, Tennessee, but *exactly* where am I?"

"You, sir, are in an area once called 'Black Oak Ridge, Tennessee.' It is now just called 'Oak Ridge,' home of the Clinton Engineering Works project."

With that, Mr. Lohorn closed up the file on Dr. Dale Hargrowe and said, "From here, please report to Room #6 in Administration Building #1 to complete your in-processing. That will be all."

As Dale stepped toward the door, Mr. Lohorn got in one last word.

"Dr. Hargrowe, Miss Kaye at the diner has reported that you stole a glass from her yesterday. This incident will be noted in your file. And if the glass isn't returned by close-of-business tomorrow, your first paycheck will be docked the 16 cents the glass cost Miss Kaye. Am I clear?"

"Abundantly, sir," Dale acknowledged through his embarrassment, glad to be leaving Mr. Lohorn's chamber of inquisition. As he marched past the receptionist's desk, he firmly plunked his coffee cup down on it, not breaking stride.

"Don't turn me in," he said to her as he walked out of Room #3.

Chapter 5-Brenda

When Dale left Mr. Lohorn's cheerful office and stepped outside, he was once again amazed at this place called the Clinton Engineering Works. He was half expecting to see Orson Wells filming a new science fiction movie in which he was just an extra. It was a civilian town, but also an Army post. It was done, but still under construction. It existed, but no one knew it was here. He saw it with his own eyes, but he could not tell anyone about it because it really wasn't here.

His head hurt.

Shaking it to clear out the cobwebs - he had not gotten enough sleep to put him back on level ground - Dale proceeded to Administration #1.

Administration #1 was the mirror image of Administration #2, not more than 20 yards away. The distinct difference was the parking space in the exact center of the building. It had two stars spray painted on the curb in front of the space. While there were military staff cars and civilian models parked in the spaces to the left and right of the one with the stars, the space with the stars was empty.

Dale entered the building, looking around for his next stop.

He saw the same layout as before, but at the bottom of the stairs at both ends of the building stood armed MPs, with white spats on their glass-black boots and steel helmets above their stoic faces. They stood at parade rest, obviously guarding the second floor. Since this was Administration Building #1, it was clear that the second floor held the brain-trust and leadership of this endeavor. Dale could not imagine what credentials it took to mount those stairs. He did not make eye contact with the guards.

Dale went down the hall to Room #6. As he was looking up at the room numbers and striding down the long hall, he heard a feminine voice call out.

"Hey!" it said, to whom, he was not sure.

"Dale Hargrowe!" the voice said.

The feminine voice came from Room #3 on the right, or odd, side of the building.

Dale sheepishly peeked in. He nervously thought that maybe Mr. Lohorn somehow sent word from his building to this one that Dr. Dale Hargrowe needed special watching for whatever reason.

"Hi, Dale," the attractive brunette from Kaye's Kafé greeted him. There were three other women in this front office, each one handling papers and running the front lines of the administration this project required. Typewriters clacked furiously, generating piles of paperwork.

Daniel S. Zulli

"It's me, remember?" she said, waving him in. Brenda noticed the other ladies in the room casting glances at this sharp-looking, masculine visitor into their work space.

"Oh, yes, from the diner yesterday. Barbara, isn't it?" Dale responded. He knew her name was Brenda, but seized this opportunity for retribution for yesterday's ribbing.

"It's *Brenda*," she replied through half-closed eyes and icy tone in her voice.

"Oh, yes—that's right. How could I ever forget you, *Brenda?*" Dale emphasized her name. He was enjoying this payback.

"Okay," Dale relented, grinning. "Let's have a ceasefire, shall we? It's good to see you again, Brenda, even if I didn't expect to find you here with the big boys."

"Deal," agreed Brenda. "It's a tie at 1-to-1. I take it you finished your first level of orientation next door?"

"Yes. My last cavity filling was almost as enjoyable. I have to go to Room #6 now to have the tooth pulled."

"That'll be with Mr. Thayer. But he's backed up now with one in his office and two more before you. It will be a while. He likes to talk."

"Say," Brenda offered. "I can take a break now if you want to get some coffee, maybe. I'll have you back in time."

"Sure," Dale said. "My last cup didn't work. I think Mr. Lohorn neutralized the intended effect."

"Yeah, he's a real charmer. I heard that underneath that grumpy exterior is an equally grumpy interior. Let me check with my supervisor over there. She's real nice," Brenda's voice dropped, "but she only got this job because her husband is a colonel here, the head of security."

"Hey, Val," Brenda tossed to the inner office where her supervisor sat. "Can I take a break for a few to show this new guy around a bit?"

Val looked up at her, looked at Dale, then back to Brenda with a nod.

"Thanks. I won't be out long."

As Dale and Brenda walked out of the front office with the four secretarial stations, they passed an attractive, peroxide-blonde's desk whose name plate read "Libby Snyder." Brenda looked back over her shoulder and mouthed, *"I saw him first,"* provoking a steely-eyed glare.

Stepping outside, Brenda offered, "There's a little cantina that's closer than Kaye's Kafé with a patio area where we can sit."

"Sounds great," Dale agreed. "I think I'm going to stay out of Kaye's Kafé for a while."

"At least until you return that glass to her!" Brenda laughed.

"Ouch! I guess this whole place knows that I'm a thief. Make that you're up, 2-to-1 now!"

27

"You look a lot better than when we first saw you yesterday," Brenda appeased. "Your bloodshot eyes looked pretty rough."

"If they looked bad to you, you should have seen them from *my* side!" They both laughed.

"Where's your twin sister?" Dale asked.

"Trudy Mac? She's in Clinton today. That's a town near here. Her job - I can tell you this -is to go around and make deals with local farmers, grocers and meat producers to help give more food for this place, like the commissary and eating places and stores. She travels a lot, to Knoxville, Clinton, Harriman - all around. They must have figured that a farm girl would be good at that."

"She looks barely out of high school," Dale mused.

"She is. Just turned 19. But don't let her appearance fool you— Trudy Mac is a sharp girl. She works hard and even though food can be scarce here sometimes, the peasants haven't revolted yet."

They arrived at the cantina. "Two coffees please," Dale requested. He concluded that winning this war would require lots of caffeine.

"Thanks," Brenda said. "We can sit over here." She directed them to a picnic table under an overhang that offered some protection from the morning sun.

"Listen, Brenda," Dale started the conversation, "I honestly don't know what to say to you. After what Mr. Lohorn said, I'm gun-shy about talking to anyone about anything. My roommate told me I took the place of some guy who talked too much. I have a million thoughts running through my head, but don't know what to do with them. This is all so strange for me. One thing I do know is that I'm here against my will. I was just getting ready to start my new job."

"I know, Dale. I got the same lecture you did. We all did. It does make it hard to make friends when you don't know who your friends are. I heard they have spies all over this place, listening to every conversation, reading all our mail in and out, watching us all the time. You should try living in the girls' dormitory where we want to talk and visit and process our feelings all the time but can't. I would imagine it's easier for you men to maintain your distances with other men, but it's brutal for us gals. We had a girl come in right after I got here, and within two days she was gone without a trace. She must have blabbed to the wrong person."

"Wow. I only have one roommate in the house we got, so I don't have to interact with him if I don't want. But whatever is going on here, I can't imagine there's ever been anything like it before."

"That," concurred Brenda, "would pass for the understatement of the year, if not century."

Changing the subject, Dale asked her, "So what's your story, Brenda? Where are you from and how and why did you get here?"

Daniel S. Zulli

"We can talk about that. I was born and raised in Cincinnati. Nothing much happened there that's noteworthy, except maybe Johnny Vander Meer throwing those two no-hitters for the Reds back in '38. We're all huge Reds' fan.

"I went to Xavier College as an economics major. My professors didn't know what a girl was going to do with that degree. To be honest, I didn't either, but I sure didn't see myself as your typical nurse or secretary the rest of my life. Even though economics is boring, I've always seen myself doing something more exciting, somehow, someway, somewhere.

"But," she took a sip of coffee, "I couldn't find work in Cincinnati so I got a job teaching elementary school right across the river in Covington, Kentucky, at a small country school. I had just been there a year when a man was going around hiring folks for this Clinton Engineering Works deal. Since he couldn't say much about it except offer us a chance to help win the war, it sounded intriguing, so I jumped at the chance to get out and see something and do something."

"But you're working now as basically a secretary," Dale countered.

"Yes, for now, but I'll be moving over to the Y-12 plant once it's built. You will too, from what I heard."

"Do your parents approve of you taking this job?"

"My mom does. Don't know about my dad."

"How so?"

"Well, he worked for the college too, recruiting. He used to travel a lot. Unfortunately, he used to like recruiting a lot of prospective female students. My mom finally got fed up with it so she left, taking us kids with her. I haven't seen or heard from my dad in a long while. Okay, so now you know about me, what's your deal, Mr. Dale Hargrowe?"

"About as exciting as you," he began. "I'm a northerner, pretty much. This is my first time being lower than Baltimore, where I grew up. I had just gotten my doctorate in physics at MIT and was about to start my first-year teaching and conducting research on fission when I got 'voluntold' I was coming here just a few days ago."

Brenda saw an opening. "So, it's really *Dr.* Dale Hairball! I'm honored!"

"3-to-1, Brenda. So much for our truce!" Not only was Brenda incredibly attractive, she was a real spitfire too. Dale was trying to not get smitten with her, but that was proving to be hard. They both enjoyed a good laugh at their little war and Dale's losing scorecard.

"Hey," Dale said, looking at this watch. "I'd better get you back before Val gets mad. I already have Kaye mad at me and I can't afford to get on every female's hit list."

As they began walking back, Brenda pointed to a three-story building about 200 yards distant. "That's the girls' dorm. Trudy Mac

29

and I are on the second floor. Look around. See all these buildings? There wasn't anything here when I first got here Now it's just about a real town, only top secret."

"My bus driver told me that there used to be some farmers and such here before. What happened to them?" Dale asked.

"Gone. They moved them all out, some with almost no notice. It was kind of sad to see families who had been here for generations displaced like that, but this war changed everything."

"I saw a parking spot with stars on it in front of your building," Dale said. "Whose spot was that?"

"That's General Groves' space. He's the man running this whole project. He comes in and out, usually in a hurry. If you ever see him, stay out of his way. Don't even look at him and do not *ever* try to talk to him unless he talks to you first. The best thing that can happen to you is that General Groves does not learn your name. I saw him chew out one of his staff members one time and it wasn't pretty. There's a major up there whose sole job, I swear, is to always keep a fresh box of chocolates in General Groves' desk. He likes chocolate and that helps keep him happy and less likely to murder someone."

"I'll keep that in mind. Thanks."

Far off to the southwest, they heard some faint rumbling. Looking over, Brenda saw the beginnings of cloud formations.

"Uh, oh," she said. "Looks like some rain will be moving in shortly."

"Why the sense of foreboding? It's just rain." Dale rebutted.

"See all this dirt?" Brenda challenged. "After a good rain, you'll be ankle if not knee-deep in mud. Just watch. This place will turn into a Tarzan movie with nothing but those quicksand bogs you used to see them fall into."

"Swell," Dale groaned.

Daniel S. Zulli

Chapter 6-Settled

When they arrived back at Administration #1, Dale asked Brenda, "Say, if you ever want to catch a movie or a bite to eat...want to do that sometime? If nothing else, you can show me around my new home." He waved his arm around the expanse that was Oak Ridge, Tennessee.

"Let me think. My social calendar is so full." Brenda pretended to be deep in thought, but after a few seconds said, "I think either one is doable."

"Great. Tell you what, let's meet here this Saturday at 5 p.m. Then you can show me where I can get some fried chicken, then maybe we can see a flick. How's that?"

"You drive a hard bargain, Dr., but I'll pencil you in. You had better be going before you're late on your very first day. Thanks for the coffee."

Brenda went back to her office and resumed her station, triumphantly passing the blonde who still glared at her. Brenda's step to her desk seemed lighter than normal.

All the offices in the Administration buildings were laid out the same: a front office where a receptionist/secretary/office aid sat, and an inner office where the head person was. Occasionally there were two desks in the inner office - as in Val's case - but for the most part, there was just the one station, like Mr. Lohorn's office.

Dale entered Mr. Thayer's front office in Room #6 and saw the two men who were before him had gone, and the receptionist - Leslie Harris, according to the name badge on her dress - waved him to a chair, saying, "Mr. Thayer will be right out. He's wrapping up the paperwork from the earlier gentlemen."

It was incredible to think that whatever this Clinton Engineering Works project was, people would be expected to produce whatever it was they were expected to produce under such bizarre conditions. Who had ever thought of not being able to move about one's work center freely? That is just not normal. Who had ever thought of not letting the workers they hired ask any questions about their jobs? That was insane. Who wrote the rule that you cannot even talk to another employee in the same outfit about their job? That was unnatural. Dale's head spun trying to piece it all together and imagine that he could be of value added under a situation as logic-defying as this.

A man's voice interrupted his mental gyrations. "Dr. Hargrowe, won't you come on in?" Dale had been so deep in thought that he didn't notice Mr. Thayer stepping out of his inner office to Miss Harris' desk area where Dale sat.

"Oh! Yes, sir. Sorry, I was just thinking about some things and didn't see you."

"I can assume what you were thinking about. Most of us here have been in your shoes. Come on, let's get down to business."

James "Jimmy" Thayer was in his mid-40s, slightly portly with a thick neck that defied a neck tie to be properly knotted around it, let alone a collar to be buttoned. He had his suit jacket off and sleeves rolled up. A cigar smoldered from the ash tray on his desk. He looked more suited to be a boss in some warehouse, supervising a crew, than a government paper-pusher.

But at least he sure seemed more genial than Mr. Lohorn, he of the grumpy exterior *and* interior.

"You've had your initial in-processing, received your badge and signed your non-disclosure form. Now you get to hear about your actual job. We all know the constraints we place on everyone make it harder - or at the least, stranger - to do one's job. You will have to rise above that, Dale. I'm going to call you Dale 'cause I hate to be so formal. You can call me Jimmy."

"Thanks. I appreciate your casualness."

Mr. Thayer chuckled. "I figured you would. After Mr. Lohorn, most people are ready to hyperventilate and pass out."

He continued. "For now, you'll be working in a trailer until the Y-12 plant is finished being built, which won't be too much longer. Your immediate supervisor will be Harold Rainey, a good guy and good manager for us. You'll be one of several engineers working under him. All you will know is your slice of the pie, not theirs. And they won't know yours. All Hal will know is what his engineers know and not another manager. *I* don't know what Rainey's job is or what his folks do. See how it works? It has to be this way."

Mr. Thayer paused to order to take a drag off his cigar. He blew a plume of blue smoke above his head.

"The bus lines here at CEW are good and you'll get around easily. All you have to do is walk down the road where your house is and wait at the bus stop. Your trailer will be at Stop #5. Look for the trailer that's labeled 'Y-12.' Don't panic, the roads will be paved before the war's over!" Thayer laughed at his little joke. "Until then, you get your pick of either dirt or mud. Pick up is 7 a.m. and you work until 6 p.m., for now five days a week. It may be more hours and six days once the plant is up and running. You begin tomorrow. Use today to finish getting settled in your quarters and get a bit of rest."

He reached for his cigar once again.

"So, welcome to Oak Ridge, Tennessee, Dale! Best of luck to you. I read your file. We need your skills and talents here. Hopefully, the good Lord willing and the bridges don't wash out, your time here - *all* our time here - will be short and we can all go home."

"Thank you, sir," Dale exhaled. He thought, yes, it would be good to go back home to his life up in Cambridge.

Dale got up, shook Jimmy Thayer's hand, then stepped out and nodded good bye to Miss Harris.

In any new and normal situation, one would naturally become more settled and comfortable. But here in Oak Ridge, the opposite happened. The more Dale Hargrowe knew, the *less* he knew. Even though he was getting more orientated to this new environment, the more he felt *dis*oriented. It seemed like up was down, black was white, hot was cold, and left was right.

As Dale ambled to the bus stop to catch a ride home, he heard the rumbling getting closer. The sky looked dark and angry. A cold front was blowing in, and it was clashing with the hot August air, producing a skirmish which resembled how Dale's insides felt.

Daniel S. Zulli

Chapter 7-Work

Brenda was right: rain in Oak Ridge generated more mud than Dale had ever seen before.

On the walk down the road to the bus stop from his house, Dale felt his feet getting heavier as the mud stuck to the bottom of his shoes like adhesive, layer upon layer, with each step.

The rain had started after Dale had gone to bed the previous night, but he did not hear a thing despite it obviously being a deluge. He needed one more good night's sleep to get him caught up from his torturous trip down and first day in Oak Ridge.

At the bus stop, he saw a new sign that was not there yesterday, a sober reminder of their mission in Oak Ridge:

WHOSE SON
WILL DIE IN
THE LAST MINUTE
OF THE WAR?

While everyone in America was affected by the war, being in academia had insulated Dale to a degree. But here, it was the war effort 24 hours a day. He had not been so conscious of some mother's son dying today, but the sign made him realize that many would.

Dale scraped as much mud as he could on the bus's bottom step, but the effort proved futile and he brought the dark red goop onto the bus like the ones before him.

During the bus ride to his work trailer, Dale saw more than one passenger car axle deep in this slop, wheels spinning and spewing out the mud yards deep behind them. Being from the north, Dale was familiar with driving in snow. It was not very hard once you learned a few simple driving tips, not the least of which was keeping some cardboard in your trunk to put under the front side of the rear tires to get the needed traction to get out of a hole of snow. But this stuff was different and was like the quicksand Brenda had called it. The more you struggled and tried to get out of it, the deeper you sank.

Riding on the bus was no picnic, either. It bumped, jostled, jerked, bounced and rocked over the many mud-filled pot holes, ruts, and divots, tossing its occupants side-to-side and up-and-down. The consensus among the new residents of Oak Ridge was that any paved road-maker could name his price and everyone in Oak Ridge would fork the funds over so that they would not have to ride like this.

The trek made many stops along the way, dropping people off as more got on. Eventually, the bus stopped at Stop #5, near the center of the site, the "reservation," as Dale had heard it called. This was his destination, as well as 80% of the bus.

The site was unusual: out in a field where trees once stood were several obviously temporary trailers, for a wide variety of purposes. Dale spotted the Y-12 trailer to which he was to report, but he also saw the line-up of trailers that offered the usual assortment of necessary living items: food trailers that were mini-diners and break areas; a post-office trailer; all-purpose ones like sewing and laundry; one for dime-store items like toiletries, stationary needs, small clothing essentials like socks, under garments, hand towels, even the latest records, magazines, books and newspapers. The latest edition of the *Stars & Stripes* was prominently displayed outside on racks. There was even a small trailer with the familiar red-and-white striped cylinder for a barber shop, two chairs out of the six designated a beauty shop for the ladies. Since this area was in its own section of the reservation, it, like other hubs of work, would have to be self-contained to give the workers what they needed to be sustained.

Dale clipped on his entry badge for Y-12 so he would not get arrested. The front-most desk belonged to Miss Rivera, raven-haired and a little older than most of the secretarial pool he had seen. She was not friendly.

"Good morning. Mr. Rainey, please?" Dale asked as cheerfully as he could without seeming unnatural.

Minus any verbal reply, Miss Rivera pushed the button on her intercom and barked. "Mr. Rainey, up front!" She went back to her paperwork.

Shortly, a tall, thin man with a shock of black hair and thick-framed glasses came out from an office deep in the trailer, went past Miss Rivera and said, "Dr. Hargrowe?"

"Yes, sir, Mr. Rainey. Dale Hargrowe."

"Call me 'Hal.' Good to have you here. Come on back and let's get going." Harold "Hal" Rainey led Dale past his stern receptionist.

Rainey's office was small and spartan, with only a metal government desk, beat-up filing cabinet and one extra chair. He waved Dale to it.

"We're glad you're here," he said. "You're replacing a man who...uh....left suddenly."

Dale figured it was the former occupant of his room.

"I understand I'm only allowed to engage you in my work?" Dale asked, seeking confirmation.

"Correct. You'll be working the day shift alongside two other engineers in your area. Two other guys work at night. It never stops here. But you cannot collaborate or discuss your work with them in any way. I'll give you what you'll have to work on. You'll leave all your work for me to inspect and up-channel every day when you end your shift."

"Understood."

"Good." Rainey inhaled and exhaled deeply. "You're in for an exciting time here, Dale, even if day-by-day it may not seem like it. We'll be moving out of this trailer soon into the Y-12 plant, and things will really ramp up then. The challenge is so much of this is theoretical, and we must put flesh and bones on this thing. This is all new. I'm sure you're feeling the urgency and magnitude of all this."

Dale nodded. "I sure am."

Rainey then reached down and pulled out a very thick folder from his desk and held it out for Dale to receive.

"No time like the present, right?" he asked with a chuckle. "You're already behind the eight ball with your predecessor's sudden departure, so you had better hit the ground running. Pour over this material. Remember, we have to go from concept to reality once the plant gets built as fast as we can. Ready?"

Brenda Andrews and her roommate Trudy Mac met for lunch back at Kaye's Kafé. They were catching up after Trudy Mac was out for the past two days on one of her food-acquiring expeditions.

"How's the food business going?" Brenda said as they sat down with their sandwiches and Cokes.

Trudy Mac looked downcast. "Not good. I can't seem to make the deals I need to feed this place. My boss - that old goat - sure wasn't happy with me this morning when I gave him my report of how yesterday went. I can't order all the food we need here; it just doesn't exist in this local area. You've been in the lines for food at the stores. If only I could turn all this mud into beef!"

"I sure don't envy you. Ever think about going back to the farm once this war is over?"

"No dice!" Trudy Mac said sharply. "No matter how frustrating this job can be, I'm not going back to that hell-hole of a dump for love nor money."

Brenda was taken back by her roommate's quick reaction to her innocent question. She changed the subject.

"Any chance of getting a different position within food services?"

"Not sure. Besides, this position pays five cents an hour better than your run-of-the-mill girl-slinging-hash job. I've had my fill of that back home, and I'm lucky to have gotten this job."

The girls sipped their Cokes. Trudy Mac asked Brenda, "Say, did I hear right about you and that new guy - Mr. Tall, Dark, and Wrinkled - going out for coffee yesterday?"

"Who needs spies around here when we have *you?*" Brenda laughed. "I swear, not only do the walls have ears, but the roofs have eyes and the doors have tongues to wag! Yes, Dale and I went out for coffee when he had time to kill before getting his briefing in my building. But that's *all,* Miss Trudy Mac!"

Trudy Mac teased. "Don't get all defensive on me now, Brenda. But it does seem like you're reacting from a guilty conscience."

"I surrender," Brenda said. "Okay, the coffee was my idea, all right? Sue me!" They giggled. "And I was right—he does look better when he's all cleaned up and rested. You should have seen the other girls in my office look at him when he walked in."

"Competition, eh?"

"Mostly from that peroxide blonde hussy, Libby Snyder," Brenda said through gritted teeth. "I have to make sure she doesn't sink her claws into Dale, that's for sure."

"If you need me to run interference for you, let me know. I learned how to corral a wild mare before I started school, so I can handle Libby Snyder," Trudy Mac both joked and threatened.

Summer eventually gave way to fall. Rain came often enough to prevent a thorough drying out of the mud, which proved to be the one constant conversation all residents could share with each other. Usually it was not in flattering terms.

Workers were crammed into every available space, be they dormitories, small "hutments" for the black workers, pre-fabricated cemesto houses of different sizes and floor plans, mobile trailers for many in transit and apartments for young married couples. Like any regular town, there were different sections of the Townsite with groups and clusters of like housing and demographics.

Dale discovered the various nooks and crannies of Oak Ridge. Jackson Square was a main hub for social life, with department and specialty stores, restaurants, a rec hall, movie theater, bowling alley, post office, and other necessities for a real town. He and Brenda enjoyed going to all the various eateries and hang outs, enjoying coffee, malts, sandwiches, especially Kaye's famous cheeseburgers. Even amid this surreal world, Brenda proved to be Dale's most pleasant diversion.

Despite getting settled, Dale had still never seen anything like this before. No one had.

Chapter 8-Y-12

The Y-12 plant opened in November 1944. The giant electromagnetic separation plant's purpose was to produce 100 grams of separated uranium-235, which had never been made before. Dale's job prior to the plant opening up was to help work out these details, to go from paper to physical object.

The hallmark of Y-12 were the massive, horseshoe-shaped electromagnets, called "racetracks." The pull from these devices were so strong that everyone who worked around them had to remove all traces of metal from their persons. Even workers with good quantities of metal in their teeth were affected.

There was not a lot of fanfare to open the plant, but General Leslie Groves did come down to Oak Ridge to address the workers who would inhabit this new facility like an army of ants in a hill.

A makeshift wooden podium was erected, with only a microphone stand on it. There were no brass bands, no mayors or dignitaries, no ribbons to be cut. Just the general and a few men with him on the podium.

General Groves was dressed in his simple khaki uniform. Even though he was only his late 40s, Dale could see that the stress of the war and this project had taken its toll on him. Yet he still seemed to have plenty of fire left in his furnace. He had a determination and tenacity about him that reminded Dale of what Brenda said about him earlier when he first got to Oak Ridge - stay out of his way, do not cross him and try to not be noticed. Dale did not want to get on General Groves' bad side. He imagined that General Groves made even Mr. Lohorn quiver with anxiety.

And, Dale noticed, General Groves did like his chocolate, as he was on the portly side. But Dale thought that he needed some outlet to help him with the stress of this massive, never-before-done undertaking. And if some chocolate did the trick, so be it.

To oversee this Clinton Engineering Works project, Dale thought, General Groves must be one heck of a leader, else President Roosevelt would not have picked him. And, all Dale saw was Oak Ridge, not even knowing if there was more to the project than this. If there was more, then it must be other-worldly in its scope and importance. Even though Dale did not like getting displaced from the comforts of his own home and career - no one did - he suddenly felt a great deal of awe and pride at being here, working on this project, during such a critical time in America's history. This time in his life needed to be cherished, not complained about, as it would never happen again. It could never happen again. The opening of this plant would be a watershed moment not only in his life, but for everyone who worked here. He savored this moment, standing in the crowd, listening to General Groves.

Dale found Hal Rainey in the crowd and stood next to him. He could see his engineering coworkers and even Miss Rivera, who still did not look happy.

The general began his remarks without any fanfare or gaudy introductions.

"Good morning, ladies and gentlemen. I can well imagine that you're all glad to finally be getting out of your trailer. So am I. The importance of this new Y-12 plant cannot be overstated. This war effort needs it, and it needs you. As of today, we will be bringing in all the workers needed to run this massive operation. As of today, we will be making all your hard work into a reality, with the goal of ending this terrible war and bringing all our boys home. So, I ask two things of you now: First, it's time to put your hand to the plow and work like never before. Everything up to this moment has merely been a preliminary. If you worked hard before, you must work harder. You must have a sense of urgency about you that you may not have ever had before. Lives depend upon your work, so once you get into this plant, get to it.

"The second thing is, I need your help. I need everyone to stay vigilant and help me keep this not only top secret, but beyond top secret. Our work here is a noble one, but sadly, there are those who want to keep us from achieving our goal. We can't let that happen."

General Groves paused to let this comment sink in.

"This work must reach its conclusion, and the sooner the better for us all. Remember, it's your son or brother or friend or classmate or neighbor or husband that's fighting this war on the front lines. Let's all do our parts and make sure our work here goes on so we can bring our boys home."

41

The crowd murmured its agreement with the general.

"I'm not one for flowery speeches, so I now conclude my remarks. It's time to get to work. Thank you very much."

The crowd politely applauded, not the type one hears when one's team wins in the bottom of the 9th, but a respectful applause. What the general said resonated in their guts and re-emphasized the importance and gravity of this project.

"Well, Hal," Dale spoke up, "I can't imagine knowing what that guy knows. The more I work here, the more incredible it gets."

"I know what you mean. If we didn't know this was critical before, we sure know it now after what General Groves said. I don't think I'd like to be him."

"Me neither. Well, let's get going and move out of our beloved trailer. Can't say I'll miss that thing."

On his way back to the Y-12 trailer, Dale stopped by the post office to check his mail. He had received a note from Brenda:

Will be moving over to your place. Done with pushing papers in Administration #1! Hope to see you around the plant. Together we'll end the war and save the world - ha!

Dale found out Brenda's new job would be working on the massive calutron machines in the Alpha section of the facility. She and a slew of other young women would sit in front of the rows of calutrons and record the data from the mass spectrometer every 15 minutes, as well as make any adjustments to keep the machines within the tolerance limits they were given.

Even though this work seemed tedious and monotonous to others, to Brenda, this would be exciting, as she was now on the "front lines" of this work in Oak Ridge. None of the ladies knew what the other one next to her was doing in terms of what numbers they were recording, what dial they had to turn to comply, or what the desired outcome of all this was.

Brenda's supervisor was Mr. Frank Sweeney, a short, chubby, balding man who habitually wore bow ties (did not dangle in the water fountains, he said), who was pleasant enough but devoid of much personality. The constant hum of the calutrons kept all extraneous conversation at a minimum. They were given good enough breaks and had a rotation scheduled whereby one girl on break would have her calutron temporarily covered by another girl who's only job was to rotate amongst the regulars. She had a higher clearance than the regular worker, as she saw the others' numbers and figures.

Dale's and the other engineers' preliminary work all the months preceding the opening of Y-12 led to the desired information that each calutron was supposed to monitor and achieve. His new work space was in a wing of the plant that now collated and compiled the data for the next level of review, again, not knowing what the final product was supposed to be or how their information figured into it. But that was the nature of work in Oak Ridge - they only knew their jobs at their level of clearance and need to know.

Soon after moving into the new plant, Dale was at Miss Rivera's desk. He spotted a young, slender man with a camera strapped around his neck passing by. Seeing someone taking pictures in a top-secret facility, let alone a top-secret town, rattled the physicist.

"Who's that?"

"Don't know his name, but unbelievably, he's cleared to do this," Miss Rivera replied. "I know it sure looks strange when we're not even allowed to *talk* about our work, and we see this guy taking pictures. I guess the brass figured that someone had to record all this work for posterity, and I guess it's him."

"I'll never figure this place out," Dale concluded, shaking his head.

Chapter 9-Anomalies

Dale worked in close proximity with two other engineers in the Y-12 trailer: Art Rossi from the University of Chicago and Louis "Big Lou" Cunningham from a laboratory near Livermore, California. Big Lou was only five feet four inches tall, but he had a head quite large enough to warrant his nickname.

It was not long after moving into the plant that Dale received the data from a certain bank of calutron machines. He examined the numbers and data carefully. Something did not seem right. It was almost unnoticeable, but there were some minute variations from what he had seen before in prior readings. All Dale could see were the numbers from the calutrons assigned to him, not the others that Art or Big Lou saw.

Dale was concerned. The figures the calutrons produced directly affected the racetrack electromagnets. That, in turn, affected the production of the separated uranium-235. A deviation, or error, from the calutrons was critical.

He left his desk and sought out his supervisor, Hal Rainey, the only person to whom he was supposed to dialog about work.

"Say, Hal," Dale said, "I know we don't have a lot of history with the calutrons and the racetracks, but I was going over the numbers today and something doesn't seem to be right."

"Let me see what you've got there."

Dale handed his paperwork to Hal. He scrutinized the data.

"I'm not seeing anything wrong," he said.

"Are you sure? I'm positive this stuff doesn't square with what I've seen before."

"That may be, but remember that you only see your piece of the pie. When I put this side-by-side with what Art and Lou show me, it looks like it's in order."

"Are you sure?" Dale repeated.

"Positive. There's nothing wrong here."

Dale was slow to respond. "Well, all right. But I'll keep looking for anything screwy."

"You're right in bringing your concern to me, Dale. I appreciate your diligence, but I wouldn't worry about it. Everything's moving along well."

That ended the conversation. Dale walked back to his station, but not convinced "there's nothing wrong here." Yes, he only saw his little piece of the puzzle, but he had the savvy to know that his little piece had to be exact in order for the whole puzzle to be put together correctly.

On his way back, Dale bumped into Big Lou at a water fountain. Dale stopped, torn between what he thought he knew to be certain and everything he had been told about not talking to anyone else. He decided to take the risk of being the next one tossed out of his room and house and sent back home.

"Say, Lou," he said.

"What's up?" the diminutive engineer looked up from getting his drink.

"I think you need a smoke break."

"I just had one."

"Time for another. Let's walk."

Dale motioned for the confused Big Lou to follow him down the long corridor, eventually bringing him outside to a patio area in the crisp air.

"You gone off your rocker, Dale?" Big Lou asked, pulling out his pack of Camels.

"Keep it down, will you?" Dale ordered. "This is serious."

"What? You gonna propose to Miss Rivera, the original ice berg? Good luck with that."

"Worse than that. Something's not right."

"I'm listening," Big Lou said.

"Just listen. You had better not blab, either. I'm taking a big risk in even talking to you, but I just told Hal, and I didn't like how it went."

Big Lou took a long drag on his cigarette as Dale collected his thoughts. At five feet four inches, Lou was a classic example of the old adage that smoking stunts one's growth.

"We get the daily numbers from the calutrons, right? I get mine and you get yours. Then we have to square all the data with the racetracks to make sure they're in sync so they can ultimately produce the 235. Have you ever noticed anything squirrelly with your figures?"

Big Lou thought. "Can't say that I have. Oh, wait. There was this one time when I thought the numbers were off a bit, but I couldn't remember what the previous numbers were so I wasn't sure."

"Did you tell Hal about it?"

"Nah, I just figured it was me. My wife back home said I'd forget my head if it wasn't attached to my shoulders."

"All right. But tell you what: if it ever happens again, let me know, okay? Hal told me there wasn't anything to worry about, but I'm not convinced. Let me know if you see anything strange, but don't tell Hal. Got it?"

Big Lou did not answer right away. He took another long inhale from his Camel.

"Want a piece of advice?" he asked.

"Sure."

"You're the new guy, right? I've been here a lot longer and seen a lot of things. You might just want do your own work and keep to yourself."

"Are you one of those spies I've been told about? You going to turn me in?"

"Didn't say that. All I'm saying is word gets around here fast, and you've just made your first wave. That's all. I gotta get back to work."

Big Lou tossed his butt on the ground and stamped it out. He did not look at Dale as he walked back into Y-12. Dale was left to wonder how to interpret Lou's cryptic warning. If he was not one of the "bad guys" who might turn him in, was he one of the "good guys?" What did he mean, he had "seen things?" What kind of things?

Dale was stumped at seeing his effort to do good work and be on the up-and-up be met with not only his supervisor telling him it was nothing, but a co-worker advising him to keep to himself. It did not add up.

Shaking his head, there was not anything more the physicist could do except go back to work. As Dale walked past Miss Rivera at her receptionist desk, she handed him a note, written in precise, feminine handwriting.

Tomorrow is Sunday. We're both off. Be outside your house at 9 a.m. I'm going to kidnap you. Ha!

—Brenda

Daniel S. Zulli

Chapter 10-Norris

9 a.m., early December. The Sunday morning sun was bright, hung in a fresh blue sky. Dale could see wisps of breath as he stood outside his home on Outer Drive. The trees have shed their leaves in anticipation of winter. But it was quiet out, a slight pause in Oak Ridge, even though the work never stopped. The faithful were at their various church services at the Chapel On the Hill.

A government staff car pulled up to the house. The stunned look on Dale's face prompted a laugh from Brenda when she rolled down the window.

"Want a lift, sailor?" she said with a musical voice.

Dale was incredulous. "How on earth did you get this thing?"

"Dead men tell no tales, my friend. Get in before they realize I stole it!"

"This isn't going to end well, but if you insist," he groaned, shaking his head.

"Okay," Brenda chuckled, "since I don't want you to have a coronary on me, I did get permission to use this car. Working at the head shed had its perks, you know. My old supervisor's husband is the chief of security. I knew the two of them were taking a bus to Knoxville to go Christmas shopping with a bunch of others, so I asked her, and *voila!* instant car. So, relax already!" Brenda patted Dale on the leg.

"I'll relax just as long as you promise Mr. Lohorn doesn't find out about this. I'm sure he'll find a regulation somewhere that I violated, like, *Riding In a Stolen Staff Car On a Sunday.*"

"My lips are sealed," Brenda agreed, passing her fingers in front of her mouth.

"Okay, so now that I'm not going to pass out, where are we going, O My Kidnapper?"

"To a really lovely spot I've heard about. I packed a lunch. We've both been doing nothing lately except work and sleep, and I thought this would be a good time for a break. I don't think you've come up for air since you got here."

"I guess I could use a good break. Thanks for kidnapping me, even if you did scare me half to death when you pulled up."

"I'll try not to push you over the edge again," Brenda chuckled. "So, for now, sit back and leave the driving to us!" She passed through the Elza Gate and hit the accelerator, pushing Dale back into his seat.

Once leaving the top-secret complex of Oak Ridge, Dale and Brenda were instantly back in rural, eastern Tennessee. There were not any more construction sites, lung-choking dirt, stern-faced MPs,

Daniel S. Zulli

warning signs, ID badges, or military-styled architecture. They saw barns, fields still covered with frost in the shaded areas, pastures, open land, horses, cows and farm houses. Even with the U.S. at war on two fronts, this scene was refreshingly far removed, despite still feeling the effects of the Great Depression in the South. But it was not at war. This was rural America at its purest. Bullets were not flying, bombs were not exploding, men were not crying out in agony for medics. This was where young boys and girls learned how to swim in creeks and play hide-and-seek in cow pastures. Women hung wash on clothes

lines and grandpas took their grandkids with them for rides on the tractor. Dale felt a massive weight leave his body as he breathed all this in. He found beauty in an old barn and fence, even if the farm looked run-down. On the farm, at least, they were thinking about getting the eggs every morning from the hens and making sure all the cows were in the pasture and the fields got plowed and crops harvested at the right time. As important as winning the war was and the work he was doing, this seemed better.

Dale was enjoying being kidnapped, especially by such a charming car thief.

Their drive was Highway 61, twisting and turning northwest of the reservation. About 45 minutes later, Brenda swung the staff car right, coming out from a wooded area, opening into a panoramic view of a massive hydroelectric dam, their road going across the dam with the water to the left and heading toward an emerald green pasture.

"Wow! This is beautiful. What is this place?" Dale asked in awe.

"Norris Dam. This just opened up about eight years ago. This was a T.V.A. project to help bring water conservation to this area. It's like Oak Ridge in the sense that before this existed, only famers were here. But from what I was told, this area flooded all the time, or else there was no water if there was a drought. So, this dam was built to make sure the right amount of water got here. Isn't it nice?"

"Sure is," Dale agreed. "Where are we going?"

"Across and down there," Brenda answered.

She drove the staff car across the dam and took the road down to the open pasture area. They could see an old water wheel, still turning. Parking the sedan, Dale and Brenda got out of the car. She took the basket of food out from the back seat while Dale got the blanket, spreading it in the warm sunshine.

"Does Trudy Mac know you took some of her hard-gotten food out of Oak Ridge? She might not like that!" Dale warned, laughing.

"She'll get over it," Brenda replied. "I just won't go and announce I did this at the A & P. Those women are out for blood there!"

"Let's see now..." Dale calculated, "so far today you've stolen a government vehicle and food from a top-secret installation. I promise to come and visit you in prison."

"And with your history of sticky fingers, I figure we'll *both* be making license plates!" Brenda was hard to gain an advantage on.

"I give up - you win!" Dale felt like he was back in Kaye's Kafé all over again, being mercilessly ribbed by this delightful and enchanting young lady. He was glad to be on her good side. Just being in her company was a wonderful experience.

"Let's get comfortable and eat all this evidence before we get caught with the goods, shall we?" Brenda invited.

Sitting down and breaking out the food, Dale said, "Works for me. This all looks great. Say, I know you probably don't want to talk about work in such a gorgeous setting like this, but how have things been ?"

"Hectic but good," Brenda replied. "I like this a whole lot more than pushing papers in Admin 1. I feel like this is really contributing to the war effort. Hey, I almost forgot: Mr. Sweeney, the big boss floor manager, asked me to be one of his mini-floor managers to run a bunch of calutrons and the girls who work them. He said he had too much to worry about to run all the various sections of calutron bays. He's making these new positions, and I guess he thought since I'm older than most of those girls and have a degree, I would be one of them."

"That's swell. I'm sure you'll do great there when you're not stealing pencils from him."

"Watch it, buster. I don't think you want to declare war on me, now do you?"

"I surrender before it even starts!" Dale laughed.

"Accepted. So, how's things in your part of the plant?"

"Good, I think." Dale took a bite of the tuna sandwich Brenda had made and packed.

"What does that mean?"

"I got some funny numbers the other day from the calutrons. These numbers impact the racetrack magnets and their production of our product. I brought this to my supervisor's attention and he didn't think anything of it. Then I went against the rules and talked to one of my co-workers about it and he basically warned me to mind my own business."

"That doesn't sound good," Brenda said. "Did he tell you this to threaten you or to keep you from getting in trouble?"

"Not sure. Maybe a little bit of both."

They ate their picnic lunch in silence, digesting not only their food but this revelation.

"Do you think you made a mistake in looking at these calutron numbers?" Brenda asked.

"No. Even though I'm the new guy at all this, I guarantee I'm right," Dale responded.

"What are you going to do about it?"

"Just sit tight and watch for now. But - I just thought of this - since you're going to be Mother Hen to a bay of calutrons, and the girls who run them, why don't you keep a sharp eye out for any hanky-panky? Let me know if you see anything wrong or smell a rat, or anything."

Brenda lit up. "Sure thing! I'm all for getting as close to the front lines as I can. I guess I'm just a frustrated soldier at heart."

"Well, just don't try and win any medals, okay? I didn't like being warned by Big Lou, and I sure don't want you getting the works too. Deal?"

"Cross my heart," Brenda motioned an X over her heart. "I'll be the absolute angel that I am."

"Yeah, an angel who steals food and cars."

"Okay, buster! You're going to walk back to Oak Ridge if you make one more crack about my car!"

Finishing their lunch, Dale said, "Speaking of heading back, we should be going. I don't want to get my pay docked because I'm having too much fun."

The drive back was quiet. Dale enjoyed the crisp, fresh air and peaceful surroundings. This was his first time out of Oak Ridge since he arrived in August. He did not realize how much he needed this break. Plus, he always enjoyed being with Brenda.

Finally, this delightful girl from Cincinnati broke the silence.

"When do you think this will all end, Dale? And what do you think about all that we're doing here? Strange, isn't it? We don't even know what we're doing, but it's supposed to help end the war."

"I wish I knew. We all want this thing to end, and for our boys to come home. Are you going back to Ohio once the war is over?"

"Don't know. Not sure. Oak Ridge has become a regular town, not just some Army outpost in the middle of nowhere, so who knows? Maybe I'll just stay here and grow old while I'm twirling dials on a calutron. You going back up to MIT?"

"That would seem logical, even though I don't know if I'll get hired up there again. I'm sure some up-and-comer has taken my position. Maybe I'll just stay here and flip hamburgers in Kaye's Kafé once it's over."

"Then maybe you can work off the glass you stole! Ha!" Brenda whacked him on the leg, then gunned the staff car, pushing Dale back in his seat. When she was not being delightful, Brenda was almost infuriating with her teasing. But Dale loved it.

They approached the Elza Gate slowly and deliberately, third in a line of cars to enter the reservation. Folks who went off the reservation this Sunday were returning. The bus line was full, as usual.

They handed their credentials to the MP, who looked them over carefully in their staff car, an unusual sight, especially with a beautiful, civilian young lady at the wheel.

But since their ID badges were in order, he let them through, even if he thought something was not right.

"Bet that made his day," Brenda chuckled.

"Yeah," Dale agreed. "He probably didn't think you looked like an Army colonel."

"Maybe I am but just undercover!"

"Take me home, before I call the MPs to take you away to the funny farm. You're nuts!" Dale laughed and gave *her* a whack on the leg.

Brenda pulled up to his home on Outer Drive. It had been a good day, despite some moments of seriousness and introspection.

"Thanks for the kidnapping, Brenda, even if I am now your partner in crime in stealing a staff car and government food," Dale said.

"Aw, I think we'd look cute in matching prison stripes," Brenda teased.

"Just as long as I get a matching neck tie for evening wear. See you around."

"Ciao!" Brenda laughed and gunned the engine, kicking up dust and rocks as she peeled away. Dale shook his head at this beautiful spitfire from Cincinnati.

Going inside, Dale saw Bob O'Neil sitting in the small living room, reading the sports page and listening to music on the radio.

"Back from your little excursion?" he asked.

"Yeah. It was fun. We went out to some place that had a really nice dam and we had a picnic. She is quite a gal, that's for sure. But I'm going to lay down for a bit and take a nap."

"If my radio is too loud, let me know," Bob said. "Oh, hey - when I came back from lunch, there was an envelope with your name on it tacked to the front door. I put it on your dresser."

"Thanks. Who's it from?"

"Don't know. All it had was your name on the outside."

Going into his room, Dale found the envelope. It simply read, "Dr. Hargrowe" on the outside. Opening it, the note only had two typed-written words on it:

BE CAREFUL

Dale's good day instantly turned bad. His mind reeled. Dale had only told two people: Hal Rainey and Lou Cunningham. Did Big Lou turn him in for talking? He did say that news travels fast in Oak Ridge. Did someone overhear either conversation? Was this a warning to keep him safe or was it a threat?

The bottom line was, someone knew something. They knew *he* knew something, and things could get worse before they got better. How much so, Dale had no idea.

The only thing he could do now, he thought, is to carry on like nothing had happened, minding his Ps and Qs along the way. He would have to both play it cool but be extra-alert, watching for clues as to who did what and why, while at the same time pretend to just mind his own business like he had been told to do.

Lastly, Dale knew he could not tell Brenda this. He wondered if he should not have asked her to help with the surveillance on his behalf. If he were being threatened, that was one thing. He sure did not want Brenda threatened as well.

It was maddening to not know who the good guy was and who was the bad guy was, if there were any. Maybe the same person was both.

Dale took off his shoes and shirt and laid down. All the cool air and sunshine had made him sleepy. He thought of Brenda and how wonderful this day had been. How he had come to Oak Ridge against his will but had found such a wonderful person. But he was not expecting to find this dilemma in a top-secret war project, either.

He fell asleep.

Chapter 11-Christmas

Dale had not gone to church since he was a teen, and even that was against his will. The only real reason he went at all was to visit with a cute blonde he had met. But since she rarely came herself, church attendance did not serve him well.

But this was Christmas Eve, in an another-worldly setting of a hybrid military base and a town that did not exist, but was home to 70,000 people. And Dale was far from his home.

Therefore, attending a church service on Christmas Eve seemed the logical thing to do.

Brenda had attended the earlier Mass and had gotten her yearly obligation out of the way.

The Chapel On the Hill had opened for business in October 1943. It was built to support the various religious needs of Oak Ridge's population. Local clergy of all flavors were contracted to lead the faithful in their different traditions.

There were several Protestant ministers who were scheduled on a rotation, one of whom being Pastor Mike Miller, a mid-30s man who normally led the flock of the Maryville Fellowship Church, a non-denominational congregation. He had the Christmas Eve service at 8 p.m. that Dale attended.

Dale sat in the back, not wanting to stand out or be noticed. He felt awkward. He did not know what to do or if he would stand out due to his inexperience in all things church. Dale was able to follow along in the traditional Christmas hymns.

He looked around and recognized several people from around town. Mrs. Taylor from the women's department at Miller's Department Store was at the piano. The choir had several familiar faces in it Dale had seen before.

It came time for Pastor Miller to deliver his Christmas message.

"Good evening, everyone, and Merry Christmas. The light snowfall outside sure makes it feel like Christmas, doesn't it? I'm very honored to share this time with you."

Dale noticed that the minister did not have fire and smoke pouring out of his nostrils and seemed pleasant enough.

Daniel S. Zulli

"My message tonight comes from the book of Isaiah, where the prophet says that God 'shall judge among the nations, and shall rebuke many people: and they shall beat their swords into plowshares, and their spears into pruning hooks: nation shall not lift up sword against nation, neither shall they learn war anymore.'

"This famous passage is very timely for us. The world has been at war since 1939, America since 1941. Even still, on this Christmas Eve, combatants on both sides are putting aside hostilities so that they can celebrate the birth of our Savior.

"The past few years have been hard. I'm sure I speak for many here when I say we are tired of war. But that begs the question: When will it end? Not just this war, but all wars. And, if it will end, who will end it? Us? The Brits? The Russians? The Germans?"

Dale's interest was piqued, as the world war was the reason he was in a town built just because of the war. He wanted to hear what Pastor Miller had to say.

"This passage from Isaiah is famous because it talks about that glorious time when there will be no more war between the nations, as their instruments of war will be turned into instruments of peace.

"But how will this happen? Let me turn to Isaiah chapter 9. This well-known Christmas passage tells us that God will have a Son - the Wonderful Counselor, the Prince of Peace. This Son will someday rule from Jerusalem when He returns, and then, Isaiah tells us, there will be no end to the increase of His government, and He will reign with perfect righteousness.

"So, when I put these two chapters of Isaiah together, it tells us that only God's Son - Jesus - will be able to bring about the conditions whereby nation will no longer war against nation, because He will be ruling instead of sinful men. I hate to burst your bubble, folks, but mankind will never bring about peace on earth and good will toward men. Oh, we can do this on a small, temporary scale, but nothing permanent or lasting. Only God can, and Jesus is the Mighty God. And it's His birth we will celebrate tomorrow. It's His first coming we honor. And it's His second coming we long for, for then, and only then, will nation no longer lift up sword against another nation. Amen.

"Would you all please stand and join the choir as they lead us in *Hark! The Herald Angels Sing?*"

Dale stood with everyone else, but his thoughts were not on the hymn. Try as he could, he could not ever remember hearing such a timely and relevant sermon before in his meager church days. What he remembered were light, pithy stories that did not apply to anything. But now, this preacher just hit him between the eyes with a message from the ancient Bible that could have been ripped from the day's headlines.

It also made him aware of a gnawing in his soul. Dale had heard from God this peaceful Christmas Eve, something he had never experienced before.

As the faithful filed out of the humble Chapel, Dale stood back so he could meet this young minister who seemed so in touch with the times.

When the crowd had thinned out, Dale ambled up to Pastor Miller.

"Excuse me," he said. "My name's Dale Hargrowe, one of the workers here. I'm afraid to admit I'm not much of a church-goer, but I really liked your message tonight."

"Thanks, Dale. I appreciate you being here."

"Say, can we get together sometime when you come back to preach? I'd like to ask you some questions, and also have a good friend of mine maybe attend one of your services with me."

"Sure thing," Mike said. "Just keep tabs on the preaching rotation and get with me after the service. I'm done with my own church by the time I come here so I'm free."

With the clouds having cleared after the snow flurry, the stars were out and the temperature was dropping. On his walk to the bus stop, Dale put his hands in his topcoat pocket to keep them warm. It was then that he felt the tiny box he had placed there but had forgotten about.

"What a dope!" he said, smacking himself on the forehead.

Instead of taking the bus back to the stop closest to Outer Drive, Dale road the transit as far as the women's dormitory area. He hopped off and strode swiftly up to Brenda's dorm, the fresh-fallen snow crunching beneath his feet. Even though Oak Ridge ran 24 hours a day, it was quiet this night. Most were in, enjoying the warmth and whatever coziness they could while missing their former homes.

Reaching the dorm, Dale realized he did not know how to contact Brenda. Males were not appreciated in and around the women's dorms. Dale walked at a respectable distance, analyzing the situation. Finally, he saw a middle-aged woman in the first-floor day room, the dorm mom, whose job it was to keep the roosters away from the hen house.

He tapped lightly on the window, not wanting to startle her.

She did not look pleased when she opened the window.

"Young man! What are you doing out there?"

"So sorry to bother you, ma'am," Dale responded in his most innocent voice, "but I'd sure be grateful if you could contact a girl who lives on the second floor for me so I could give her a Christmas present. Her name is Brenda Andrews and she's in room 212."

Daniel S. Zulli

The dorm mom's visage softened a bit. "I'll see if she's in." She closed the window. Dale could see her going over to a switchboard-looking device and flip a switch. It was getting very cold outside, he thought. Dale blew hot air into his hands and stamped his feet.

Finally, Brenda came down, wearing her top coat over her pajamas.

Meeting him at the front door, Brenda said, "Dale Hargrowe! What on earth are you doing out here? Building snowmen?"

"I think all the snowmen went inside. It's too darn cold out here even for them. But, hey, I just came from Christmas Eve service at the Chapel, and I heard a really good message. I'd like you to come with me sometime to hear this guy. Then I asked him if I could visit with him after the service, so we could talk about things. I'd like you to do that too. Maybe we could all get lunch together."

"Uh, sure. That'll be fine. Is that what you got me out of my nice warm bed for?"

"I forgot again!" Dale said, slapping himself a second time on the forehead. "I came here to give you this little present and to wish you a Merry Christmas. Merry Christmas. Open it."

Dale handed Brenda the little package. He looked at her in the glow of the dorm window. She looked radiant in the soft light. Brenda wore little to no makeup, but did not need any. She was just an incredible example of femininity.

"I got it at Henebry's Jewelry Store. The pickings were pretty slim by the time I got there, but I hope you like it."

Brenda unwrapped a small bracelet with twelve stones on it, one for each month of the year. Her eyes widened.

"Oh, Dale! It's beautiful! Thank you so much!"

"Well, I just think the prettiest gal in Oak Ridge should have the prettiest bracelet. And I didn't even steal it!"

Brenda laughed and hit Dale in the shoulder. "You're a nut! But thanks so much, Dale. I'll be the envy of every girl in the dorm."

"Well, I need to go now. Even though it's Christmas tomorrow, it's a Monday and I have to work. Good night."

Dale reached down and gave Brenda a quick peck on her red cheek, then turned and walked down to the bus stop, leaving Brenda speechless and holding her present.

Dale had heard a good message at Chapel and had given his present to a wonderful girl. For the moment, he was not missing being back home in Massachusetts.

Chapter 12-Innocence

During a lunch break in early January, Dale made his way over to a small sandwich and beverage counter in Y-12. He saw the main receptionist for his area, Miss Rivera, sitting alone on a stool, working on a malt in stony solitude. Dale did not recall ever seeing her smile. She was all business, which did not seem to include any fun or levity.

Dale bought a Coke and approached her. "Hey, there, Miss Rivera, mind if I join you for a few minutes?"

"Suit yourself," Miss Rivera replied in her usual non-friendly manner.

"Thanks. Say, I haven't really ever had the chance to talk to you before. I would imagine you've been here since day one. Where did they shanghai you from?"

"I was working at the main Project office in Manhattan," Miss Rivera answered. "I'm from New York City; all my relatives are up there, and I was able to get a job in this deal when it came available. Then they handed me a train ticket and told me to report here within one week."

Dale nodded his head. "Sounds familiar. I imagine that coming down here was a shocker to you too. How do you like being here?"

"I hate it," she said, straight-faced, with brutal honesty and without any attempt at subtlety. "I'm from the big city and now I'm down here in this cow pasture with the Hatfields and McCoys, drowning in either dust or mud. I had a nice apartment and now I'm in the women's dorm with a roommate who talks nonstop when she's awake, and snores louder than these bulldozers when she's asleep. I used to go out to wonderful night clubs and listen to the great bands and dance all night. Now, all I can do is go to the rec hall in Jackson Square and listen to the bands on a jukebox while fending off lonely GIs."

Dale easily saw why Miss Rivera was never in a good mood. The big city girl had her life interrupted by the war as he did, only she did not take it as well. He could also see that any attempt to warm her was futile.

"As soon as they tell me I can go, I'm on the first train north. Any other questions for me, Dr. Hargrowe?" Miss Rivera challenged.

"No. I...uh...just wanted to come over and say hi. I guess you'd like to finish your malt without me bugging you, so I'll just be on my way now. Have a...uh...good day, Miss Rivera." Dale sheepishly ended their conversation, glad to get out with his hide.

Daniel S. Zulli

He picked up his Coke and made a hasty retreat. This would be his one-and-only attempt at getting on the good side of Miss Regina Rivera. Dale concluded that she did not have one to get on.

As Dale assumed a safe distance from the stern receptionist, Trudy Mac entered the snack area, carrying a full complement of papers in a huge binder, and a clip board. A pencil was behind her ear, poking out of her strawberry blonde hair.

"Hey, there, Dale!" she called out. "I saw you sitting over there with Miss Sunshine. Whatcha doing?"

"Taking a little break before getting back to my numbers," Dale replied. "Yeah, Miss Rivera is a real charmer. She got the short end when they hauled her down here. She's our main secretary. What are you up to, Trudy Mac?"

"Making my rounds. I have to go into every place that serves or sells food products, take an inventory of what they've used in the past week, then order what they need. Then, I compile it all, try to go into all the local towns and see if I can beg, borrow or steal from them to keep this place from rioting. I swear, Dale, these wives here are out for blood - mostly mine - if they can't get what they want for their houses or cafes. I'm sure you've seen the lines at the A & P and the Tulip Town Market. You'd swear the front lines of the war were in the grocery stores!"

"Yes, from what I've seen, it's every man or woman for themselves in those places. But it seems you're the person to make it all work, somehow. You have a lot of contacts in the surrounding towns?"

"Yeah, and they all run when they see me coming!" They both shared a laugh.

"Well," Trudy Mac said, "I've got an army to feed and you have a war to win, so it's time for me to get on back to the supply room. I should have been issued a GI helmet for this job. Wish me luck."

"Will do," Dale nodded. "Be careful out there."

That night, Dale sat in the living room of his house. His housemate, Bob O'Neil, sat in the other chair, reading the *Knoxville New Sentinel*. Dale composed a note to Dr. Tupper back home.

Dear Dr. Tupper,
    Sorry I haven't written for a while. Suffice it to say, we've been very busy. We're moving right along. On another side note, I've met a very nice girl down here, a real peach.
    But this place is really hopping. Hopefully we'll be able to wrap things up soon and come home. Maybe I can convince my new friend to dump the Cincinnati Reds and become a Red Sox fan. I hope you're well up there and that you've gotten top dollar for my old office if you've rented it out. Take care and God bless. (Something we all could need.)
                    Your friend, Dale

59

Chapter 13-Calutrons

Brenda Andrews was diligent at her new job as floor manager for her bay of calutrons. During each shift, the ladies waited for Brenda to give them their forms to fill out to record the various readings the machines produced. *Gosh, they look young,* Brenda thought. Most of them looked like they should be in their high school gym, preparing for a prom or dance, instead of doing this top-secret work, in front

of humming, stark cold machines with blinking lights and twitching dials; either that, or safe at home with perhaps a baby or two in tow. But they were game, as she was when she had to man her machine before becoming a supervisor.

Brenda arrived at one young lady's station, a buxom girl with a mound of fiery red curls on her head and a noticeably snug blouse that was unbuttoned one button too low.

When Brenda handed the red-head her paperwork, she was blunt. "Hike it up another notch there, honey," she said. "Save all that for when you're with the GIs in the rec hall." She left her with, "And make sure the clothes fit tomorrow, too."

Brenda was not there for a personality contest. No wonder Mr. Sweeney wanted her to work the floor and supervise the other women. She was perfect for the job. She imagined that his bow tie would shoot off his neck if he had seen this exchange.

The calutron girls did their work, dutifully recording the data every quarter hour and making all the necessary adjustments on the dials. Brenda collected the forms from her charge of girls and funneled them up to Mr. Sweeney at the end of the shift for review and processing.

Maggie Hancock, from Asheville, North Carolina, was one of the young women who would rotate among the calutron bays and spot the other girls so they could take their breaks. They were all on a rotating break schedule. Maggie had a higher clearance which would allow her to see all the other girls' data on their calutrons, something that the single calutron worker was not allowed to do.

In addition to Maggie, there were other rotating girls who did the same thing in the bays assigned to them. This way, there was the 24-hour per day, seven days per week manning of all the calutron machines and bays. This work never took time off.

During Brenda's breaks, she met the other women in her position. They tended to be a little bit older, some married or with more education or work experience. This was Oak Ridge's version of Rosie the Riveter - women who did not work in smelters, or factories, or munitions assembly lines, but who manned this newfound technology in a closed, top secret environment. They were trying to win the war with their 100% effort.

In late January, Maggie Hancock came to Brenda one afternoon as she was making her rounds in Brenda's bay, cornering her away from the rest of the girls.

"Say, Brenda," Maggie started, "is there someplace we can talk?"

"Sure thing, Maggie. Is there something wrong? You look a little worried."

"We need to go somewhere, please.

Brenda's first thought was that Maggie had one of those "girl issues" that many times happen, such as a roommate problem, a guy problem, some health concern - any number of which could cause her to look distracted and want to talk.

They moved out of earshot of the other women.

"Okay, Maggie, what's up?" Brenda asked.

"Something's not right," Maggie said.

"How do you mean?"

"I've been noticing that some of the numbers on a couple of calutrons aren't looking like what I've usually seen."

Brenda looked concerned. "How so?"

"I know what they should be reading by now. One machine in your bay, one in the next bay, and two in some of the other bays have shown numbers that just aren't right, and I don't like it."

"Can you name the girls who run those calutrons?" Brenda asked.

"I don't know," Maggie offered. "I've moved around so much and there have been so many girls in and out on different shifts, that I'm not sure I can. I've filled in for Sally McBride on the swing shift when she was sick, and that was in her bay, not yours. But with all the 24-hour operations, I can't keep track of each girl who works with which machine."

"I need to ask you again, directly: Are you sure what you saw isn't normal for that machine?"

"Look, Brenda," Maggie rebutted, "I've done this enough to know what to expect. Even though the calutrons are different, I know what each one I've worked at should read. It's like this: you were a school teacher, right?"

"Right," Brenda agreed.

"And how many kids did you have in your class?"

"25, give or take."

"And they were different, correct?"

"Correct," Brenda agreed again.

"My point is: each kid had a personality normal for him or her, even though they were all different. So, if a normally outgoing kid suddenly became quiet and withdrawn, you'd know that he'd be acting different, even though another kid might be quiet and withdrawn in his normal state, right?"

"Okay, I see your picture. You know what's normal for each calutron you've worked, even though each of the machines are different and have their own tolerance levels. Am I getting it?"

"Bingo," Maggie said. "I know these machines like you knew your kids, and I can tell you some of them haven't acted normally on too many occasions for me to like it."

As she was talking to Maggie, Brenda was thinking in the back of her mind about what Dale had asked her to watch out for - anything out of the ordinary that might be suspicious enough to warrant investigating. She knew she would have to tell Dale about this. What *he* would do about this new information, Brenda was not sure. The nagging problem was that this new news did not smell right; there can only be so many "coincidences" before they become a pattern.

Brenda was silent as she tapped her pencil against her chin, deep in thought. Finally, she said, "Okay, I tell you what. Try and recall the calutron number and the dates you noticed the variations in the data, as best you can, and give that to me."

"What are you going to do?" Maggie asked.

"I have to tell someone who might be interested in this new development. I don't like it. But you have to do two things: One, keep quiet. I don't want you involved in anything that could cause you trouble. The second is to keep your eyes peeled if it happens again, and that includes which calutron and who works on it the most."

"Is all this bad?"

"Not sure. Maybe. Maybe not. But I would rather be safe than sorry. There's more to this than I can tell you right now, Maggie. But you did right in telling me. Is there anything else?"

"This is enough for me! I'm really worried."

"Just go about your business and keep me informed of any more strange scoop. Okay?"

"Got it."

"Okay, get back to work so no one gets the heebie-jeebies from seeing us talk like this."

Brenda had to get word back to Dale. She had not seen him in a while due to the non-stop pace they were working. She fired off a note to him and gave it to Mr. Sweeney to pass along.

Once Brenda completed her shift, she dragged herself to her room, feeling drained physically and emotionally. She found Trudy Mac on her bed, reading a movie magazine.

"Hey, there," Trudy Mac called, when Brenda opened the door. "How was work in the salt mines today?"

Brenda was slow in replying. "Good...interesting." She was deep in thought and not her usual vivacious self. Even when she was tired after a long day, Brenda was always in an upbeat mood, with a joke or quip on the tip of her tongue. She was not that way tonight.

"Hmmm," Trudy Mac said. "If I didn't know better, I'd say you have something going on. Something happen between you and Dale?"

"No," Brenda replied, "although I almost wish that were the case. That I could fix."

"Spill it. What's going on?"

"I have to be careful with this..." Brenda was hesitant to say anything, as that was against everything she had been trained not to do. But since she knew Trudy Mac so well, she could trust her.

"But..." she continued, "some strange things have been happening at work and one of my girls brought to my attention today."

"Wow. Like what?"

"Some of our machines have been making really offbeat readings that aren't in the normal range they should be." She felt this was nebulous enough to not be breaking her security clearance.

"For real? Is that bad?" Trudy Mac asked.

"Not sure. Could be. I don't know yet."

"What are you going to do about it?"

"Dale had some strange things happen to him too, a little while back. He told me to let him know if anything unusual happened to me as well, in my area of Y-12. So, I have to get in touch with him. I think he'll have to let someone above him or us know about it."

"When are you going to see him?"

"I wrote him a note saying tomorrow night. That gives him time to make any adjustment in his schedule to meet with me."

"Where will this meeting be at?" Trudy Mac asked.

"I told him to meet me at the Grove. They're showing the new Rita Hayworth movie, *Tonight and Every Night*. This way, we can visit in the dark and connect the dots on this stuff."

"That's a good plan. If nothing else, you two Charlie Chans will have a nice night out. Looks like you could use some R & R to take your mind off things."

"Yeah," Brenda agreed, "I could use a good laugh. I hope this thing goes away. I'm going to bed. My head hurts."

Brenda arrived at the theater early. She felt like she was walking on pins and needles. She had barely slept the night before, and work was a blur. She went through the motions, but her mind was so distracted she had a hard time focusing, and was worried that the other girls would recognize she was not her usual self. Brenda wondered if she was being watched by whomever or *whoms*-ever might be responsible for tampering with the calutrons in order to get the false readings. She did not like this at all. She had not expected to actually see anything amiss, that Dale's asking her to was pretty much hypothetical. This had unnerved her.

Where is he? Brenda's mind demanded.

When Dale showed up a good 10 minutes before the movie started, Brenda was ready to go off like a firework.

"It's about time!" she hissed, controlling the urge to yell.

"What?" Dale protested. "We have plenty of time to get our tickets and get a seat." He could see she was perturbed at something.

"I've gotten our tickets. Let's go." Brenda grabbed his arm and almost dragged him through the turnstile into the theater.

"Over here," she said, pulling him to the uppermost and deserted corner of the theater.

"Why do you want to sit way up here?" Dale asked. "There are plenty of good seats down there," he said, pointing to the middle front of the theater.

"Sit," Brenda ordered.

"Okay, okay. I'm sitting." Dale gave up. "Now, do you want to tell me what's going on before I call the padded wagon on you?"

"Quit clowning, and keep your voice down," Brenda warned. "This is serious." The newsreels came on, giving the latest news on the war effort, and made enough background noise so Brenda could whisper without being overheard.

"Do you remember telling me about that monkey business at your job with someone changing your numbers to something else?"

"Yeah, when we went on that picnic."

"Has anything happened since then?" Brenda cross-examined.

"In fact, yes. I told Hal Rainey about it."

"And do you remember telling me to watch out for anything out of the ordinary?"

"Sure do. Has something been going on?"

"Yes. One of the girls under me, who floats the floor and fills in at all the calutrons to break the other girls, came to me the other day and told me she's been getting some goofy readings on a lot of the machines, numbers that couldn't happen without someone intentionally tampering with the dials to produce phony readings. She said it's happened too much to be just a freak accident."

Daniel S. Zulli

"And you are sure you can trust her to report this accurately?"

"Yes. She's been very reliable and swore she knows these machines and what they should be reading, just like you know."

Dale was silent, thinking.

"What do you think?" Brenda asked.

"I think all this adds up to something not good. I'm worried about someone - or *someones* - is trying to sabotage what we're trying to accomplish here. I don't know if it's an enemy spy or an inside job. If the calutrons are being tampered with to produce fake numbers, then the end product will be bad, or delayed, or incomplete or just wrong, and won't work. I've heard talk of 'the gadget,' and all this makes me think someone doesn't want this gadget to work. He or she is tampering with our work to produce false information that would make the gadget defective or ineffective. You were right in telling me."

Brenda clutched Dale's arm and drew close to him, not in the usual girl-boy way at the movies, but in a scared, frightened way.

"I can't believe this is happening," she murmured. "And I'm scared. We were warned about blabbing our work to those who didn't need to know, but that was to people on *our* side, trying to keep this work safe. I never thought we would have enemies here, trying to mess up our war effort and everything we're trying to do!" She squeezed his arm tighter.

"I know. This is too far-fetched to comprehend. But my only conclusion is the bad guys have infiltrated Oak Ridge, and now we're both involved in this mess." For a moment, Dale thought that this wouldn't have happened had he stayed at MIT in nice, quiet Cambridge, Massachusetts. He did not ask to be thrust into this project in the first place, and he sure did not ask to be privy to a potential spy ring with international implications. Finally, he did not ask for, nor did not he want a woman for whom he had fallen hard to be involved with something that might be dangerous. It was bad enough that he might be in danger someway. Dale sure did not like the thought of this wonderful woman next to him being exposed to harm as well.

"Hey," Dale softly said, trying to calm Brenda, "let's finish the movie and try to redeem this night. I'll tell my boss tomorrow that this is getting bad. But let's enjoy ourselves tonight, shall we?"

He looked down his right shoulder at her. She was not moving, her head resting against his upper arm. Dale could see her shoulders move up and down slightly with precise timing. Since Brenda had been so keyed up and stressed the night before and all day, she had fallen asleep in this dark theater, too weary to fight it anymore.

Chapter 14-Alarm

The next day, before he went to Hal Rainey, Dale swung by to ask Big Lou Cunningham one last time if he had seen anything amiss and finally confront Art Rossi if he had noticed anything. He was taking a risk by questioning his fellow engineers so openly, but he had no choice.

Both men said that all had been normal, nothing was wrong.

Dale took a deep breath as he approached his supervisor once again to let him know that something with massive implications was going on. No longer could he call these occurrences anomalies. They were not. They were intentional, the end result being to sabotage their work which they believed would end the war. Far too much was at stake, and at the risk of exposing himself and - worse - Brenda, to harm, Dale had to speak up.

As usual, the unfriendly Miss Rivera was manning the pathway to Mr. Rainey.

"I need to see Mr. Rainey as quickly as possible," Dale spoke directly, minus any small talk.

"He'll be back shortly, Dr. Hargrowe," Miss Rivera responded, in her non-pleasant manner. "He's in a meeting with some higher-ups over at X-10. You can wait if you want."

"Thanks. I will."

Dale sat down in the reception area that Miss Rivera controlled. But having his nerves fraught with anticipation and worry, he found himself pacing. He noticed a coffee pot on a counter, but his senses were on high-alert. Artificial stimulants were the last thing he needed. He was deeply worried that he had stumbled upon something that might get very big and very ugly quickly, not to mention risky and dangerous.

"You all right?" Miss Rivera asked. "You look like a cat in a dog pound."

"Me? Oh … yeah, I'm all right. Just have a lot on my mind, that's all." Dale tried to deflect the situation by appearing calmer than he was, but the concerned look on his face betrayed him. "Say, when did you say Mr. Rainey was getting back? I could come back if I need to."

"He'll be here any minute now. Just sit tight and relax." Miss Rivera actually seemed nicer now, noticing that he was unusually keyed up about something. Her voice had a smoother tone to it.

"Thanks. I'll sit down and not wear your floor out," he said, with a slight grin.

Daniel S. Zulli

Even though it took a short twelve minutes for Hal to arrive, to Dale, it seemed like an hour. When Hal came through the door, Dale bolted to his feet.

"Hal! Glad you showed up. I need to speak with you."

"Sure thing, Dale. Come on in. Miss Rivera, unless it's FDR or General Groves - or my wife," he laughed - "hold all my calls."

"What's going on? You look like you've seen a ghost. You're not wanting to quit and go back to MIT, are you?"

"I almost wish it were that simple," Dale responded. "But I'm afraid it's a lot more complicated than that."

"I'm listening."

Dale picked his words carefully. "I tried my best to not imagine the worst. I thought they had been a bunch of random flukes, but not when you add them all up."

Hal was tapping a pencil on his desk, listening to Dale explain. "What kind of 'flukes'?"

"Look, I've already come to you before with something I saw. You said it wasn't anything. But then another person who works with the calutrons had someone come up to her and tell her a bunch of screwy things were happening. And, I've had some anonymous person leave me a warning note at my house, I assume to quit nosing around. Something's going on here, Hal. I think it's an intentional attempt to forge or alter or change our work that would produce a faulty or delayed finished product, I'm assuming on the gadget. Someone, or someones, is intentionally tampering with this work."

Hal Rainey studied his engineer.

"I hear what you're saying," he finally said. "If what you are saying is true, then we have a problem here."

"Right," Dale agreed. "You've got to elevate this as high as you can get it."

"Agreed. Okay, here's what you need to do: Keep this quiet. If word of this gets out, people are going to panic and be so distracted that we'll never get anything done. I'll bring this up to my higher-ups and let them take it from there. What we'll do is work as normal. Don't say anything to spook anyone out. But, we'll keep our eyes peeled and see if we can spot this person or persons who may be doing all this. Let me know if you notice any reoccurrence of this fudging on the data. Sound good?"

"Good deal. Thanks. This has really gotten to me."

"You did the right thing, Dale. Why don't you take the rest of the day off and get some rest? Maybe go bowling or catch a movie or something? I need my best engineer running on all cylinders, okay?"

Chapter 15-Chapel

As Dale stepped out into the crisp winter air, he remembered he wanted to take Brenda to a service pastored by Mike Miller at The Chapel On the Hill. With nothing else to do in terms of solving this mystery of potential sabotage, Dale caught the bus up to the Chapel to see the service schedules and preaching rotation posted on the outside the Chapel.

He was in luck. Mike Miller was up at bat this coming Sunday, at the 11 a.m. non-denominational service. That would give him time to contact his wonderful friend and tell her about the service. Dale would meet her at the Chapel.

The liturgical service was filing out as Brenda got there. She looked sharp and very feminine in her winter coat and hat. She was wearing the bracelet Dale had given her at Christmas. Dale could feel his heart flutter a bit when she walked up to the main doors.

"I've never been to this type of church service," Brenda remarked. "I won't get called out for coming for the first time, will I?"

"Well, if you do, I'm sure I will too," Dale tried to reassure her. "This is new to me as well. But I think you'll like this preacher. He wasn't all hell-fire-and-brimstone at the Christmas Eve service, and I liked how he put things. From the looks of this crowd going in, I think we'll be able to blend and not be noticed as amateurs."

Dale and Brenda recognized some fellow workers in the newly-organized choir, not realizing they were church folk or that they could sing. Other familiar faces were in the congregation. The choir director led them in hymn number 72, *How Firm a Foundation*. Dale and Brenda felt awkward, not knowing it, but by the last verse were able to plug along with the rest.

After a few preliminary announcements, Scripture reading and responsive reading, Pastor Miller strode up to the pulpit with his Bible.

"Good morning, ladies and gentlemen. It is good to see you today on this cold but sunny day. My congregation in Maryville sends their greetings.

"My text today is from the book of Esther, specifically chapter 4, the end of verse 14. Here, Esther's uncle Mordecai tells the young slave girl who had just been appointed queen, and who was about to risk her life trying to save her people, the Jews: 'who knoweth whether thou art come to the kingdom for such a time as this?'

"This is the context: The Jews were in captivity in Persia, under King Xerxes around 465 B.C. Because King Xerxes placed the scheming Haman to a high position, and the Jews did not honor him the way he wanted, Haman tried to get the king to exterminate the Jews. The only problem was, this young Jewish girl, Esther, caught the king's fancy, but he didn't know she was Jewish. So, now, as queen, Esther is about to go into the king's presence, which was only allowed if one had an invite, which she did not have at the time, to plead for her people. Esther realizes that she might lose her life in the process. It is here that Mordecai tells her that she has been placed in this circumstance, at this time, to do a work of God on behalf of her people. She had been placed there 'for such a time as this.'"

Dale looked at Brenda. Having this historical context caused the message to have more meat on it. It was unlike the nondescript sermons and homilies he had heard in his youth.

"My main point is this," Pastor Miller continued. "God is sovereign over the affairs of human history. He has no Plan B. We are not puppets without a free will, but God is sovereign and nothing catches Him off guard. And this includes the good and the bad.

"Take this war, for instance. Did the bombing of Pearl Harbor catch God off guard? No. Take the building up of Oak Ridge. Is this a mistake? No. How about each and every one of you here? Were you planning on spending a winter of 1944/45 in lovely northeastern Tennessee?" Many in the congregation chuckled at that.

"I bet if I were to ask everyone here if a year ago you had thought you would be here, I wonder how many would say 'yes.' And yet here you are, just like Esther - placed in a situation you never imagined in your wildest dreams you would be in. But I say to you, like Uncle Mordecai: Who knows? Maybe God put you here for such a time as this, to do something wonderful for Him."

Dale was paying attention before, but this really caused him to sit up. Not that he felt like a biblical character, but he suddenly identified with Esther in the sense that he was in a strange land similar to hers, and out of all the people in it, only he - with Brenda's help - was aware or interested in some nefarious plot to sabotage the work in Oak Ridge. Was he placed here by God's design, like Esther, to do some work on His behalf, on America's behalf? Was he too here for such a time as this?

The preacher continued.

"What we need to do is be willing to be used by God, even in the seeming smallest of situations, because He has placed us in them. We walk by faith and not by sight, and so it takes faith to understand that God has put us where we are when we are by His providential and sovereign hand. This is God's Plan A for you. He has no Plan B. Sometimes we do not know what the plan is until it is over, but, rest assured, God has a plan and we are all part of the situations in which He has placed us. Trust God to use you. Amen.

"Would you all stand as the choir leads us in *Standing On the Promises,* hymn number 48? Thank you and God bless you."

Dale gave Brenda a quick glance. She looked as stunned as he.

"Wow," Brenda whispered as everyone else sang. "This is new to me."

"Yeah, me too. I need to talk to him some more. Want to invite him to lunch?" Brenda nodded in agreement.

As the congregation was filing out and doing the customary hand-shaking and "Nice sermon, pastor," Dale and Brenda hung back until they could speak with Reverend Miller without a crowd around them.

"Excuse me, Pastor Miller," Dale said. "I don't know if you remember me from the Christmas Eve service, but I talked to you briefly then. I'm Dale, and this is Brenda, the friend I told you about."

"Good to see you again, Dale. And pleased to meet you, Brenda. I'm glad you came today."

"Say, we really enjoyed what you had to say. If you haven't had lunch yet, can we invite you to some of the finest cuisine this side of the Elza Gate? Brenda and I would like to visit with you, as you gave us a lot to think about."

"Sure, I'm all done with church at my place, so I'm game. Where are we going?"

Brenda chimed in, "You have not lived until you've had a cheeseburger from Kaye's Kafé. They're so fresh, the cows are still in back, waiting their turn!"

"How can I turn down an invite like that?" Mike laughed.

Daniel S. Zulli

Chapter 16-Discussion

On the bus ride back down to Area 1, Pastor Miller saw a sign that he hadn't noticed before.

**HOLD YOUR TONGUE
THE JOB'S NOT DONE
SILENCE STILL
MEANS SECURITY**

When the bus stopped near Kaye's Kafé, Brenda announced, "We're here. Fall out!"

Dale grinned at Pastor Miller, as if to silently say, "Yes, she is this vivacious all the time. Get used to it."

Kaye's Kafé, like most every facility in Oak Ridge, was busy non-stop. There was not a time gap between breakfast and lunch, lunch and dinner. Civilians and GIs filled the diner. They were eating whatever their schedule dictated, be it breakfast or a midnight snack. Some were getting off duty, others just coming on shift.

Kaye had different shift supervisors and assistant managers providing oversight around the clock when she was not there. Dale saw that Kaye was working today.

"Hiya, kid," Kaye said to Brenda, then nodding to Pastor Miller, "Who's your friend?"

"This is Reverend Miller, from Maryville. He did the Christmas Eve service and now regularly preaches at the Chapel on the Hill."

"Hi, reverend," Kaye said. "I was at that service. Good to see you again. What will you folks have?"

"Three of your best cheeseburgers and three R.C.s," Dale said.

"Coming right up."

They found a table. There was no such thing as a quiet corner this time of day, so they plunked down at the first available spot.

When the cheeseburgers were ready, Kaye brought them and the Royal Crown Colas to their table, expertly balancing all on a tray. As she sat Dale's drink down before him, her hand lingered noticeably on his glass. She glared down at him and whispered, "Thou shalt not steal."

"What was that for?" Pastor Miller asked.

"Uh...nothing. It's just a...uh...private joke we have between us," Dale answered with a slight red glow to his face. Brenda gave him a polite kick under the table, rubbing it in.

"Tell us about yourself, Reverend Miller," Brenda asked. "You have a family there in Maryville?"

"Call me, 'Mike,'" he said. "No, I don't have a family. Still single, but looking."

"Come to the rec hall any Saturday night, but watch out for Libby Snyder!" Brenda laughed.

"What?" Mike asked, not getting her joke.

Dale cleared his throat, changing the subject.

"Anyway, thanks for coming with us to lunch. Brenda and I really enjoyed your message. We both have nominal church backgrounds, so it was pretty new. I liked your Christmas Eve message as well. It got me thinking what you said how mankind will never bring about world peace, only God can. Can you explain that some more, because, as you may have guessed, everything you see here is because of a war."

"Sure. And thanks for the lunch. Let me ask you this: Do you have any siblings, either of you?"

"I have an older brother," Dale said. Brenda answered, "I'm sandwiched between an older sister and younger brother."

"Good," Pastor Miller continued. "So, remember when you were growing up in your households. As the kids got older, the rules for you guys changed, right? The older ones got more privileges than the younger ones, but as you all got older, there were rules that you had to follow, right? And they changed, right?"

"Right," Brenda agreed. "My older sister could go to a school dance when I couldn't. Then I could while my younger brother couldn't."

"So once your older sister got old enough, the rule was: Be home from the dance by a certain time, while you didn't have to obey that rule because it didn't apply to you, right?"

"Correct," Brenda said. Dale was intrigued, even if he was a little lost.

"Did you guys ever keep all the rules or did you disobey them?" Pastor Miller asked.

"Trust me - both my brother and I broke the rules, for which we paid handsomely," Dale answered, laughing.

"Ditto for us," Brenda said.

"Okay, here's why I asked this. Imagine this world is God's household, and as it grows older, like you kids, your parents - like mine - had age-appropriate rules for you, and they changed from era to era. And, every one of you kids broke the rules. Trust me - I have three older sisters and I know what I'm talking about! My dad's big rule was to come home at night at the exact time he said, and not a minute late. Boy, there was heck to pay when we did come in late, especially when we were in someone else's car and couldn't control our time. That was rough.

"So, in the history of the world, God had different rules for different eras, for different demographics. And in each one of these eras, we broke the rules. For instance, in the Garden of Eden, God told Adam and Eve to tend the garden and to not eat from tree of the knowledge of good and evil, right?" Dale and Brenda nodded yes.

"But they did not obey, and what happened next?"

"They ate the forbidden fruit and God expelled them from the Garden," Dale said.

"Correct. But let's say that Adam and Eve obeyed God perfectly. Then, Adam and Eve could take credit for maintaining a perfect paradise, right?"

"Right," Brenda was following his logic.

"Moving on with the kids getting older, God told Noah after the Flood that humans were to rule the world with human government. God said that if anyone sheds another man's blood intentionally, that his blood shall be shed too. That means that humans were to police themselves.

"But what happened is that man tried to build a tower all the way to heaven, which was in effect moving past his humanity and trying to achieve godhood. So, what did God do then?" he asked.

"He scattered the nations and confused the languages," Dale answered, feeling pretty impressed that he remembered that Sunday School lesson.

"Right again. You guys are pretty good!" Pastor Miller laughed. "This brings us to the church age. I wish the Christian Church - all who truly believe in Jesus - would end war by evangelizing the world. I would love to take credit for that. But it just will not happen. Just think of all the war and carnage that has happened since the first century, after Jesus died. Our own country was born out of a war. We had the Civil War. We had World War I; now we're in World War II.

"After World War I, we started the League of Nations in 1920, with the goal to maintain world peace. Did it work? No, because here we are again. Did the Armistice of 1918, ending World War I, lead to peace? No. In fact, it was one of the things that led to Hitler's rise. Did Hitler keep the Munich Agreement of 1938 with Chamberlain? No, again. And, after we defeat Hitler and Tojo, there will be wars in other places in the world, some involving us and some not. The guns are getting more efficient, the bombs are getting bigger and deadlier, the scope of warfare is involving more people. Do you see my point? Mankind is sinful and evil, even though there are nice, law abiding people. But the Bible is clear when it says that men love darkness more than they love the Light. And that our hearts are wicked and corrupt and desperately wicked. We hate to admit it, but it's true."

Dale countered. "So, you are saying it's impossible for mankind to lay down its arms and live peacefully, like it says in the Bible: 'The lion will lie down with the lamb'?"

"I know it sounds very pessimistic," Pastor Miller responded, "but look at the first sins of Adam and Eve. They didn't have a sin nature like we do now. They lived in perfect relationship with God and in harmony with their surroundings in the Garden. Everything was perfect. Yet they sinned by disobeying God. With us, we have a sin nature, making it impossible to keep God's laws. Only Jesus could do that because He was sinless. So, no, we can never totally live in a condition like you mentioned. Let me illustrate it this way. Do you lock your doors and windows at night when you go to bed?"

"Yes."

"Do the police in your town have guns and weapons?"

"Yes," Dale admitted again.

"Why is that? Because," he answered his own question, "there are bad people out there who want to break into your home and steal what belongs to you, even perhaps your life, and these bad people need to be stopped by the police. My point is: while you would *like* to live in a peaceful world, you are realistic enough to know that it's not going to happen and you take measures to protect yourself."

Dale silently admitted that Mike was right. It wasn't pessimism but realism.

"Further, since man couldn't maintain the paradise he once had, nor can man ever usher in paradise - by that I mean a sinless state in perfect communion with God - God alone can and will do this Himself. I guess it's like the old saying, 'If you want a job done right, do it yourself.' That was the point of my message Christmas Eve. God will do this when Jesus returns and sets up His millennial kingdom from Jerusalem, as prophesied in the Bible."

"So even once this war is over, it really won't be over?" Brenda asked.

"Hate to say it, but no. That's the sad part. But the good part is we know for sure that one day God will end all wars. The book of Revelation states that one day there will be no more pain, no more death, no more sorrow, and then we'll have that perfect Eden-like state that we had in the beginning, in the New Jerusalem. And, the Bible says, God alone will get the credit and the glory. We sure can't."

Dale and Brenda sat there in silence, taking it all in and trying to connect all the dots in their minds. To comprehend Genesis through Revelation at lunch over cheeseburgers and sodas was a lot to absorb; it was like trying to drink from a firehose - only a few of the many drops of water actually got down the throat as it was overwhelming.

"Well," Dale spoke up, "Brenda and I sure do appreciate your time, Mike. You really gave us plenty to think about. I would love to disagree with you, but you showed us from history that mankind sure hasn't done a very good job of stopping evil and wars and such."

"And I appreciate this nice lunch, Dale. You're right, Brenda - these are great cheeseburgers. Please thank Kaye's cows for me."

Dale went over to the register to pay for the meals, making a point to gesture to his glass left on the table to Kaye, who still glared at him. Pastor Miller should preach on forgiveness one of these days, Dale thought, and he would make sure Kaye had that Sunday off so she could attend.

"If you show me the bus stop I need to go to, I'll catch the bus by myself to the gate. My car is parked outside. Thanks again for the lunch, guys. I really do enjoy coming into Oak Ridge. It is quite the place, that's for sure. I'll make sure to pick up the pace at our prayer meetings at my church, and pray for you all here a little more fervently."

"Our pleasure, Mike," Dale answered. "Brenda and I will do our best to make your services. With the nature of our jobs, we cannot promise that, but we'll try."

Daniel S. Zulli

Chapter 17-Threat

Dale decided to take the long walk back to his house. The air was crisp and helped him clear his mind. And the exercise would certainly do him some good.

As he walked he looked around at Oak Ridge. It was still growing. In addition to Y-12, two more massive plants had been built, X-10 and K-25. Dale had no idea what they were working on, but he wondered if they, too, were experiencing security breaches like his plant was. Were there others like him who had discovered discrepancies in their work? Had others reached a conclusion like his? If not, he thought, he could not believe that of all the people who were working here, that he and Brenda were the only ones who might have stumbled upon this mystery.

Was he placed here by divine providence for such a time as this? The very thought of it was so strange since he had not given God so much as the time of day his entire life.

Dale stayed deep in thought and was surprised to look up and discover that he had found his way home, more on autopilot than cognizant awareness. He felt like a homing pigeon who worked on some innate instinct and not intentional thought.

That evening, when the winter's sun had gone down, Dale and Bob O'Neil were sitting in their living room. *You Always Hurt the One You Love* by the Ames Brothers was softly playing from their small tabletop radio. Dale was reading the Sunday edition of the Knoxville *News Sentinel,* while Bob was checking out the latest issue of *Baseball Digest.*

"I can't believe it!" Bob exploded.

"Believe what?"

"My Dodgers will be opening the season at Philadelphia!"

"What's wrong with that?" Dale asked.

"I can't stand those bums!" Bob protested. "Those Phils have the worst fans. Makes us in Brooklyn look like real class acts."

That provoked a slight chuckle from Dale. Bob's devotion to his Dodgers was amusing.

"I just can't wait for Ted Williams and Johnny Pesky to come back," Dale said. "I'll be behind home plate at Fenway so fast your head will spin!"

They heard the car suddenly pull up to the house, brakes squealing to a stop, indicating the driver had been going at a high speed.

"Who's that?" Dale asked. Bob's chair was closest to the front window that looked out on Outer Drive.

Before Bob could look out the window through the blinds and give an answer, a brick came crashing in, showering Bob with shards of glass. The car accelerated rapidly, causing the tires to screech with a horrific noise, adding to the cacophony of noise.

Dale jumped out of his chair and snapped the front door open. Unable to spot the car in the darkness, he asked Bob, "You okay?"

Dale's housemate was wide-eyed, feeling himself over for injuries. "I think I'm all right. Good night! What was that all about? Maybe a Phillies fan heard me!"

"Don't think so, partner," Dale responded. He picked up the brick. A note was wrapped around it. Even though he could not tell his housemate what was going on, Dale knew this was about him.

Reading the note to himself, it read:

```
You were told to be careful. Don't stick your nose
where it doesn't belong.
```

The two men made a makeshift window with cardboard and tape. Dale convinced Bob to let him handle this incident. He would report it to the head of security - Val Hutchinson's colonel husband, the senior-ranking MP - and it would be investigated. He would also report the broken window to the head of housing so it could get fixed, using the story that some boys were out throwing a baseball and one got away from them. Baseball was a popular pastime in Oak Ridge with many different leagues, so a wayward throw, even in winter, would be believed.

Once they got the house cleaned up and they settled in for the night - not an easy task - Dale's thoughts went to Brenda, and how to keep her safe, especially since she was his first confidant in the altered information dilemma as well as now personally involved in it with her calutrons. He was not sure he would tell her about this incident.

Despite the chilly air that had come into their house, Dale broke out into a cold sweat at this new, more serious threat.

Chapter 18-Disclosure

Colonel Wesley Hutchinson worked in the Security building. Starched MPs came in and out continually, scurrying about their duties. A fair number of civilians worked there as well. Typewriters clacked furiously, sending papers flying in various stages of processing. Much smoke filled the room, mingling with the smell of stale coffee. This office ran on nicotine and caffeine.

Dale entered the Security building at 0700 on Monday. He approached the first MP who manned the front desk.

"Excuse me, Sergeant....Stowell," he read the name badge on his shirt. "I need to see Colonel Hutchinson right away, if possible. It's urgent."

"Have a seat, sir," the sergeant replied. "I'll see if the he's available."

"Thank you."

Sergeant Stowell departed into the inner office. Dale could see the colonel through the door's glass as he looked out at Dale and gave a "What now?" look. But the colonel shrugged and followed the sergeant out.

"You wanted to see me?" Colonel Hutchinson asked, trying to be professional, but not liking being disturbed, especially first thing in the morning. He looked worn and tired, the result of too many work hours and too great a responsibility, with too few men.

"Sir, I am truly sorry to ask for your time. I know you're a very busy man. But I have something very urgent to tell you and it cannot wait."

The colonel glanced at Sergeant Stowell as if to say, "Please screen these people better," but waved Dale into his office.

Colonel Hutchinson lit up a cigarette.

"I'll get right to the point, sir," Dale began. "My name is Dr. Dale Hargrowe. I work in Y-12, as does a good friend of mine. I got here last August. On several instances, my friend and I and a co-worker have discovered that our work has been compromised and our data intentionally altered. I truly suspect a person or persons is trying to sabotage our final product. We think it's an effort to thwart, delay, or ruin this thing we're working on.

"Further, I have been threatened twice, once in the fall, and now again last night." Dale produced the two warning notes. "The first one wasn't so bad," he said, "as it was nailed to my door. This second one was pretty bad. It was attached to a brick and thrown through the window of my house. So, obviously someone who's involved with this thing knows that I know something. I've told my supervisor and he said he's reported it. But now, I have come to you to elevate this. I've never been threatened before, but I've never been involved in a top-secret, war-ending project before, either."

Dale concluded, "Whatever is going on can't be good, sir."

Colonel Hutchinson puffed on his Salem, tapped it out in his full ashtray, then pulled out another one and lit that one as well.

"So, you're telling me there is a spy-sabotage ring here in Oak Ridge? Right under our noses? And that my men and the entire security team has not detected it, but you have?" he challenged.

"Yes, sir. I know it sounds strange, and in no way am I inferring that you and your men are not doing an efficient job. But if I were a betting man, I would place my money on an inside job, with people who have access to all our facilities. And, these warning notes I'm getting sure don't sound like someone is merely looking out for my best interest."

"I'll look into it," Colonel Hutchinson said, resigning himself to yet another task, "even though my men are maxed out with normal, day-to-day operations."

"Colonel," Dale said, "I sure wouldn't be coming to you if I were not convinced something bad is taking place. I'm not as concerned for my well-being as I am this project. However..." he paused.

"What?" the colonel asked.

"I'm concerned for a friend of mine, a girl who used to work with your wife in Administration #1, but now works in Y-12 with the calutrons. She's a close friend and I'm very concerned about her welfare. I'd like her to be involved with this as little as possible. If I got a brick this time, I'd hate to see the warnings get elevated and for her to be caught in the cross hairs. Her name is Brenda Andrews, and she doesn't deserve this." Dale thought of the irony of Brenda telling him she came to Oak Ridge because she wanted something more exciting than teaching elementary school in Kentucky. He wondered if this were exciting enough for her. Excitement was one thing; danger was another.

"I can't place a guard on her, son," the colonel said. "My advice to you is to tell her to stay as far away from this as possible, and to watch her step."

"I understand, sir. I'll tell her."

Dale caught the bus to Y-12. Everything appeared normal. He met up with Mr. Sweeney and asked him to relay to Brenda that he needed to see her at her first opportunity. He would meet her in their mutual break room.

The look on Dale's face betrayed his anxiety. Without a word, he took Brenda's elbow and escorted her a secluded section of the hallway. The humming of the calutrons muffled their conversation.

"Okay, Dale," Brenda started, "what's up? It doesn't take Sherlock Holmes to see you have something on your mind. What's wrong?"

Dale did not answer.

"What happened?" Brenda said, raising her voice. "Dale Hargrowe, you had better not be in any trouble!"

"I might be. I hope not."

"Tell me!" Brenda ordered.

"Okay, I didn't want to tell you at first, but now I have to. When we came home from that picnic out at Norris Dam, a note was addressed to me, telling me to be careful. I wasn't sure how to interpret it. It was either a warning to keep me safe or a warning telling me to back off. But then, last night, I got a brick thrown through my window, with another warning to keep my nose out of this business. Word gets around here quickly, and someone knows I've been putting two and two together and coming up with a rotten four."

Brenda gasped. "Oh, no!"

Dale tried to reassure her. "Look, I'll be okay." He knew that was hollow at best. "But the main thing is you have to be careful. I don't want you involved in this affair at all. I went to Colonel Hutchinson this morning to tell him about the brick, and he said he can't protect you, which I know he can't. Have you talked to anyone to where someone might think you know something like I do?"

"No. Of course not," she said. "The only person who knows I know anything is Maggie Hancock, the girl who told me about the funny calutrons. And I trust her. I hope I can, anyway."

"That makes sense. But you really have to be on your guard now. I don't like how this thing is going. More and more people are finding out about this, and it all comes back to us. And nothing had better happen to you."

Dale mused. "This reminds me of what Mr. Lohorn said at my in-processing, about not trusting anyone, because anyone could be an enemy. I sure never thought it was possible. Everyone seems so nice and trustworthy. I hate the thought of someone being a spy trying to catch one of us talking."

"What next?" Brenda asked.

Dale inhaled deeply. "I sure wish I had a plan. But seeing how this has never happened to me before, I don't. The only thing to do is to continue to do our work, and trust the ones that we have been telling this to will get to the bottom of it all. I'd rather do something - like take some action - but I'm a scientist, not John Wayne or Clark Gable." He sounded defeated.

"Listen, buster," Brenda admonished, "You may not ride on a white horse, but you've done more than the average Joe would have done. I don't know if Pastor Miller would agree with me because I don't know that much about God, but maybe He sent you down here to Oak Ridge to do something great besides adding up figures with your Number 2 pencil. You've done just fine." Her words were encouraging. They gave each other a quick but firm hug, then spun around and went back to work.

Dale felt reassured he had such a wonderful ally in this predicament. Brenda was truly a one-in-a-million woman. He was glad he was on her side.

Chapter 19-Assault

When Brenda came home from work that evening, she found Trudy Mac lying on her bed, a hot water bottle on her stomach.

"What happened to you?" Brenda asked.

"I don't know," Trudy Mac moaned. "I had lunch in Harriman today and it seems to be rebelling against me now. I feel like New Year's Eve and a bachelor party all rolled into one!"

"Do you need anything?" Brenda offered.

"Would you mind going down to the drug store for some Bromo-Seltzer? I promise not to die before you get back."

"Sure thing. Here - use this trash can if your head falls off." Brenda put the can next to Trudy Mac's pillow in case the big one hit.

The Jefferson Fountain drug store was in Jackson Square, several blocks away. Brenda decided she could make better time by hoofing it rather than wait for the next available bus. She quickly walked to the store and bought the medicine.

The sun was down by the time Brenda headed back to the dorm. Shadows were deep and thick. She cut in between the buildings of the townsite, bypassing the main roads. This way, she could diagonal back and shave off some time and distance.

Brenda was behind Miller's Department Store when a figure sprang out from a doorway behind her. A rough hand clamped over her mouth as the man pinned her arms to her body with his other arm. Brenda attempted a scream and tried to struggle, but could do neither.

"Listen, girlie," the unrecognizable voice behind her head warned in a low and menacing tone, "tell lover boy to back off, or it might not be good for his health. Or yours."

Brenda's assailant gave her a firm shake. "You understand what I'm saying, girlie?" Brenda nodded affirmative as best she could. His large hand covered her mouth and up to her nostrils, barely giving her room to breathe. Between the sheer terror and her blocked nose, Brenda felt herself getting light-headed.

"When I let go of you, you run and don't look back. You got that, girlie?" Brenda attempted a weak nod.

Daniel S. Zulli

The man released his iron grip on her, and ordered, "Go!" Brenda bolted forward, suppressing a scream against all her natural instincts and ran unlike any time in her life. Her package from the Jefferson Fountain dropped, breaking the glass bottle, and spilling its contents in a foam of sizzle.

She doubted that her feet ever touched the ground.

Brenda flew up the stairs to the second floor of her dorm. She barged into her room, wide-eyed and panting, both from the exertion of running and from the assault.

"What on earth happened to you?" Trudy Mac asked. "You see a ghost?"

Brenda did not answer at first. She collapsed on her bed and began to sob uncontrollably.

"A man - " she gasped for air. "A man attacked me and threatened me and Dale!"

"What?" Trudy Mac bound out of bed, sending the hot water bottle flying off her stomach.

Trudy Mac grabbed her roommate by the shoulders. "Are you all right?"

"I'm not hurt," Brenda began to slowly compose herself. "Oh, my stars! I've never had anything like that ever happen to me! I'm not hurt physically, but I can't swear my heart rate will ever get back down to normal."

Trudy Mac talked in a calm tone. "You say this person threatened you and Dale?"

"Yes. He told me to tell Dale to back off from asking questions about this phony data situation. Or else he and I could get hurt."

"That is terrible! What are you going to do about it?"

"I don't know yet," Brenda replied. "I always wanted more excitement than what life had to offer back in Kentucky, but I'm not sure this is what I had in mind. I sure wasn't expecting to get assaulted in the dark and threatened. Or, even worse, the guy I like being threatened. So, I'm not sure what I'm going to do."

"Brenda," Trudy Mac said, "look, I'm glad you're safe, but if I can give you a word of advice or caution..." she hesitated.

"What is it, Trudy? Go ahead, give me a word of caution. What's one more?"

"I know how you feel about Dale, and how you wouldn't want him to get hurt by being involved in this whatever..." Trudy Mac hesitated again.

"Out with it, kid," Brenda insisted. "After what I've been through tonight, I don't think anything else will rattle me."

85

"All right. I'm just not sure you should be risking your neck for him. It's enough that you have to be extra careful to protect your own now."

"What are you saying, Trudy Mac? Why wouldn't I want to make sure Dale doesn't get hurt?

"I'm not saying you shouldn't try and prevent him from getting hurt. But I am saying maybe you should put your well-being first and Dale's a distant second."

"Why?" Brenda said, getting a little defensive.

"Look, I wasn't going to tell you this for fear of you getting your heart broken. But now I'm more worried about your *neck* getting broken! Tonight was just too close a call. But not too long ago I went into Y-12 to take inventory. I saw Dale there in the break room, and he looked like he was getting cozy with that mean old receptionist."

Brenda's eyes narrowed. "What do you mean, *cozy?*"

"They were sitting real close to one another. There were plenty of empty places to sit but he was right next to her. Then...I didn't want to tell you this, but I saw Dale put his hand on that girl's knee when he was talking to her."

"Trudy Mac, no! I can't believe this. Are you sure?"

"Sure as I'm standing here. They saw me come in and Dale took his hand back and they acted all casual-like, as if him sitting next to her with all them empty seats was normal. I pretended like I never saw anything and went about my business, but I saw what I saw. Oh, Brenda, I'm so sorry!" Trudy Mac said, remorseful. "I sure never wanted to tell you this, especially now when your nerves are frayed to the end, but I just want to make sure you don't risk yourself for a guy who may not feel the same way you do, maybe even two-timing you."

Brenda backed away slowly from Trudy Mac, eyes staring blankly, this being too much to absorb. The memories of her father cheating on her mother those many times flooded back to her in a torrent of pain. To think Dale could be as low ripped at her heart in a terrible way.

After the narrow escape at being assaulted and threatened, Brenda's system had reached its limit for being able to cope. She could not put two thoughts together in her head, much less speak. She slowly sat down on her bed, sitting upright at first, then falling toward her pillow. Still fully clothed, Trudy Mac pulled the blanket at the end of her bed over Brenda. Then she walked softly to the light and turned it off, exiting the room to leave Brenda to her thoughts. Sleep would be the best for her. She could not process any more information, good or bad.

She had reached her limit of excitement.

Daniel S. Zulli

Chapter 20-Rejection

Dale by-passed Miss Rivera without saying a word to her and went straight into Hal Rainey's office. She was too caught off-guard to protest.

"Sorry to barge in on you, Hal," he said, closing the door, "but what's happened with your report to your superiors?"

"I funneled the news to Joe Blaine, my boss, who said he'd pass it on to the district manager," Hal replied. "After that, there's nothing else we can do. We have to let them handle it. Look, Dale, I know you're pretty spun up about this - and you were right to come to me - but we have to let the experts handle this from here on in. You've done good. But this place is crawling with security pros whose number one job is to ensure that this project works with no complications. I know you want to see some action now, but I know from experience that these types of things are best worked quietly, behind the scenes. The goal is to not let the bad guys know we're on to them, then catch them when they slip up. If you go around raising a ruckus, they will know that we know, which will scare them. It's best to let them trap themselves in the act. Do I make sense?"

"I hear what you're saying, Hal, but I just can't shake this feeling that something's really rotten in Denmark. Is your boss Blaine going to get things moving?"

"I'm sure he will, Dale. Like I said, he knows how to work these things. You don't have to worry. Word will get up to the brass in Washington so fast your head will spin. And trust me, once General Groves gets wind of this, you'll see plenty of action. The best thing you can do now is to get back to work and leave the detective work to the pros. You've done all you can do."

Dale knew that he had to calm his emotions down and trust in what Hal said, even if he wanted something to happen now, if not sooner. Dale did not want any more bricks thrown through his window. Further, he did not want the gadget compromised at the expense of this tremendous war effort. Whatever it was, it had to succeed.

Finally, he wanted Brenda to be safe. More than anything else, he did not want to drag her into this dilemma any more than he already had. This alone made him want a quick resolution to this mystery.

What Dale did know was this thing was really eating at him.

When he left his boss's office, Dale ran into Art Rossi in the hallway.

"Hey, Artie," Dale said, "everything still all right? Nothing unusual going on?"

"Not a thing, except Lou's down to only a pack a day. Is he all right?"

Dale chuckled. "Hope he is! Say, just let me know if anything out of the ordinary happens. *Capisce?*" Dale used Art's native Italian.

"*Capisce,*" Art nodded.

Dale tried to return to his work and pretend things were all right, but he felt like he was the only one on the Titanic who knew the ship had hit an iceberg and things were going to get bad. Dale knew Hal's advice had wisdom to it, but at the same time it did not *feel* right. Dale had been too personally involved to merely go back to work as if this was a small bump in a road. It felt like heading for a cliff and no one else - aside from Brenda - saw any need to get excited.

Dale thought he should go see Brenda, if, for nothing else, then to get a friendly wave from her.

He went to where he could see her bays of calutrons. The girls were dutifully working them, paying close attention to their dials and knobs. The held clipboards with their paperwork in one hand, pencil in the other. When they made a knob adjustment or read the dials at the precise times, the girls marked on their paperwork.

Dale scanned the rows of humming calutrons. He could see other floor supervisors who were Brenda's counterpart in their bays. After a few minutes, he noticed her by the last machine in the far bay. Brenda was engaged in her work, being the professional she was. She was making her rounds to her girls, picking up paperwork for processing and delivering the girls fresh forms, managing her area.

Dale waved once, twice, hoping she would see the movement within her peripheral vision. Finally, after a few waves, Brenda did look up at him. He expected that she would smile and wave back, even in the midst of hard work. But she did not. Even though they were a good 25 yards apart, Dale could see that Brenda did not look her usual, engaging, vivacious self.

Brenda's eyes were rimmed with red, her brow furrowed. Her normally lovely mouth was lined in a serious mood that Dale had never seen before. She looked like she was down a few pounds, as if she had not been eating. She looked like she needed sleep.

Dale smiled and waved again. This time Brenda saw him, but the look in her eyes had lost all their usual luster and warmth. She quickly looked down and directed her attention to the nearest calutron girl, concentrating on her work.

This hit Dale hard. Even if she were not feeling well, the Brenda he thought he knew would have smiled and waved back at him. This was unexpected. For the life of him, Dale could not figure out what was wrong or what had gotten into her. He knew she had been worried about the warnings to him, but he had not expected her to merely turn away from him. Dale was perplexed. He could understand numbers and calculations, but not women. His Ph.D. in nuclear physics did not help him now.

This rejection and cold shoulder from Brenda added to the mystery of the possible sabotage of their top-secret project. Dale's head reeled. He would have to connect with Brenda and try to sort this out. Not only was she his only true confidant in this affair, she had reached a place in his heart that had not been reached before.

Dale needed her.

As Dale tried to sort this new development out, Miss Rivera approached him on the bay overlook.

"Dr. Hargrowe," Miss Rivera called. The hum of all the calutrons forced her to talk in a louder tone than normal. "Mr. Rainey told me to tell you that you need to report to Administration #2. Someone named Mr. Lohorn wants to see you."

"Do you know what for?"

"I don't, but it sounded pretty serious. Are you all right?" Miss Rivera touched Dale's forearm as she said this.

Brenda happened to glance up from the calutron floor to see the raven-haired secretary deliver her message to Dale and touch him on his arm.

Brenda felt a new stab in her already-broken heart. The girl manning the calutron where Brenda was at noticed the reaction on her face.

"You all right, Miss Andrews?"

"Not feeling too well, Carrie. I...need to take a break." Brenda abruptly turned and left the girl looking at her, never having seen Brenda look that way before.

Before departing Y-12 for Administration #2, Dale cast one last look down at Brenda, just in time to see her bolt her position on the floor. A wave of total helplessness overcame him when he saw Brenda have this sudden reaction to, what, he did not know.

Daniel S. Zulli

Chapter 21-Redirection

The bus ride to Administration #2 was dreadful. Not only did Dale not want to see Mr. Lohorn again, but the situation with Brenda stripped him of all vitality. He felt like a convict walking his last mile to the chair. The pit of his stomach felt like a volcano right before the final eruption.

Dale and his fellow passengers exited at the bus stop closest to the heart of Clinton Engineering Works. Numbly, he strode to Administration #2. His feet were moving, but his mind was not telling them to. His autonomic nervous system was keeping him upright and causing him to place one foot in front of the other.

He made his way to Mr. Lohorn's office of doom. Mr. Lohorn had gotten a new receptionist/secretary. This was not unusual, as many young ladies had sought employment in Oak Ridge, and moving them around to different positions was commonplace.

"Please tell Mr. Lohorn that Dr. Hargrowe is here to see him. Thanks." Dale sat down, trying his best to not look like a third grader being called into the principal's office, guilty before the charges were even read.

The young lady entered Mr. Lohorn's office, announcing Dale's arrival. He could hear the muffled exchange between them.

"He'll be right with you, Dr. Hargrowe," she said, pleasantly enough, although he knew that she knew this was not a social call. Howard Lohorn did not make any of those.

From the inner sanctum, Mr. Lohorn's voice called out, "Tell Dr. Hargrowe to come in, please, Miss Kaminsky."

Not needing Miss Kaminsky to repeat the directive, Dale got up and walked into the office, ready to place his head in the noose for Mr. Lohorn to kick the chair out from beneath him.

Shutting the door, Dale sat down, again, not needing a prompt. If it were possible, Mr. Lohorn looked less happy than he did during Dale's in-processing.

"I'll get right to the point, Dr. Hargrowe," Mr. Lohorn said, not needing any pleasantries to begin the conversation. "The reports on you all, to the letter, say you've done nothing but outstanding work the entire time you've been here."

"Thank you, sir," Dale replied, at least glad for one positive thing.

"However,"

Here it comes, Dale thought.

"...as of late there have been some concerns about your ability to focus on your job. You apparently have been involved in some

Daniel S. Zulli

incidents that have concerned the leadership here in Oak Ridge. For instance, am I correct in saying that you have been threatened, even to the extent that your home has been vandalized?"

"That is correct, sir." *Bad news does travel fast around here*, Dale thought again.

"And, is it also correct that you have made several inquiries to your co-workers about possible compromises in their work?"

"That is correct," Dale acknowledged.

"Further, have you also involved some of the women who work with the calutrons, to such an extent that even one of them was personally threatened?"

"Yes, sir. Wait. What did you say? Who was threatened?" Dale became suddenly more alert.

"Allow me to give you the bottom line: You, sir, are walking on very thin ice. If it were not for the sterling quality of your work, you would be gone before nightfall. I briefed you on this, as you signed and which is in your folder." Mr. Lohorn raised up Dale's folder which contained everything on him and about him, beginning with the stolen glass from Kaye's Kafé.

"You cannot continue to go about causing any more disruptions, Dr. Hargrowe. If, as it has been documented, you have raised concerns about the direction this project is going, then you are being hereby served that you are to be 100% mindful of your work, and to let our security specialists handle any irregularities, real or imagined. Are you understanding what I am saying, Dr. Hargrowe?"

"Yes, sir, I am. But can you tell me which female worker has been threatened?"

"I cannot. That, frankly, is not your concern. What *is* your concern is that you need to tread very lightly and carefully from this point on. Any more incidents will not serve you well."

And just like Dale's in-processing briefing with Mr. Lohorn in August, he concluded with, "Do you have any questions for me?"

This time he did not. "No, sir."

"Then you are dismissed," Mr. Lohorn said.

As Dale approached the door to open it, Mr. Lohorn added, "Be careful, Dale."

Dale walked out. It was not until he got outside of Administration #2 that it dawned on him that Mr. Lohorn called him "Dale" for the first time, even sounding concerned for him. Dale shook it off. His main thoughts were now on the woman that Mr. Lohorn said had been threatened. It had to be Brenda. Sure, it must be her. Who else would it have been? There was a chance it was Maggie Hancock, the one who told Brenda there was some funny business going on. But Dale would bet the farm it was not her, but Brenda.

93

Dale skipped the bus and walked home. All told, this was a day straight from the dark place. Dale could not imagine how it could have been worse.

What he did know, when he had put all the pieces together, was that he was somehow privy to and the center of some mysterious goings on here in top-secret Oak Ridge. Further, he was now a marked man, the focus of suspicion by those whom Dale was serving to the best of his ability, the very ones he was trying to help. It was not enough for Dale to become the enemy of whomever had threatened him, but he was also on the hit list of his friends, or the ones he thought were his friends. The bottom line was: he did not know whom his friends really were.

Dale remembered how Mr. Lohorn said to be no one's friend, trust no one. Anyone could be an enemy. As he ran down the list of names and faces that he had shared work and life with since he first got here, Dale was more confused as ever as to whom his friends really were. Maybe no one was.

Most of all, he thought of Brenda. Of all the people he needed on his side, apparently, she was not. She had gone from snuggling in his arms at a movie theater to looking away from him in pain when she saw him.

As Dale walked, trying to compose his thoughts and next actions, he looked over and saw the bus terminal. A group of drivers huddled in front of a bus, taking a break between runs. They were having an animated conversation, punctuated with laughter and good-natured ribbing.

"So, I says to my wife, 'Baby, I'm going bowling tonight and that's just the way it is!'"

"What did your wife say?"

"Nothing," the first man said. "She just took my bowling ball and tossed it out the window!" The group of drivers doubled over, howling. It was clear these men, like most of the black workers in Oak Ridge, had their own sub-culture, from their jobs to their living conditions to the schools for their children.

Dale recognized the driver that had brought him to Oak Ridge from Knoxville that very first day, Mr. Earnest Eugene Cummings.

Daniel S. Zulli

Seeing Mr. E. made an idea pop in Dale's head. He approached the drivers.

"Say, Mr. E., remember me? You gave me my first bus ride in from the station in Knoxville back in August."

"Sure, I remember you, boss," Mr. E. said with a straight face. "I remember you just like I remember every one of the ten thousand others I've brought here!" All the drivers burst out again in belly laughs, knowing that this guy had been had.

"Okay, you got me," Dale grinned. "But I need a favor. Got a minute?" He motioned with his head for Mr. E. to step away from the other drivers.

"What's up, boss?" Mr. E. asked. "Am I in trouble?"

"No, but the way things are going, I might be," Dale responded. "But I need to get off the reservation quick-like, and I don't have a ride."

"Where do you need to go?"

"To a church in Maryville. I have to see their pastor who has preached here at the Chapel. I need to see him."

"Gotcha. But my route is only between here and Knoxville."

Dale nodded. "I know, but is there any way you could swing a deal with another driver, maybe, so you can take me? I'll pay you for your time. Look, I really need to see this guy."

"All right now, let's see..." Mr. E. mused, rubbing his chin. "Okay, I'll tell you what. One of those drivers over there is just getting off - Flathead Harris - and he owes me a favor 'cause I brought him home drunk one night and got him to bed before his old lady caught him. She was looking for him all over town. He's just getting off and he has a car parked at the terminal. I'll get him to cover my bus route and I'll drive his car to take you to Maryville. Will that work?"

Dale was thrilled. "That would be swell, Mr. E.! I wouldn't be troubling you if it weren't important."

"No sweat, boss," Mr. E. said. "You had just better hope that Flathead has some gas in that old jalopy. Otherwise it's going to cost you my tip *and* his gas!"

Chapter 22-Guidance

Arnold "Flathead" Harris's 1934 Plymouth Coupe showed its age. Not only did it make more noise than a car normally should, pieces threatened to fall off at every pothole and rut. The roads to Maryville were the same as all the others in this area in terms of having seen better days. Mr. E. drove with caution, not wanting to lose either the car or any part of it along the way.

The Maryville Fellowship Church was a modest building. It was not dilapidated, but it did show the effects of the Great Depression. The Clinton Engineering Works project may have infused government money into Oak Ridge, transforming it from a sleepy farm community to a bustling, industrial-military complex, but that money had not spilled into the surrounding towns, the one exception being Knoxville, the main town outside Oak Ridge, where the CEW citizens went and played. Maryville had not yet been the beneficiary of that money.

"Here you go, boss," Mr. E. said. "How long do you think you'll be?"

"No more than an hour," Dale replied. "Do you want to come in while I talk to the pastor?"

"No, thanks. I saw me a watering hole about a mile back. I think I'll go over there and wait and be back in an hour. I could use me a little pick-me-up, if you know what I mean."

"Understood. Have one for me too, Mr. E. And thanks for this lift. I needed it more than you'll ever know."

As he walked up the church's steps to the front door, it suddenly dawned on Dale that he had no idea if Pastor Mike Miller would even be in. Coming here was a complete shot in the dark which, hopefully, would not result in a total waste of time. But, if he reasoned correctly, if God or some small, inner voice put it into his heart to talk with the pastor, then surely coming unannounced would not backfire on him. Surely.

Upon entering, Dale was struck by the humble, worn look of the church. It was the perfect country church. Dale imagined the congregation sitting in the pews - good people, simple in their lives and faith. Dale felt warm in his soul. It felt *real,* more real than what he remembered church being from when he was a boy. If there was one thing Dale needed at this tumultuous time in his life, it was something real. Something sure. Between the loss of Brenda's friendship and not knowing who the good guys were, he felt adrift at sea. If ever Dale needed Brenda, it was now.

Not only did he need a friend, he needed guidance.

Daniel S. Zulli

A middle-aged lady with a quaint bonnet on her head interrupted Dale's mental wanderings.

"May I help you, sir?" she asked.

"Yes, ma'am. I am very sorry to barge in on you like this, especially so late in the afternoon, but I would like to see Pastor Miller, if that would be possible. I work in Oak Ridge and I met him there when he did some church services for us."

The woman smiled. "You're in luck, even though we don't believe in 'luck' here. Reverend Miller was just getting ready to go home for the day."

Mike Miller stepped out from his office. "Thanks, Miss Ruby," he said. "I can take it from here. I know this guy; he shouldn't be too much trouble," he said with a wink.

Miss Ruby turned and left the small church, leaving the two men alone.

Mike waved Dale into his office. "Come on in. How have you been? What brings you out to Maryville? Looks like you have a lot on your mind. How's your friend, Brenda?"

Dale looked down and mumbled. "I wish I knew. There's a lot of things I wish I knew right now."

"Tell you what," Mike said, "you just talk and we'll see where we end up."

"Thanks. There's a lot going on, none of which is good."

"I know it's all classified, but is there trouble at work?"

"Could be. I've gotten messed up in something big and no good. I cannot tell you the details, but there is some hanky-panky going on with our work, and what we're trying to accomplish. I've seen it firsthand. And, I've been threatened because I've been trying to expose it and get it fixed.

"If that weren't bad enough - this is the worst part - something's happened to Brenda. She wouldn't even look at me today. We used to be on really good terms. I really like her and I thought she felt the same about me. But when I tried to wave to her to get her attention and just say hi, she looked terrible and turned away from me like I was the devil incarnate. So, between me being warned and threatened and treated like a pariah at work, Brenda's giving me the freeze. Mike, I don't know what to do, or which end is up, or what is going on. All I know is: nothing's going right and it seems like my whole world is crashing down on me."

Dale added, with a lopsided grin, "So can you fix it for me?"

"Sure thing. Let me pull out my magic wand here and I'll *poof* it all away!" Dale had to chuckle at Mike's joke.

"Well, my friend, you do have a lot on your mind. Sorry about all of this drama your having. It doesn't sound good."

97

"Is there any cure, Doc?" Dale asked, using medical imagery.

"I don't know. We might have to operate." Mike was so easy to talk to, Dale thought.

"Sorry. Couldn't resist," Mike continued. "But really, the answer is yes and no. Let me do the No first. Our actions have repercussions and consequences. Perhaps - and I don't know this for sure - you're experiencing the consequences of your actions. It does say in Proverbs that when our ways are pleasing to the Lord, that even our enemies will be at peace with us. So maybe your ways haven't been too pleasing. That's possible.

"But we also know that bad things happen to good people. It rains on the just and unjust. So, the Yes part of my response it that even in a dark time when everything's going wrong - whether we brought it on ourselves or not - God will walk with us through the valley. He never promised we wouldn't have bad times, but He did promise He would be with us *in* the bad times. So, while I can't guarantee to fix your work dilemma and make Brenda like you again, I can guarantee that God will be with you if you want to walk with Him on His terms."

Dale listened intently.

"The Bible says that God resists the proud but lifts up the humble. Maybe if you were to go back to Brenda and apologize for whatever you did or she thinks you did, you could win her back to your side. Since I have never been married, I won't swear that I know that much about the feminine make-up. But, I have done my share of marriage counseling to know that eating some humble pie never hurt anyone. I'm not saying you're guilty of anything, but if Brenda even *thinks* you are, trust me - you are!" That produced more chuckling and head shaking.

"I hear you, Mike. I sure wish I knew what happened to get her so upset with me. So, where do I go from here?"

Pastor Miller reached toward the shelf behind him. "Here, take this Bible. Start reading. You can't do things God's way unless you know what that way is. Start with the book of Proverbs. Let me quote chapter 3, verses 5 and 6 for you: 'Trust in the Lord with all thine heart, and lean not unto thine own understanding. In all thy ways acknowledge Him, and He shall direct thy paths.' Also, read the Gospel of John. If you want to know the way, that book will tell you. Finally, let me pray for you and ask God to fix things at work and with Brenda."

They both bowed their heads as Pastor Mike Miller asked God to be with Dale during this dark period of uncertainty and potential danger, both to himself and the work that was being done in Oak Ridge. Mike asked God to go before Dale and divinely intercede to bring all Dale's issues to a satisfactory conclusion. Most of all, Mike prayed, that God would reveal and bring glory to Himself by using this difficult period in Dale's life to do so.

When Dale lifted his head, he felt the streams of tears on his cheeks. His soul felt relieved without being able to say why. Coming to see Mike paid off.

"Thanks, Mike," he said. "Even though I'd sure like to hop on the next train back up to Massachusetts, I feel better about facing whatever it is I'll be walking into in Oak Ridge. I'll start reading and will try to connect with Brenda an attempt to sort through this. Man!" he declared. "Life was so good and easy up there. What did I get myself into?" They both laughed as Mike slapped Dale's shoulder.

"I don't know, Dale. But you sure have a knack for finding trouble, from stealing Kaye's glass to this!"

"Would you please forget about that glass?" Dale hollered, exasperated. "I can't believe my whole life has been defined by one stupid glass!" They laughed some more. This good-natured ribbing relieved the tension.

Mike looked out his window, spying Mr. E. pulling up into the gravel parking lot in Flathead Harris's car. "I think your ride is here. I have to get home and so do you. Take care, Dale. I'll be in prayer for you."

"Thanks, Mike. I sure could use it. I'll try and get to your chapel service more often. Thanks for your time today."

Chapter 23-Turmoil

Dale was exhausted - physically, emotionally, spiritually. This was more than what he signed up for. In fact, he thought: he had not signed up for *any* of this. It just happened *to* him. If he, as was a possibility, had been sent to Oak Ridge for such a time as this, he sure did not feel up to the task. He more wanted to tell God to get someone else.

Still, something tugged at his spirit to not throw in the towel, especially if Mike said that God would be with him even in this difficult time. Dale concluded that he could not very well sit back and watch this massive war-ending undertaking get torpedoed by a person or persons. That would never do. He could never live with himself if he did not try and solve this enigma, even at the risk of his career and/or well-being. The next brick through the window could be aimed at his head. It might even be worse than a brick. This was a chance he would have to take.

Further, Dale had to somehow make things right with Brenda. First, he had to find out what had turned her warmth for him into a block of ice. There had been no signs of cooling off their relationship in any way. Then, he had to make sure she was protected from any potential harm or further involvement in this mystery at work.

Dale's face must have betrayed his inner turmoil. Mr. E. had been glancing back in his rear-view mirror at his passenger.

"What's up, boss?" he asked. "Having a hard time of it?"

"You have no idea, E.," Dale answered.

"What's going on, if you don't mind me asking?" Dale's congenial driver said.

"Pretty much everything. Everything was going so well for me back home, before I got the call to come here. It's all shot to pieces now."

"How so?" Mr. E. probed.

"For one, I didn't want to come here. Second, work has turned into a quagmire of trouble. Third, the girl I thought liked me, and I sure do like, has suddenly given me the deep freeze. It's a mess, all the way around."

"That pastor help you out some?"

"He did, although I still am new to all things related to God." Dale looked out his window as he said this, indicating the struggle between his earthly training and natural world view, and the spiritual void he was feeling. "Even though the pastor has certainly opened my eyes to some things, it's still hard to see God in all this. I would have thought

He'd be busy in Europe or the Pacific and the war than messing with little old me down here."

Mr. E. chuckled. "May I give you a piece of advice, for what it's worth, boss?"

"Sure. Might as well," Dale said wistfully.

"I'm the first to admit that I'm not exactly the poster child for the church, but my daddy was a deacon and we all were there every Wednesday and twice on Sundays. I learned the words to *Joshua Fit the Battle* before I learned my first cuss words. But I know enough to tell you this: the Man upstairs is never not here, and He has no Plan B. The devil, he thinks he can mess with God, but he can't.

"You coming down here was no accident, even if it was with you kicking and screaming. Nothing's an accident. You riding my bus that first day was all planned out. I was s'posed to be off that day, but another driver took ill, so I filled in for him. And now here you are in this car with me driving you to see the minister, and me telling you about the Father. Y'all think that's just a coincidence?"

"You'll make a good lawyer when you retire from bus driving, E.," Dale said. "I sure can't argue with you."

"Another thing," Mr. E. continued. "Look at me. You think it's been easy for us down here? My granddaddy was still on the plantation when Lincoln freed us. I'm not trying to make you feel guilty and all, but here's my point: He never stopped believing in the goodness of God. Now here we are in the middle of this terrible war. People ask: Where's God? Well, He's in the same place He's always been - on the throne. He was on the throne when we were still being auctioned. He was on the throne on December 7. And He's on the throne today even though you're going through a tough spell right now.

"No, you coming here was no accident, boss. I don't know everything there is to know about women; just ask my wife!" Mr. E. howled at this own joke. "But I betcha your gal will see the light and see that whatever's going on with her never amounted to much and that you're the real deal. And even if your job is all messed up and things don't work out, God's still God and you ain't escaped His notice 'cause He was too busy with Hitler."

Dale took all this in and added it to what Pastor Miller said. Between the two of them, he certainly got some spiritual insight this day. Dale also thought that, despite Mr. E.'s lack of formal education, he was profoundly knowledgeable with rubber-meets-the-road theology. It made sense.

Mr. E. announced, "We're here at the gate, boss. Get your ID ready."

They produced their credentials and proceeded to the bus terminal. All the other drivers were back on their routes except Flathead Harris, who was waiting in front of Mr. E.'s bus, wanting to go home for the day.

"'Bout time, E.!" Flathead called when they pulled up. "My wife's gonna have my scalp for coming home so late!"

"Yeah?" Mr. E. countered. "If I hadn't bailed you out and got you home when you were sloppy drunk before she found you, she woulda had more than your scalp. She woulda had your butt!" Mr. E. broke out in a good belly laugh. Flathead scowled.

"All right, E., you got me. But we're square now, so gimme back my wheels so I can get on home."

"Thanks for your car, Mr. Harris," Dale broke into their banter. "Here's five dollars for gas and your trouble."

"Yes, sir!" Flathead said. "Anytime you need a ride, mister, you just call on Flathead Harris now."

"Hopefully I won't be having any more emergencies, but if I do, I'll give you a holler. And, don't worry," he said over his shoulder, walking away from the two bus partners, "Mr. E. kept your car under 90!"

Mr. E. roared with laughter at his friend's expense.

Daniel S. Zulli

Chapter 24-Transfer

Trudy Mac was in her room, folding clothes fresh out of the dryer. Just getting a dryer in a woman's dorm was a victory, as it did not have enough to fully accommodate the ladies. She was humming and dancing to Louis Jordan's *G.I. Jive* coming from her table radio, moving from her bed to her dresser and back again. As she was doing so, Brenda came in with a brown paper bag of groceries.

"You're in late," Trudy Mac said.

"I stopped by the store and got some things," Brenda said, unpacking the sack.

"Anything good?"

"You bet. I got just the perfect thing for when things are lousy - chocolate ice cream! If you're nice, I might even share with you." Brenda pulled out a spoon from a drawer and plunked down on a chair, ripping open the cartoon of the emotionally-deadening substance, gobbed a bunch on her spoon and shoved a huge hunk of chocolate into her mouth.

"Hey, easy there!" Trudy Mac said. "You don't want to get fat."

"Who cares?" Brenda mumbled with mouthful of ice cream as she scooped out another mound.

After his shift was over, Dale swung by the women's dorm to try and talk to Brenda to not only apologize for whatever-it-was that set her off, but also to tell her about his visit with Pastor Miller in Maryville.

The dorm mom recognized him.

"Can you please get a message to Brenda in 212 that I'm down here?" he asked.

"One moment," she said, going to the phone.

Trudy Mac answered the intercom. Brenda had just stepped down the hall to the latrine at the end of the hallway.

"No, ma'am," Trudy Mac said. "She hasn't come in from work yet. I haven't seen her. You're welcome."

Dale was not deterred. The next day he stopped by to see Mr. Sweeney and ask if he could fetch Brenda. He did not want to talk to her at work, but Dale did not have much choice. He had read several chapters of Proverbs the night previous and wanted to tell Brenda about the beauty and joy he felt as he read the Bible, really for the first time. Dale was impressed with the timeless truths he discovered by reading what he did.

Mr. Sweeney seemed stunned that Dale would ask to see Brenda.

"Didn't she tell you, son? I would have thought you'd be the first to hear."

"Hear what?"

"She transferred over to X-10 yesterday. It was real sudden. She must know people in high places."

"What? I can't believe it!"

"I sure hated to lose her too. She was one of my best area supervisors. I had to pull another gal from her station to fill in temporarily until I train another to take her place. I'm sorry, son."

Dale walked away from this conversation as defeated as he could remember ever feeling. Not only did Brenda refuse to return a friendly wave and then turn her back on him, her suddenly getting transferred seemed to complete her rejection of him. Dale may not have been a genius when it came to women, but this was pretty obvious—she wanted nothing more to do with him. The worst thing was he could not figure out why, nor could he try and fix things.

Dale ambled back to his work area, shell-shocked. He thought about what Mr. E. had said about God not having a Plan B. But, he mused, he's not God and he needed a Plan B now because his Plan A had been shot to pieces.

Chapter 25-X-10

The X-10 Graphite Reactor used neutrons emitted in the fission of uranium-235 to convert uranium-238 into the new element of plutonium-239. Brenda's job was to assist with pushing fresh slugs of uranium into the rows of rod-shaping channels. She was merely a floor worker, the lowest-rated position. She did not care about the decrease in pay; she only wanted to be mentally occupied enough to keep her mind off of Dale and his apparent two-timing of her with the raven-haired vixen in Y-12.

Brenda enjoyed being in the thick of Oak Ridge's mission, and making a quantifiable contribution to the war effort. While every job in Oak Ridge was in support of ending the war, this felt like the front lines to her and not merely some tertiary role. She liked getting sweaty and grimy during her shift.

In her baggy overalls and gloves and goggles, Brenda felt glad to not be projecting a feminine appearance which could make her attractive to someone. She was taking herself off the market and every little bit helped. When she was fully garbed for work, she was almost unrecognizable as a woman.

During a lunch break, Brenda was carrying her tray to the table of a couple of other X-10 girls. Brenda was fast making friends, both men and women. However, during times like lunch breaks, each gender tended to congregate together.

As she moved toward her table, Brenda overheard a conversation amongst a table of men.

"I tell you, it happened again," one man said to the men.

"Aw, your screwy, Eddie," another answered. "You're just getting forgetful in your old age."

Daniel S. Zulli

"No, really. I may not remember where I put my keys, but when it comes to my tools, I don't forget that. On Monday, I left my stuff right where I always do - on the top shelf in my locker. Tuesday when I came into work, they were missing. That never happens to me. And that wasn't the first time either. It happened a few weeks ago. My whole day was fouled up and that set our work back by a couple of days, until I could get more tools."

Brenda stopped to interject herself into the conversation. "Are you sure about this, Eddie?"

"Sure, I'm sure. Like I said, I can't remember what I had for lunch yesterday, but I know where I put my tools." Eddie punctuating his remark by tapping on the table as he spoke.

"Has anyone else had anything weird or unusual happen to them?" Brenda addressed the whole table of six men.

"It did me," another man spoke up. "I never said anything because I didn't want anyone to think I was screwy like Eddie." The other men laughed at Eddie.

"What was it that was strange?" Brenda asked.

"All my gear and clothes in my locker were all messed up one day. They weren't missing, but everything was ruined, cut to shreds. I thought maybe someone was playing a stupid prank on me, so I didn't say anything."

"Did having your stuff ruined affect your work? I have a reason for asking this, in case you guys are wondering why I would care."

"As a matter of fact, it did. I couldn't do my work in the fission room until I could get new gear. It really slowed work down. I thought that whoever did this had a crummy sense of humor. My boss wasn't laughing, that much I can tell you."

"Thanks," Brenda responded. "Anyone else?" They all nodded negative.

"Okay, look, guys," Brenda offered. "If anything odd or out of the ordinary happens to anyone else, let me know, okay?" The men all grunted affirmative. "Swell," she said.

Rats, Brenda thought to herself, proceeding to her table. *Of all the nutty things to happen to me, this is the last thing I wanted.*

A girl at their table noticed that Brenda seemed perplexed about something. "What's wrong? Your cat die?"

"What? Oh, nothing. I just have to call on someone I wish I didn't have to. You guys go ahead and eat without me. I'll meet you back at work."

Brenda took her tray to the receiving area of the lunch room and went directly to the main secretary of that section of X-10.

"Say, Annie," she said, "let me have a pen and paper, would you, please?"

With the stationery, Brenda fired off a terse note:

Meet me at the rec hall at 7. Work is not right.

Brenda sealed the note in an envelope and wrote "Dr. Hargrowe" on it, then handed it back to the secretary. "Annie, I need a huge favor. Can you get this lickety-split over to Y-12? It's very important."

"Sure thing. I'll get a runner."

Brenda was torn between not wanting to see Dale anymore and her desire to not see anything happen to their work. Unfortunately, he was the only person to whom she could turn. Whether anything happened after that, she could not control it. But she had to make the effort. She purposed to not get emotional or carried away with sentiment. Dale was merely a resource.

Daniel S. Zulli

Chapter 26-Intrigue

Dale was in his boss's office, not happy with the answers he was getting.

"Hal, look," he protested, "I don't like how this is going. If fact, it's *not* going. That's the problem. Nothing's been happening with our situation here. By now, all the security folks should have found out something or the someone who's doing the something."

"I know you're frustrated, Dale, but you've got to slow down and not be so anxious."

Dale raised his voice. "'Not be so anxious!' I just got a note from Brenda Andrews in X-10, and she said there is some strange stuff happening over there too. Hal, this is getting bigger by the day, and you don't seem to be worried about it!"

"I'm just as worried as you are. I just know that getting all worked up isn't going to solve the issue. My advice is you don't get yourself all in a lather and just go about your work. In fact, you need to focus on your work a little better, Dale. You seem to be distracted."

"I, uh...have had a lot on my mind lately. Sorry if I seem preoccupied. I'll knuckle down better."

"Good. Okay, get back to work." Hal dismissed him.

Walking out, Dale was still not satisfied. He knew, or thought he knew, that the security folks were engaged in all the oddities that he and Brenda have reported. But call it instinct, call it his gut, call it divine prompting, Dale just was not settled. He wondered if what Brenda wanted to tell him would make things worse.

If that were not enough, he would be seeing Brenda again, the first time since that day on the floor of Y-12, when she turned from him and right before she quit. Dale had no idea how he was going to handle this. His stomach was full of not just butterflies, but bees and gnats and every type of critter that buzzes and flitters about.

Dale tried to concentrate on his work, but did not do a very good job at it. When he got done with his shift, he was not sure of what it was he had worked on. His body went through the motions, but his mind had not been fully engaged.

He fairly flew to the rec hall. Dale was nervous. This place was not right for a heart-to-heart talk with Brenda. He imagined she knew this, which is why she picked this setting to finally see him.

Dale jumped out of his chair when she came in. "Brenda! I sure am glad to see you again. Look, I don't know what went wrong, but I sure would..."

Brenda cut him off. "I didn't come here to try and patch things up, so I'll make this quick." The stern look in her eyes pierced through Dale's heart.

"During lunch today at work, I overheard some guys say that they've had some whacky things happen to them too. They sounded intentional because it slowed their work down far too much to be a coincidence. My guess is our gremlin has moved over to X-10 now."

Dale controlled his urge to speak in a loud voice. "That's bad! I've been to Hal Rainey and then Colonel Hutchinson and back to Hal. They said they were on it. But nothing's happening to convince me that they are. And now this. It's just not stopping. The more I hear, the more I'm sure someone is trying to sabotage Oak Ridge and the gadget. I don't like this at all."

"What are you going to do now?"

"Not sure," Dale mused. "I've been warned by more than one person to mind my own business. I got called into Mr. Lohorn's office again. That was fun."

Brenda managed a slight smile. "I bet you felt like you had been to the principal's office, right?"

"The principal, the superintendent, Mother Superior, you name it. I've been told to mind my business and skip the detective stuff. Only problem is, the detective experts don't seem to be finding the whodunit."

Dale tried to change the subject. "Say, Brenda, I went to see Pastor Mike Miller in Maryville recently. He really helped me. He gave me a Bible and I've been reading it. You should -"

Brenda cut him off. "Look, this isn't the time nor place for hearts and flowers. I'm glad you saw Mike and are doing better. Wish I could say the same for myself. Maybe we'll talk more someday, but not now."

Brenda abruptly got up and walked out, leaving Dale staring at her back. He was disappointed that he didn't get the chance to make things right. He felt drained of all energy.

Despite Brenda's rejection, Dale hatched a plan. Seeing how his career and reputation were already on the line, and that the woman he thought had feelings for him apparently either didn't or got over them, he had nothing else to lose. And after hearing this latest news of intrigue in another plant, Dale decided to move. For his plan to work, he needed another person. He knew whom to ask.

Chapter 27-Bob

When he got home on Outer Drive, he approached his housemate. "Bob, I need some help, and you work in X-10. Interested?"

Bob looked up from his sports page. "What do you mean?"

Dale explained. "I know you've been here longer than me, since almost the beginning of Oak Ridge. But we've been working on something so big no one can even mention it, but it's something which can end this stupid war. But all our hard work is in jeopardy from forces that want it either delayed or broken. Remember that brick through the window a little while ago?"

"I'll say I do. Whoever tossed that thing could throw a fastball better than Ralph Branca!"

"It was a warning to me to keep my nose out of this thing because I was getting close to uncovering what was going on, and whoever's doing it didn't want me to find him out."

Dale was worked up, pacing in their living room. "Up until now, most all this bad stuff was happening in Y-12, where my friend Brenda and I work. Only now Brenda works in X-10 and she just told me some monkey business is happening there, too. This is where I need your help, Bob."

"I get you. But have you told the authorities and they're looking into this?"

"I have, and they are," Dale agreed. "I think they are, at least. I've gone to my supervisor more than once and to Colonel Hutchinson, the head of security, and they told me they're on it, but I'm not seeing any results. And, it's still going on if I'm reading what Brenda told me right."

"So, you're really positive some hanky-panky is going on with our stuff?"

"Positive. Way too much has happened for me to think it's all a coincidence."

"And you need my help to help catch these guys?"

"Bob, I wouldn't ever involve you if I didn't need your help," Dale said, with resolution in his voice. "And I need to tell you there might be some risk in this."

"Look, Dale," Bob replied, "I've worked far too hard to have someone come in here and foul up all our hard work. I'd love to find out who tossed that brick in my window so I can - as we say back home - 'moider da bum!' I'm in."

Bob might be a scientist in his own right, but he was as blue collar as they come. He never backed down from a good scrap.

When Dale reported to work the next morning, he immediately looked up Maggie Hancock, the woman who first reported to Brenda that she had noticed irregular computations on several calutrons.

"Maggie, I'm Dr. Hargrowe, from the research division. I believe you reported some unusual readings from more than one calutron to Brenda Andrews, is that correct?"

"Yes, I'm the one."

"Since you first reported that to Miss Andrews, have you noticed this happening anymore?"

"In fact, yes, on calutrons 4 and 7 here in this bay, and on 1 and 6 in the next bay over. Dr. Hargrowe, I don't like this one bit. And with Brenda - Miss Andrews - gone, I haven't told her replacement about this because she's so green and doesn't know the history of these things. I feel helpless just sitting by and watching what I know to be wrong!" Maggie was keyed up.

Dale answered her in a soothing voice. "Maggie, you've done great, and I really appreciate you taking an interest in these unusual occurrences. I agree with you: I don't like it myself. If you suspect anyone of being the culprit behind this, please let me know immediately. Will you do that?"

"Sure thing, Dr. Hargrowe." Maggie felt relieved she wasn't bearing this load by herself.

"Swell. I'm going to switch my hours to the night shift so I can keep an eye on things better. You just keep watching the day shift for me, okay?"

"Sure thing."

Leaving Maggie, Dale went to Miss Rivera and left her a note to give to Mr. Rainey:

Need to coordinate with some folks on the night shift for a few days.

It was a gamble, but Dale was rolling the dice to see if he could catch someone in the act of tampering with the calutrons. He couldn't stay on the night shift forever but could milk his "excuse" to Hal for a few days. Dale knew that Hal trusted him enough to not need an explanation for this sudden move.

Dale had Bob be on the lookout in X-10 as well, especially the locker room. He did not know if Bob would discover anything, but knowing Bob, he'd find a way. He had plenty of street smarts from growing up in Brooklyn. If there was a rat to be found out, Bob would find him.

Chapter 28-Discrepancy

Bob went to the X-10 plant, where he worked. He hung around the locker room area where the men would suit up for their shifts. He shuffled about, pretending to be about his business, dealing with various industrial items needed for work. Bob found it easy to find empty lockers and various pieces of equipment loosely strung in the room with which he could fiddle. Bob felt like he was back in his native Brooklyn as a teenager, milling about malt shops and record stores, whiling away the summertime hours with his friends.

Bob also walked around all the places in X-10 in which he was authorized, pretending to be busy working, but in reality, scoping out the plant for anything that looked out of place.

Dale was in Y-12 by 10 p.m. that night. He could easily look down upon the main floor of calutrons, even if some of the female workers were obscured by being on the other side of their machines. He hoped he could catch something - anything - out of the ordinary in terms of calutron worker that seemed out of place or doing anything suspicious.

With a thermos of coffee, a sandwich and some paperwork, Dale made himself comfortable for the night, staying out of the main calutron area but within its line-of-sight. He looked like he was going through his work on a lonely midnight shift, thus drawing no attention to himself. The calutron workers paid him no mind, not knowing that he was observing them.

The young ladies did their jobs professionally and efficiently. They adjusted their knobs and dials and recorded their information like they had been trained. The women who had the job Brenda once held made their rounds and monitored the girls. They took their breaks on time. When one went on a break, there were the floaters like Maggie Hancock who went from calutron to calutron, filling in for the girl.

The shift was orderly, precise, demonstrating the months of precise routine it had become. With this precision, Dale thought, it should be easy to spot any irregularity.

The shift wore on. Dale's appreciation for the well-oiled machine that Oak Ridge had become grew. This work never ended. It would not end until this world war was over, and whatever it was they were making was made.

Y-12 made any bee hive look clumsy and improvised by comparison.

Being on his first midnight shift was difficult. Dale's body hadn't adjusted to it like the regular midnight shift workers had. This was normal for them. Day was night and night was day. There were no windows in the calutron bays. They did not know it was dark outside, and that they should normally be in bed. The industrial lighting was the same during the day as it was during the night.

But Dale's interest in finding a solution to the sabotage dilemma kept him on edge. That and his thermos of coffee. He went to the break room to refill it around 2 a.m.

Everything continued as normal. Dale spied nothing wrong.

Until 3:30.

One calutron girl went on break as per her schedule. At the same time, the regular floater went on break too. The two of them left together to go have a smoke and a snack in their break area. To fill in for the both, another girl came in from the bay of calutrons next to theirs. She was short and wore glasses. Her dark-hair was pulled back in a bun. She took up her stool when the regular girl and the floater left. Call it intuition, but Dale locked in on her as she was a new face to come into this bay.

The girl appeared to be doing her job. She also adjusted her dials and knobs without any appearance of impropriety. Dale had no idea of how the calutrons should be set, so he didn't see anything obviously out of place. But he still observed her.

Like clockwork, the regular calutron girl and the floater came back from their break. The floater moved away to the next worker that was going on her break in another bay. The regular took her place in front of her machine. The substitute floater departed the area and moved on to another. Dale watched her leave.

The regular girl picked up her clipboard the sub had used. Then she looked up at the dials on the machine. Then she looked down on her clipboard again. Then back up to the dials. Dale could tell she read something on her paperwork that did not square with the calutron. No one else had done this.

The girl flipped through her other paperwork. It seemed like she was comparing other data she had been recording during the shift. Finally, she waved over to the floater who was filling in at another machine down the row.

The floater stood next to the regular and listened to her story. Dale saw the regular point to her paperwork, point up to the dials, and in an animated fashion seem to describe that something was amiss between the two.

Dale didn't need his coffee to put him on alert. He left his little hideout area and came down to the floor of calutrons. This might have been what he came to discover, perhaps the key to unlocking this mystery of false information that threatened to subvert the work in Oak Ridge.

He came upon the two ladies at the calutron. Since the machines produced a noticeable hum, he could not hear their conversation until he got close to them. When he came close, Dale heard the regular say to the floater in a very thick Southern accent, "Look, I know this ain't right, Darla. I've never had these readings before, and I know what the numbers should be."

"Excuse me," Dale addressed them. "My name is Dr. Hargrowe. I happen to notice you two seemed to be having an issue here. What exactly is going on?"

The women were too flustered to check Dale's restricted area badge or ask why he was there.

"I just came back from my break," the Southern girl said, "and I saw these figures and compared them to my calutron. I can tell you this ain't right. Something fishy happened when that girl filled in for me."

"Do you know who she is or what her name is?" Dale asked.

Both shook their heads. The floater offered, "I've seen her around before, but she goes all over the calutrons, filling in when everyone else goes on their breaks."

"Where do you think she would be now?"

"Hard to say," Darla, said. "She could be in any other section of calutrons or in another section of Y-12."

"Okay, thanks." To the Southern girl, he said, "Record the information as you found it. Then note next to it what you would have expected it to be if it read normally. Mark it with an asterisk so we can go back to it later and compare notes, all right?"

She nodded in agreement.

To Darla the floater, he said, "Do you have an extra clipboard I can use?"

"Sure. Take mine. I'll get another."

Dale took her clipboard, loosened his tie and rolled up his sleeves, giving the appearance of working the floor on this shift. This was the break he had hoped to get - finally putting a face onto what had been going wrong with this project. His goal now was to walk around Y-12 until he ran into the substitute calutron girl again.

Daniel S. Zulli

Chapter 29-Pursuit

Dale began his pursuit. He wasn't challenged as he walked around Y-12. The girls would look up at him, but Dale would look over the machines and the workers, make notations on the papers on his clipboard, appear satisfied with what he saw, then move on, seemingly being about his official duties. His clearance badge was in full view, but no one thought to examine it closely. On occasion, he would ask a calutron girl how things were going, to which they would answer respectfully enough that things were fine.

He did a good job of pretending to know what he was doing.

Dale continued his perusal of Y-12. Everything looked normal. Everyone was about their business, as they had been trained to do and had spent months doing. Calutrons hummed. People scurried and moved about and did their jobs with military precision.

Not finding his quarry, Dale approached one calutron girl in the most extreme part of the plant.

"Say," he said, at once getting her attention, "I need to find one of you calutron gals and get a message to her from back home, something about her mother. She goes around substituting and filling in. I forgot get her name," he said, tapping his clipboard as if trying to recall her name. "But she's short with dark hair and glasses. I've got to pull her off shift and see if I can get her home. Have you seen her?"

"You must be talking about Abby Felton," the calutron girl said, trying to be helpful. "I haven't seen her in a while. Last time I did, she was in the C wing, working over there. Gosh, I hope everything's all right!"

"I hope so, too," Dale responded, not stretching the truth. "I hope it will all be better soon. Thanks for your help."

He left the B calutron wing and headed over to the C Wing of Y-12, which was devoted to the electromagnetic "racetrack" area, where the Beta racetracks used enormous amount of copper for the magnetic machines. There were 36 calutron tanks in C wing; B wing had 96 Alpha calutron machines. It was, therefore, quite easy for someone like Abby Felton to move about, filling in wherever there was a need. If she were indeed the one of perhaps many workers tampering with the calutron settings with the intent on sabotaging the Clinton Engineering Works project, Dale could see how this was the perfect setting for it to be done.

This time it was riskier, as his own restricted area badge was color-coded for B wing, and not C wing. He silently prayed that he could spot Abby Felton before he was challenged.

But there was nothing quite as convincing as *looking* like he belonged there. He kept to himself, looking down at his clipboard, not peering around like a country tourist in Times Square for the first time looking up at the skyscrapers in awe. New York City locals can spot a tourist a mile away. Dale did not want to stand out like that. He cast just enough glances up from his clipboard and note-taking to be able to look around for the short, dark-haired girl with glasses.

It was getting near 4:30. The new shift would come in at 6 a.m. Dale hoped that he could find his prey before the shift ended.

He did.

She was working at a calutron at the end of the bay of eight machines on both sides. Dale gave her credit. Abby Felton was professional and poised. If she was Oak Ridge's version of Mata Hari, she looked good.

Dale's heart started to race. He had to consciously remind himself to play it smooth, to not let his excitement tip her off that he was coming her way to catch her.

He came up upon worker after worker, looking like he was inspecting each girl's work and checking up on them.

His heart almost stopped when one girl said, "Say, you aren't our regular floor boss. Who are you?"

"I had to fill in for him at short notice…uh…Kathy," he said as suavely as he could, noticing her name badge. "I think it was something from the cafeteria that did not agree with him. He'll be back tomorrow." Dale said, hoping he would not have to produce his name. He also hoped this regular man would not suddenly show up.

Without waiting for Kathy's approval, Dale moved on, away from her and closer to Abby. Kathy wasn't totally satisfied with Dale's answer, but she turned from looking at him back to her calutron.

He was just one calutron away from Abby. Again, Dale stopped by the last remaining girl's machine. He did not talk to her, just nodded and made a few notes. He left her with, "Good job."

He made it to Abby Felton's calutron.

"Hello, Abby," Dale politely said. "How's business on the old gal tonight?"

"Everything's running smooth as silk, Mr. - " She paused. "I'm sorry, what was your name, sir?"

"Let's take a break," Dale said, his tone not as polite. "Come with me."

Dale held her elbow firmly enough so that Abby could not break free, but not dramatically enough to warrant looks from the other girls.

"Hey, what's up, mister?" Abby protested. By this time, they had moved far enough away that, combined with the hum of the machines and racetrack, no one heard her.

Dale got her alone in a corner. "I know what you've been up to. I know that you're the one - perhaps there are more - who has been fudging data on the calutrons and messing with their dials so as to give false readings. I know that you've been doing this intentionally, trying to throw off this project. Why?" he demanded.

Abby's eyes grew bigger. "Look, mister, I didn't mean no harm, but I needed the money. My pappy's very sick back home in Clarksville. What are you going to do with me?"

"You're in big trouble, Abby," Dale warned. "I don't know what all you can be charged with, but if I were the judge, I'd put you away for a long time."

Abby started to melt and tear up. She repeated, "What are you going to do with me?"

Dale ignored her question. "Are you working alone or are you doing this for someone else?"

"All I know is I do this for some guy named as Ted. He's the one who contacted me, and said he'd pay me if I did this for him. That's all I know."

"Do you see him regularly?"

"Once a week."

"When and where?"

"Behind the main post office. He hands me the money - ten dollars cash each time - and I drop it in the mail to go back home."

"When will the next time be?"

"Tomorrow night at 10, before my shift starts," Abby said.

"Okay, here's what I want you to do. You're in this deep, kid, and you had better do as I say or else it will go worse for you when you stand before the judge. Do as I tell you and it might go better. You hear me?"

"Y...yes, sir," Abby said, choking back the tears. "What do you want me to do?"

"First, you have to play it cool. You can't let this Ted guy suspect for a second that I know. You just meet him as normal, like nothing ever happened. That's all I want you to do. You got it? You meet Ted at 10 and do everything normal."

"Okay, sir. Look, I'm real sorry if I caused any trouble. It's just that I needed the money for my daddy."

"We'll deal with that later. I need to get to whoever hired you in order to get to the bottom of this. Oh, and another thing: from here on in you don't mess with these calutrons ever again, you hear me, Abby?" Dale's tone indicated how serious he was. "I'm going to get you removed from Oak Ridge, but until I do, you had better not tamper with these machines again, or fudge with the data. And I can find you again if you don't do exactly like I say and meet Ted tomorrow; so, there's no place you can run, Abby. Now git."

Dale released the terrified girl and she bolted. Dale walked back to the calutron in which he had caught Abby. The regular girl had just come back from her break.

"Hi, there, Miss…Rawls," Dale said, casting a quick glance at her name badge. "Abby had to take a sudden break. She was feeling a little light-headed. She was just gone a minute before you arrived, so don't worry about finding your calutron unmanned. Just make sure everything is a-okay with your dials and readings, all right?"

"No problem, sir," Miss Rawls said.

Dale left C wing. His work on this night shift was done. He felt accomplished toward finding the solution to this enigma. From Y-12, he caught the bus back home. He needed to compare notes with Bob.

Dale wanted to sleep, but had to wait up for Bob to get in and report on how his night at X-10 went, as well as coordinate the evening's meeting between Abby Felton and the one who was paying her to tamper with the calutrons.

Around 7 a.m. Bob came in, looking like a rumpled towel tossed into a corner.

"Nothing!" he complained. "Not a single thing happened. Last night was longer than a double-header in the middle of July!"

Dale grinned. "Sorry 'bout that, Bob. I deeply appreciate your effort, though. But I hit pay dirt."

Bob perked up. "How so?"

"I finally saw and caught up with the girl who's been messing with the calutrons to get bogus readings. There may be more than one, but at least I got one. She was being paid to do it because she said she needed the money. She said a man pays her weekly, and—this is the best part—she's meeting him tonight to collect her money. It will be at 10 o'clock behind the main post office in the townsite. If we can catch him, we might crack this deal. You in?"

Bob was enthusiastic. "Am I! Wild horses couldn't keep me away. I want to catch the bum who caused me to stay up all night looking for him!"

"Great. But if you feel as bad as you look, I suggest you hit the rack and gear up for an interesting night. I need some sleep too."

Dale was satisfied with his night's work. He was finally getting somewhere with this mystery.

As he was lying down, he suddenly realized he had forgotten his coffee thermos back in B wing.

Chapter 30-Death

That night, Dale stationed Bob about 25 yards to the far side of the alley behind the post office, tucked away between two buildings. He ensured Bob could see clearly any movement as well as see Dale for any signal from him.

Dale went on the opposite end. He desperately hoped that Abby had not gotten too scared to meet for her money, or else had given any indication that a trap was being set for Ted. She was young and frightened, and was facing who-knew how much legal trouble. Even if she hadn't said anything to Ted, her demeanor might give her away.

The best-case scenario would be if she did not have to see or talk to Ted, merely meet at the prescribed time for the money exchange. The worst-case scenario would be if neither showed up. But, since Dale knew Abby's name, at least he felt like he could accomplish something by tracking her down afterward.

Dale shook his head as he hid in place. He had been able to put 2 and 2 together and come up with Abby and Ted. How come all the "experts" had not been able to do the same?

It was 9:45 p.m.

Being on the midnight shift the night before got Dale used to hearing every second of his watch click by. This made it easier for Dale to endure these last 15 minutes. It seemed like his heart rate mirrored his watch; he could feel one and hear the other both moving together. Even though behind the post office was relatively quiet this time of night, Oak Ridge was active 24 hours a day. Two people like Ted and Abby causally passing through would not arouse suspicion.

At 9:57, Abby entered the alleyway on the side closest to Dale's position. She walked casually behind the stores and shops toward the post office.

To Dale, she did not appear to be nervous or anxious, but it was dark enough for him to not be sure. The street and store lights cast irregular shadows on the scene.

A man showed up at 9:59 at the other side of the alleyway, closer to Bob's hideout. His hat was drawn low, obscuring most of his face. Both hands were set in his suit coat pockets.

Dale could feel anger well up inside him. The very thought that someone could be selling out the war effort in Oak Ridge caused his blood to race. Even if Abby did what she did to help her ailing father, that was not enough cause to hinder or halt this critical effort involving thousands of dedicated people who were giving it their all.

Dale looked closely as the man, who had to be Ted, drew nearer. Even in the gloom, Dale thought the man looked familiar. What was it? Dale wracked his brain. Oak Ridge was a closed community, and people had seen most everyone else at one time or another: waiting in line at the store, at the movie theater, the bowling alley, the new swimming pool - somewhere. Where was it?

Then it hit him. The ton of bricks that is normally associated with this feeling seemed light in comparison to what Dale felt. He had seen this man at the Pastor Mike Miller's church service at The Chapel On the Hill. He was positive. Ted had even helped take up the offering, which went to paying the various ministers their stipend for doing the services. Dale remembered looking up at Ted when he came to his pew with the offering basket as he was on the end of the pew with Brenda to his right. Ted the usher in church was also Ted the traitor!

Ironically, both times Dale had seen Ted, money was involved. Dale remembered the Bible passage which stated that the love of money was the root of all evil. He could only imagine what Ted was being paid to be a part of this nefarious activity. The $10 he was paying Abby was probably peanuts to what he was getting. It made him sick to his stomach.

Abby and Ted walked closer together. Their routine was perfected. When the two finally got within five yards of each other, Dale saw Ted pull a bill out of his left coat pocket. Abby extended her left hand, received the money, then slipped it into her purse. Neither said a word. Abby was being paid for her week's worth of treacherous deeds. Dale could easily imagine how Abby would then walk to the front of the post office, put the currency into an envelope, and place it in the drop box to go her father. It was slick.

Dale had seen what he wanted - to catch them in act. He had told Bob to wait until he made his move. As Ted walked closer to Dale's end of the alley, Dale began to step out nonchalantly, as if he too were on an evening stroll.

Bob wasn't as patient.

Just as Ted passed the money to Abby, the man from Brooklyn could not control himself.

"Hey, you!" he yelled at Ted, not wanting him to get away. Bob's shout shattered the stillness of the night. Abby jumped several feet and let out a blood-curdling scream.

Frightened, Abby turned and ran, bumping into Ted, who knocked her to the ground. Instantly, Ted started to run. Dale had no choice but give chase.

"Stop!" Dale shouted.

Ted looked both ways, then ran in between Dale and Bob into an alley perpendicular to the one that ran behind the post office.

Dale and Bob joined together in the middle of the alley to give chase. As they ran, Dale saw Ted dip his right hand into his coat pocket and pull out something. Dale saw a gleam of metal then heard the sharp *pop!* of a pistol.

The first shot careened off a trash can. Bob yelled, "Come back here!" Despite being shot at, both Dale and Bob were fueled by the desire to catch Ted. The odds of Ted getting an accurate shot off as he ran seemed remote.

Ted fired again. Dale heard the shot hit the brick of a building next to him. An instant later he felt a sharp punch in his right side, knocking him to the ground. Placing his left hand on his side, Dale felt the warm ooze of his blood.

Another shot made Dale look up from his seated position. He glanced over his shoulder to where Bob had been, only to see his friend crumple to the ground.

Dale forgot about Ted.

"Bob!" Dale shouted. "Bob, are you all right?"

Dale stumbled to Bob, about 10 yards behind him. He couldn't tell how serious his own injuries were. It felt like some ribs had been broken but he didn't know if the ricocheting bullet had caused any internal damage. He was in a lot of pain.

Dale reached Bob. He was face down. Even in the darkened alley, there was enough light to reveal a pool of blood was growing beneath his friend.

When he pulled Bob over, Dale could see spurts of blood coming from the side of Bob's neck. Ted's wild shot had severed Bob's carotid artery.

"Bob, no!" Dale wailed. This was not what he had planned on. They were going to catch Ted and get to the bottom of this affair. This was not supposed to happen.

Dale clamped his handkerchief around the wound, but Bob had already lost too much blood.

He looked up at Dale with empty eyes. A gurgle came from Bob's lips as he tried to speak. Blood spurted out of his mouth. Dale held Bob's head close to his.

"Catch that bum. Catch..."

Dale felt the last bit of life leave Bob O'Neil's body. It became limp. Dale held him close and sobbed.

"Oh, God, no! I'm so sorry, Bob!" he cried. "I'm so sorry!"

Dale could hear yelling and footsteps. Then he felt himself grow weak. His grasp of Bob grew looser as he slumped to one side, unable to keep himself upright.

As blackness engulfed his consciousness, Dale pictured that sunny fall day when he went to Norris for the picnic. He saw Brenda.

Daniel S. Zulli

Chapter 31-Fallout

When Dale awoke, he saw nothing but white.

In a fog, he tried to piece together the last events he remembered with what was happening now.

He couldn't move his right arm.

He closed his eyes and groaned. He remembered his good friend and roommate, Bob O'Neil, from Brooklyn, lying in his arms and slipping away into eternity. His plan had backfired and it caused Bob's death.

Dale was alive but didn't care to be. What had started out to be a noble mission ended in disaster. His wounds would heal, but Bob's would not.

And, Ted the traitor from church had not been captured. It had been a bungled job from beginning to end.

Dale had never felt so alone and helpless. Bob was gone and the girl he thought was his closest friend had left him. He wondered if he would lose his job and possibly his career. Perhaps he might lose his freedom if someone decided to press charges against him. During war time, that was a real possibility. What they were doing in Oak Ridge was serious enough to easily find an offense against him. Catching Abby Felton may have all been for naught if the powers-that-be decided that Dr. Dale Hargrowe was the one at fault, which led to someone's death.

A starched nurse escorted Hal Rainey in to Dale's room.

"Don't be long," she said.

"I won't. Thanks." The nurse left.

Hal stared down at Dale, who would have shrunk into the mattress if he could have.

Finally, he spoke. "Boy, Dale, you've gotten yourself into a pickle now."

Dale's throat was parched and dry. "I know who's been tampering with the calutrons and who hired her," he croaked. "We almost had them. Bob and I - " he stopped. At the thought of Bob, Dale could not continue with the lump in his throat and ache in his heart.

"I know, Dale. He's dead."

Dale closed his eyes. "Hal, I didn't mean for this to happen. But he started shooting at us when we were chasing him. We almost had him."

"The MPs are looking for the guy. Don't worry, they'll get him. In the meantime, must get better and then we'll have to figure out what to do with you. Dale, if you had only let Colonel Hutchinson and his boys take care of this, none of this would have happened."

"That's just it, Hal," Dale protested. "They weren't doing anything that I could see. When I get out of here I'm going to see him to tell him what I found out. I know the girl's name who was messing with the calutrons."

"That'll be fine. I'm sure he'll be interested. But get some rest now and we'll see you when you get back on your feet."

"What about Bob? Will there be any funeral for him?"

"We have a team working on that. They're collecting his belongings from your house and everything will be taken care of. You'll be informed."

Hal left, leaving Dale with his thoughts. Even though the morphine was deadening his physical pain, it could not erase his memory of holding Bob O'Neil as life departed from his body. No narcotic would ease the sorrow in his heart which he would have to carry with him until he met his Maker.

When the nurse came by Dale called out for her.

"What happened to me?" he asked.

"You took a bullet in your side. You're very lucky it was a ricochet and not a direct hit. You have three broken ribs and a collapsed lung. Fortunately, the doctor got the bullet out and there isn't any internal organ damage. You'll heal up and be out of here in a week. Sorry about your friend," she said.

"Me too."

"Get some rest now," she instructed and left.

Dale closed his eyes and started to drift off in a morphine-induced haze. He was determined to tell Colonel Hutchinson about Abby Felton and the plot he uncovered. But Dale still had some more questions. Was Ted the mastermind? Were there more operatives trying to subvert their efforts in making the gadget? For all Dale knew, Abby was back at work, fiddling with the knobs and dials on the calutrons even as he lay there.

As soon as he got out of the hospital, he would tell everyone about Ted paying Abby to do this terrible deed. He would find Ted and make him pay for killing Bob. He would get to the bottom of this, once and for all. He would...

He never finished the thought. Sleep captured him and held him in its grip.

"Dale," a feminine voice said.

It was not the regular nurse. Maybe it was the night shift nurse. A new one.

"Dale!" she called out again. Dale felt himself be shaken.

"Hey, sleepy head - wake up," she said.

127

It wasn't easy, but Dale became conscious. Opening his eyes, he saw Brenda Andrews sitting next to him, shaking his left arm.

"Did you get the number of the truck that ran over me?" Dale asked in a self-pity tone.

"I heard what happened. News travels fast here. What on earth were you thinking?"

"I almost had him, Brenda. *We* almost had him. I finally caught the girl who was fudging on the calutrons and I had set a trap to catch the man who was paying her. But then it didn't go well."

"I'm so sorry about Bob," Brenda offered. "But, how are you doing, you big lug?"

"I'll recover. Not sure my career ever will. I might be back on the first train to Boston when I'm out of this place."

"That's possible. But even if they do ship you out, you did a good job of trying to salvage our little operation here. You did more than most anyone else would have done."

Brenda's words felt comforting. Dale didn't think he would hear anyone in Oak Ridge pay him a compliment over his involvement in trying to solve this dilemma.

"Listen, I know you're not 100%," Brenda said, "but we have to resolve a problem just as big as the bogus calutron deal. And since I have a captive audience, you're not going to bolt on me until we do, *capisce?*"

"Doesn't look like I have much choice," Dale sat up with a grimace. His head was becoming clearer. "In fact, that sounds like a swell idea. Seeing how I'm already beat up, another go-around with a crazy dame shouldn't hurt me anymore."

"And in this corner," Brenda mimicked the nasal tone of a boxing announcer in the ring, introducing a prize fight.

"Let me start," Dale said. "What in the world got you so mad at me? For the life of me, I can't figure out what I did to deserve the wrath of God."

Brenda was indignant. "Are you kidding me, buster? You really don't know?"

"No," Dale answered with a firm voice. "And since I can't decipher the top-secret code you females talk in, please enlighten me."

"Okay, I will. You were caught red-handed making time with that girl from your office, the head receptionist."

Dale was stunned. "*What?* Are you serious?"

"As a heart attack, *Dr.* Hargrowe. Red-handed."

"And by whom, may I ask?" Dale felt like a defense attorney. He was on trial, actually.

Daniel S. Zulli

"By Trudy Mac. She came into the plant one day and saw you sitting next to Miss Home-wrecker, and saw you get real frisky with her."

Dale wracked his thoughts. This was insane, he thought. He could not for the life of him place this incident. He did know it never happened.

"When was this?"

"Several weeks ago."

Dale started to remember when he talked to Miss Rivera that one day in the break room, and seeing Trudy Mac come in.

"Okay, wait a minute," he said. "She's got it all wrong. I sat next to Miss Rivera all right, but only to make small talk with her. But I never made a pass at her at all, Brenda. I swear."

"So, what did Trudy Mac see?" Brenda challenged.

"I don't know, but I never did anything wrong. I was just talking to her because she's always so miserable. In fact, she hates me. She hates everyone. She hates being here in Oak Ridge. She's a real mean queen. I remember Trudy Mac coming in and we chit-chatted for a minute before she did her work. But trust me - there is nothing between me and Regina Rivera."

"You didn't touch her knee, or any other part of her?"

"No! I wouldn't touch her with a ten-foot pole. She would probably take it from me and beat me with it, anyway."

"So, there's nothing between you and her?"

"Not a thing," Dale protested. "Never was, and never will be. Look, Brenda, I'm crazy nuts about you and have been since I first rode into this cow-town. I can't believe you'd think I'd sneak behind your back with another gal. I swear, you're the only one for me. And trust me - I sure can't handle any more!"

Dale's sincerity finally warmed Brenda's heart and she melted, hearing what she needed to hear.

"Oh, you big lug!" Brenda cheered. She reached over to give Dale a hug but inadvertently grabbed his right side.

"Ow!" Dale hollered. "Ease up before you break more ribs!"

"Sorry!" Brenda said through laughter mixed with tears. "Dale, you don't know how much agony I've gone through these past weeks. I thought I was going to die when you waved to me on the floor. I was crushed into a thousand pieces seeing you there."

"But why would Trudy Mac say what she did?" Dale queried. "I don't get it."

"Me neither. But Miss Trudy McIntyre and I are going to have a serious pow-wow over it."

Dale's room had a window that looked out into the front parking lot. He and Brenda heard a car roar into it and screech to a halt.

129

Looking out the window, Brenda saw an olive-drab colored government vehicle. It had two stars on the front license plate. From the back seat poured Army Colonel Wesley Hutchinson, chief of security in Oak Ridge, and a civilian whom she did not recognize. The major, whose job it was to make sure there were chocolates in the general's office, got out of the driver's seat and scurried to the passenger seat to open the door for General Groves, who looked both tired and rip-roaring angry.

The entourage stormed into the hospital without asking for either help or directions. They headed directly to Dale Hargrowe's room.

"This is him, general," the civilian man said.

"Are you Hargrowe?" General Groves roared.

"Yes, sir, I am," Dale responded, swallowing.

"What do you do here?" General Groves continued in a loud voice.

"I'm an engineer in Y-12, sir."

"And what's this I hear that you've been doing detective work, getting a man killed along the way?" The conversation wasn't going well and Dale didn't think that it was going to have a satisfactory conclusion.

"Sir, I can explain," Dale said.

"Please do," General Groves said, with false politeness, "although I seriously doubt it will be to my liking."

"General, I uncovered a plot to sabotage all our work here in Oak Ridge. Someone was intentionally falsifying the information the calutrons were putting out to either delay or damage what we're working on. And you don't know how sorry I am that my roommate was killed. He was helping me and was a very good man."

"So, you think you could do a better job of uncovering this plot than my security team?" General Groves demanded, nodding his head toward Colonel Hutchinson. "Do you?"

"Yes, sir. No, sir," Dale stammered. "I mean, I didn't think they were getting any results. It was still going on. I raised the issue with a lot of people, but nothing was happening. I ... I took it upon myself to see if I could help the investigation. I didn't mean any harm, sir."

"Well, Hargrowe," General Groves raised his voice, "your impudence has gotten a man killed and caused a huge mess! As soon as you're back on your feet and out of this hospital, I want you out of Oak Ridge and on the first train back home. Do you hear me?"

"Yes, sir. I understand."

Dale sunk low in his bed. If he could have fallen through the mattress, he would have.

General Groves turned and stormed out of the room. The major and civilian followed. Colonel Hutchinson stayed behind, looming over Dale's bed. After the entourage entered the car, it flew rocks and kicked up dust as it departed.

Dale was apologetic. "Colonel, I didn't mean to get ahead of you guys, but I thought I could do some good following a hunch I had, and - "

Colonel Hutchinson cut him off. "We were following our own leads, Hargrowe. We almost had this case wrapped up before you interfered. But what did you find, so we can compare notes?"

"I found a girl named Abby Felton, who was being paid by a man named Ted. I never got his last name, but I remembered him from a chapel service I attended one time. He was there. He works somewhere in Oak Ridge. He was paying Abby to tamper with the calutrons and produce false readings in order to slow the project down, if not ruin it. I don't know if Abby was the only person involved in the actual sabotage or not."

"That's all I need to know, Hargrowe."

Colonel Hutchinson abruptly turned and left the room.

Silence filled the room. Dale closed his eyes and felt as low as a man could feel. Everything he had worked for with every good intention was now gone.

Brenda broke the mood.

"I told you it wasn't good for the general to learn your name."

Dale grinned. Even in defeat, Brenda could lift his spirits with a precocious wisecrack.

Chapter 32-Questions

Brenda was fit to be tied when she stomped into the head office of the firm that had the food management contract for Oak Ridge. Trudy Mac worked in a small office with barely enough room for a desk and filing cabinet to the right of the main secretary's station.

Not bothering for a courtesy check-in with the young lady at the front desk, Brenda, spied Trudy Mac through the open blinds in her office, marched through the little swinging door that partitioned off the main area and went into Trudy Mac's office. She shut the door firmly and closed the blinds.

Startled, Trudy Mac stood up, wide-eyed. "Brenda! What on earth are you doing here? You look like you just backed into an electric fence on a rainy day."

"You betcha I have, Trudy Mac," Brenda said with a take-no-prisoners tone in her voice. "You owe me some serious explanations, roomie. So, sit and start talking."

"What are you talking about?" Trudy Mac either truly did not know, or was feigning ignorance well.

"I just came from Dale's hospital room," Brenda said. "Even though he's been on my hit list lately, I had to see him after I heard he got shot. And, we had to clear the air about why he was on my hit list in the first place, about what you told me."

"What did he say?"

"He told me his side of the story. He said he was only talking to that secretary that day because she's so unfriendly, and that he didn't put the moves on her like you told me. He said he had no feelings for her whatsoever, that she was meaner than a wet hen all the time and he was only trying to make polite conversation with her. So, what gives? Why did you say he was two-timing me when he wasn't?"

Trudy Mac began to tear up. "Oh, Brenda! I'm so sorry. I didn't mean to cause any trouble. It's just that I … I was jealous, I guess, that you had found a nice guy when so many of us single girls haven't yet. You met Dale as soon as he got here, and there are thousands of us running around, trying to find Mr. Right and we haven't! Brenda, I'm so sorry," she repeated. "I guess I was acting like a silly school girl who just lost the guy she wanted to take her to the prom to the competition. I didn't mean to do you any harm, really."

Trudy Mac pulled out a tissue and started to dab her eyes. Brenda stared at her thoughtfully, not 100% sure of her honesty but not having enough evidence to prove her wrong. This was a serious breach of female etiquette, and Brenda was trying to process Trudy Mac's explanation as well as seeing if their relationship could be restored. "Okay, look," Brenda said, "I'm going to put you on probation. If you ever pull this stunt again, Trudy Mac, your stuff will be out the window so fast you'll think a tornado hit our room. Got it?"

Trudy Mac sniffled and smiled weakly. "Got it. I promise to behave myself."

Chapter 33-Delay

Dale was unceremoniously discharged from the hospital after his week recovering. He could feel the stares of the hospital staff as he walked through. Even though his right arm had not been injured, it was in a sling, keeping him from moving it and interfering with his ribs and right lung healing.

He had to report to Mr. Lohorn's office again, this time to initiate paperwork for his exit from Oak Ridge and back to Cambridge. Being called back into Lohorn's office, especially for this reason, was the ultimate humiliation. It was in this office that Dale had received his initial briefing and warning about obeying all the strict rules. Then, he had been called back to it with a warning to behave himself. Now, Dale had to see him a third time, admitting that he had not behaved. Now he had to pay the price.

"Mr. Lohorn is expecting you, Dr. Hargrowe," the front desk receptionist said, trying not to look at him, as if she knew what he was there for.

"Thanks," Dale murmured. He entered the sanctum.

"Close the door, please," Mr. Lohorn said, not looking at Dale but down at his paperwork. The tension in the room was thick.

Finally, Mr. Lohorn quietly spoke.

"I've been instructed to process you out of Oak Ridge, Dr. Hargrowe."

"I know. Do what you have to do."

"I'll do just that," Mr. Lohorn said, "as soon as I can locate your file."

"Excuse me? Could you please say that again?"

"I said, Dr. Hargrowe," Mr. Lohorn repeated, "that with all the files and paperwork of the tens of thousands of people who have come and left Oak Ridge, I cannot seem to find yours."

"And what does that mean, if I may ask?"

Mr. Lohorn continued to look down at his paperwork. "It means that your leaving here may not be as quick as some folks would like."

"I don't understand, Mr. Lohorn," Dale said.

Mr. Lohorn finally looked up. "Dr. Hargrowe, what I am about to say pains me to no end. I wish it were not true, but alas, it is."

Dale did not respond. He didn't know what to say.

"I know what's been going on," Mr. Lohorn finally said.

"You do?"

"Regretfully, yes."

"Why haven't you said anything?" Dale questioned.

"Because I cannot," Mr. Lohorn said, his voice indicating sadness. "They say confession is good for the soul," he continued. "I've lived with this for many long months now, and even though you cannot grant me absolution, I have to confess to you now."

Dale sat there, speechless. This conversation was going far from where he had thought it would go.

Mr. Lohorn began slowly, deliberately.

"I was in Knoxville one night. I had been working about 15 hours a day, seven days a week, and I needed a much-deserved break. I normally don't drink except wine with my dinner, but this night I went to a bar to unwind. One drink led to another, and before I knew it, I was outside, getting some air and trying to clear my head.

"Simply put, Dr. Hargrowe, in my drunken stupor, I had a moral failure. I saw a young person and made an inappropriate advance."

"You made a pass at a girl?" Dale asked.

"Yes, only it wasn't a female," Mr. Lohorn hung his head.

Dale was stunned. He could not believe what he was hearing.

"If it were possible to get things worse, it got worse," Mr. Lohorn continued. "This person was conspiring with the people who are involved in this nefarious business in which you have involved yourself. I know this because I myself caught one of their members talking about it to another one night in a coffee shop. When I confronted these men, one said that he knew what I had done that night in Knoxville, that he knew the young man I had accosted. He said if I knew what was good for me, I should keep quiet."

Mr. Lohorn's voice quivered, "Dale, my wife stayed back in Syracuse when I came here so our two kids could finish high school there. I have worked long and hard to get where I am today. My reputation is immaculate. I have never done anything like that before in my life. Even now I don't understand it. If word got out of what I had done in my terrible lapse of judgment, I would be ruined. I couldn't bear that. So, I kept quiet. I kept quiet while these people were working on destroying our work, on ending the gadget. This has gnawed at my soul for months!"

Dale could see that Mr. Lohorn was on the verge of cracking under the strain of this weight. Holding all this in had taken its toll on this stoic, reserved, matter-of-fact professional, who didn't have a single stain on his stellar record. Mr. Lohorn put his head in his hands, his shoulders heaving from his labored breathing. It was heart-wrenching for Dale to have to see this. He forgot about his own career plight.

"Mr. Lohorn, I'm so sorry this happened to you. But what does this mean for me? You said you wouldn't toss me out of here because you can't find my paperwork. I don't get it."

Mr. Lohorn inhaled deeply and looked up.

"It's quite simple, Dale," he said. Mr. Lohorn only called him "Dale" when he wanted to relate to him on a personal level. This was the second time.

"I know what you have done to try and catch these people. I know how close you came. And I applaud you for that. I also know that this thing is bigger than we all imagine. I can't confirm anything other than what I know for sure. But I know that you are the only one who is truly trying to catch these scumbags." It was strange to hear Mr. Lohorn speak in such an earthy manner.

"If I can redeem myself in any way, if I can do anything to help you solve this enigma, if I can atone for my sins in any capacity, I want to do it. I am going to take my time 'finding' your paperwork so you can be free to continue in your pursuit of these traitors. Since you have been relieved from your work, you now have the time to do so. You can keep your security badge and continue to move about. Dale, I want you to catch these miserable, rotten, Benedict Arnolds and get them put away so long they'll forget the sun ever shone." Mr. Lohorn's face became firm, resolute. Dale could see him straighten up with conviction and resolve.

"Mr. Lohorn, I can't tell you enough how grateful I am that you're doing this. Between you and me, I don't think the one girl and the man bribing her are the only ones involved. I have some hunches I'd like to act on. I smell a rat big-time here, and you're giving me the opportunity I need to really get this going. And don't worry, sir, I will never breathe a word of what you just told me to anyone. You can bet on that."

"I do not know how long I can look for your paperwork, Dale," Mr. Lohorn said, "but I'll delay as long as I possibly can. Good luck to you, son."

A few days later, Colonel Hutchinson filed a report to General Groves that Abby Felton had been caught at the bus station in Clinton, trying to flee Oak Ridge and go back to Clarksville.

She also gave him the name of Ted Hildebrandt, who worked in the new K-25 plant - the third of the major plants in Oak Ridge - as a lower-level technician involved in the gaseous diffusion process. Upon investigation, it was revealed that Ted Hildebrandt had connections with a group of people back at the University of Chicago that had Nazi sympathies.

Abby Felton was merely someone whom Ted Hildebrandt hired to subvert the work on the gadget. He was determined to be the sole operative and not part of a larger organization.

Colonel Hutchinson was pleased to report that he had been following tips and clues that were leading to Abby Felton separate from Dale's investigation, and had been hot on her trail. He had interviewed several women who worked on the calutrons in Y-12 and the trail was pointing to this one, lone girl as the person who was tampering with the machines.

Colonel Hutchinson declared to General Groves that the case had been solved and was now closed.

Chapter 34-Suspicion

Howard Lohorn was very capable when it came to bureaucratic mumbo-jumbo. When Colonel Hutchinson inquired every so often regarding Dale's status, Mr. Lohorn's red tape-ese satisfied the colonel and continued the delay. Mr. Lohorn was the supreme paper-pusher and knew how and when to find, as well as to *lose,* files that were being moved from desk to desk and office to office.

The funeral service for Bob O'Neil was held in The Chapel On the Hill. Since Bob was Catholic, the rotating priest - Father McNally - presided. Dale sat in the very last pew, coming in only when the service started. He felt bad enough without being looked at and fingered as the man responsible for Bob's death.

Bob's parents and brother came down from Brooklyn for the service. They placed a picture of Bob on the casket, as well as the team picture of the 1944 Brooklyn Dodgers taken in the outfield of Ebbets Field. Bob's ex-wife did not attend. They had no children.

When the service was over, Dale was the first to exit the premises.

Bob's body was shipped by rail back to his beloved Brooklyn and interred in the Holy Cross Cemetery.

An Army officer was appointed to assist the family in collecting Bob's belongings from his and Dale's house on Outer Drive. It wrenched at Dale's heart to see them remove Bob's stuff and then face a half-empty house. Dale was allowed to stay until he officially got evicted from Oak Ridge. He doubted if he would ever forgive himself for Bob's death. Even though Dale was always the "new guy," he had grown close to this personable Dodgers fan.

Dale and Brenda had some catching up to do.

On this Saturday evening, McCrory's 5 and 10 Cent Store in Jackson Square was a bee hive of activity. Customers milled about. A group of teen-age girls were leafing through new records that had just come in. They were trying out *The Trolley Song* by Judy Garland on the little turntable dedicated to customers who wanted to hear a record before buying it. An Army private was looking at birthday cards for mothers.

Dale and Brenda were in a booth, sharing malts and catching up. Brenda, however, found herself doing most of the talking, with Dale not as engaged as she thought he should be. It was clear he was deep in thought.

Frustrated, Brenda said, "I normally would ask, 'A penny for your thoughts?' but my rates have gone up. I'm charging a nickel now."

Dale looked up from his malt.

"Oh, sorry. I suppose I should be more in tune with my very pleasant company, but it's not adding up."

"What's not?" Brenda asked. "Catching Abby Felton and Ted Hildebrandt wasn't good enough for you?"

"No," he said. "I can't tell you everything, as I've been sworn to secrecy by someone who shared some information with me. But I can tell you this: it's not over yet. I'm just waiting for the next event and trying to figure out what to do about it, or stop it before it happens."

"Well," Brenda said, firmly, "I think it's over. All I know is no one's attacked me ever since Ted Hildebrandt got nailed and sent up the river."

Dale looked startled. "So, *you're* the female who was attacked? What happened, and when?"

"A little while ago. I went to the drug store to get some medicine for Trudy Mac, and some goon grabbed me from behind and told me to tell you to back off. We weren't talking during that stage, so I never got the message to you. Looking back, I figure it was Ted Hildebrandt. I never saw him when I ran. He told me to not turn around."

"Were you hurt?" Dale asked, wide-eyed.

"Not physically. My nerves didn't fare too well. Between me thinking you were two-timing me and that incident, I was pretty well shot."

Dale was incredulous. "And you didn't think to tell me this?"

"Like I said, I wasn't thinking too well at the time. And, I moved over to X-10 and didn't want to talk to you anyway."

Dale thought. "I guess it could have been Ted Hildebrandt. I'm just glad you're all right."

"So, am I off the hook now?" Brenda asked with a smile and twinkle in her eye.

Dale hesitated. "Well…" Brenda threw her straw at him.

"Tell me exactly what happened that night," Dale instructed. Brenda could see the wheels were turning in his head, even if the car to which they were attached was spinning in the mud.

"Trudy Mac told me she wasn't feeling well when I got in. She asked me to get her some bicarbonate soda at the drug store. On my way back, some gorilla grabbed me from behind and warned me to warn you to mind your business."

"Which way did you come back from the drug store?" Dale questioned.

"I didn't want to wait for the bus so I cut behind all the stores."

"Didn't you think it was strange he was there? How did he know you would be out walking all alone in that direction?"

"Look, after he grabbed me and let me go, I didn't question anything except the fact that I was alive and unharmed. I was so scared I couldn't have come up with my middle name if I were asked."

"What is your middle name, by the way?" Dale asked.

"Leah. Why?"

"Never mind. You said you were going to talk to Trudy Mac about why she told you I was two-timing you with Miss Rivera. What did she say?"

Brenda stuck a new straw in her malt.

"She said she was jealous of me finding a decent guy when 99% of the female population in Oak Ridge would like to. I guess she wanted to break us up so you could go back on the market."

Dale shook his head. "I never will understand women."

He tapped his fingers on the table. "You said one time you never told anyone what I was doing in terms of investigating this deal. Is that right?"

"That's right."

"Are you sure? Did you ever spill the beans to Trudy Mac in any way?"

Brenda was getting frustrated at being on the witness stand. "I don't know! I don't think so. Maybe I said one thing to her. I don't remember! What are you driving at?"

"Not sure. There's still so much that's not adding up. I mean, what are the odds of that goon being behind the stores the one time you happened to walk there? I think he knew you'd be out alone and he followed you there in order to accost you. And I know that this is bigger than just Abby Felton and Ted Hildebrandt. I know it." Dale grew silent and thoughtful, staring out into McCrory's but not looking at anything.

"Did you offer to get the medicine or did Trudy Mac ask you?" he finally said.

Brenda thought. "If I remember right, I asked her if she needed anything. Then she asked me to go to the drug store and get her some stuff."

"So, she was the only one who knew you were going into the townsite?"

"Yes," Brenda admitted. She didn't like where this conversation was going, but it seemed to be heading toward a conclusion that she didn't like. They both sat there in thought, not speaking.

"Okay," Dale finally said. "I'm not totally sure what to do next, but I have a bit of an idea of something of a plan to start with, especially while I'm in limbo."

Daniel S. Zulli

"What would that be?"

"Not telling you. Sorry, Brenda, I can't afford to have you attacked again. The less you know, the better off you'll be. Besides, no sense getting both of us shot at and fired and kicked out of here. Just say nothing around your very interesting roommate, especially about this conversation."

Brenda nodded. "But, you promise to include me if you need the help, right? I've gone through this much with you and I'm not about to let you get into trouble all by your lonesome. Besides, I think we can agree that you need someone to watch over you, seeing how you can't seem to keep yourself out of trouble!"

This time, it was Dale who threw his straw at her.

The next day Dale went down to the bus terminal, waiting for Mr. E.'s run to show up. What he had in mind was thoroughly far-fetched and a long shot, but he didn't know what else to do. The waiting was driving Dale half mad, since he knew there was more nefarious activity at work in Oak Ridge and he didn't have much time to solve it. He had to try and act again, even if his first attempt led to disaster. Mr. Lohorn's stalling on his discharge paperwork gave him the window he needed to try something new.

Fortunately for Dale, Mr. E. was as precise as a Swiss watch. He came in right on time.

The passengers departed Mr. E.'s bus and went in the terminal to do what they had to do. When the last one got off, Mr. E. stepped out to stretch his legs and take a quick break. Dale was waiting for him.

"Hello, Mr. E.!" Dale greeted him with a cheer. "Just when you think you've seen the last of me, I show up once again."

"Hello, boss man. Let me guess, you need to go back to church again. You been misbehavin'?" Mr. E. howled at his joke.

"Well, yes and no," Dale laughed back. "It's a long, sad story, my friend. No, I don't need to go back to church today, although I wouldn't turn down any divine intervention. But I do need another favor. This time it's pretty big and could be very important."

Mr. E. eyed him suspiciously. "Uh, oh, boss. I'm not sure I like that look in your eye. Whatcha got going on?"

"Another $10 for you, that's what. You need to get ahold of Flathead and have him switch with you so you can have someone drive your bus while you go into town for me and do some recon work. You can borrow his car or take your own. You in?"

"For $10, I'll *shoot* old Flathead!" Mr. E. grinned. "I can take my jalopy. Tell me when and where and who."

Dale produced a picture of Trudy Mac that Brenda had slipped out of their room.

141

"Actually, this will be the easiest $10 bucks you'll ever make. All I want you to do is follow this girl into town when she leaves next. I'll find that out for you. She goes into these surrounding towns to work with local food producers to order and buy food that we eat here. I want you to trail her and tell me exactly what she does and who she talks to. If nothing happens out of the ordinary this first time, I want you to do it again until I'm satisfied with what you're finding. It's a ten spot each time you trail her. Can you do this for me?"

"Are you serious? You're talking to the king of sneaking around town. My wife doesn't know half the places I've been to! And I know these roads like the back of my hand. Don't you worry none - she won't give me the slip."

"Great. The next time you see me here is when I know she's going into a town, whether Knoxville or Clinton or Oliver Springs, or wherever. You make the arrangement with Flathead and have him be ready to make the switch with you so he can take your bus route. We clear?"

"I gotcha, boss man. I won't let you down."

Dale had nothing to do but wait until he heard from Brenda. He hated to involve her, but, obviously, she was the logical choice to find out when Trudy Mac was off on one of her excursions into town. They were regular, but not 100%, so Brenda had to coyly ask for the information without drawing undue interest from her roommate.

Dale didn't like inactivity. He was living on borrowed time and didn't know how much of it he had. Being alone in his half-empty house was almost unbearable. Dale played his radio, but that too reminded him of Bob O'Neil, who habitually had it on. Bob's favorite programs were *The Adventures of Ellery Queen* for a detective drama and *Amos & Andy* for comedy. Of course, when baseball news and scores came on, that was Bob's number one priority.

But now, having the house to himself gave Dale time to read the Bible that Pastor Mike Miller gave him. True to what Mike said, the book of Proverbs was especially helpful, as it gave Dale insight into life that he never had before.

Proverbs 9:10 caught Dale's eye. He underlined it: "The fear of the LORD is the beginning of wisdom: and the knowledge of the holy is understanding." If there was anything he was lacking now, it was wisdom. He didn't know which way to turn to completely solve this dilemma. He was hoping trailing Trudy Mac would pan out, but that could easily turn into a dead-end street.

God hadn't been a big factor in Dale's life. He was entrenched in the sciences and didn't think God belonged in that world. But Dale was slowly coming to the realization that human resources were finite at best and many times wrong at worst. *This couldn't be all there is,* Dale thought. *Surely man doesn't have all the answers,* despite the smug certainty he saw from his professors. Dale had to conclude that man wasn't the top of the heap. This work in Oak Ridge was proving it. Thousands of people were desperately trying, 24 hours a day, to tap into some force that was there but beyond man's ability to control. They were dealing with the atom, so small it could not be seen, yet so powerful that it was unlike anything ever before experienced.

Who made the atom? Where did it come from? Something so specific surely was not the product of random chance. If intelligent men could not figure it out, then it must have come from some source far more intelligent. The atomic world existed, yet man couldn't see it. It stood to reason that if man could not see the atomic world, then a spiritual world could exist as well.

So why not God?

Dale was discovering that denying the existence of God did not fill the void deep down in his soul. If being in perfect control meant that he had life all figured out, then he most certainly was not in control. Ever since he was plucked from his sanitized world back in Cambridge and sent down to the unknown in Oak Ridge, Dale felt like he had lost all control. He was being moved and bounced around like a buoy on the ocean. Some force was in charge, and Dale realized it was not him. He was being moved from Point A to Point B. The only problem was, Dale didn't know where Point B was, or where he was on the continuum, or even if he was headed for Point Z.

Maybe he wasn't so smart after all, he concluded.

Maybe Proverbs 9:10 was the key: knowing about God was the starting point of wisdom.

Despite all this uncertainly gnawing at his heart, Dale felt like this quiet time of introspection and soul-searching with the Bible Pastor Mike had given him was for a reason and very profitable.

Chapter 35-Trail

The ringing of the phone almost gave Dale a heart attack. He wasn't sure if he had been merely deep in thought or deep in sleep. Whatever he was, the jarring noise sprang him to alertness.

Trying to sound composed but doubting he did, Dale answered the phone.

Brenda sounded excited. "Hey! Trudy Mac will be leaving tomorrow morning at 0800 for Clinton. She'll be gone most of the day and return around 2. Can your contact be ready to go tomorrow?" Brenda's voice displayed her enthusiasm.

"He said he will be," Dale answered. "I'll get to the terminal first thing and wait for him. He should be there at 7:15 at the latest, with his first run in from Knoxville. Thanks, Brenda. Trudy Mac doesn't suspect anything, does she?"

"If she does, she didn't get it from me. I was as cool as a cucumber when I asked for her schedule."

"All right, then," Dale said. "Let's see what tomorrow brings, if anything. If nothing else, this is sure getting your pulse racing."

"You know it!" Brenda laughed. "This sure beats 25 first-graders with runny noses any time!"

"Well calm down and get some sleep. Where are you calling from, anyway?"

"A pay phone outside Administration #1."

"Be careful when you walk back," Dale admonished.

"I will be. It's all lit up and out in the open. I've sworn off dark alleyways for Lent," Brenda said with a chuckle.

"Good work, kid," Dale said. "Good night. Love you."

"Night," Brenda replied. She paused when she hung up the phone receiver. She realized that Dale had just used the "L" word for the first time. She repeated what he said: "Good night. Love you," just to hear it again.

As she began her trek back to her dorm, Brenda replayed, "Good night. Love you." all the way back.

Dale was back at the bus terminal at 7 a.m. His take-out cup of coffee from Kaye's Kafé was warm in his hand and tasted good going down. The caffeine wasn't necessary to prompt him alert; he barely slept due to thinking about this day's activities.

Mr. E. pulled up at exactly 7:15. In a world full of doubt and uncertainty, it was good to have something Dale could count on. He grinned at the sight of the jovial bus driver.

Daniel S. Zulli

"Hey, there, boss man!" Mr. E. hollered cheerfully when the last passenger debarked. "Is it show time today?"

"It is, my friend. It is indeed. Everything all worked out with Flathead?" Dale didn't want a glitch in his finely-laid plans.

"You betcha," Mr. E. responded. "All I got to do is go in and tell the dispatcher to fetch him over here, and he'll take my bus while *I* take your $10!" Mr. E. was a never-ending source of jokes and good-natured ribbing.

"Great," Dale said. "Here's the skinny: she's going into Clinton today, leaving at 8. Do you know what bus takes that line?"

"I know them all. I'll just hang back and watch the bus pull out of here, and it's a piece of cake to follow it into town. I got her picture with me so this will be a cinch."

"Great. When you get back, just switch back with Flathead. I'll meet you back here at 4 so you can give me the low-down on what she did. Sound good?"

Mr. E. grinned. "You're the man with the plan, boss!"

Dale saw an opening to rib Mr. E. "Oh, and I promise to not tell your wife that you were chasing some young blonde around Clinton when you should have been at work."

"Hey, now. If you tell her that she'll charge you $20 to not kill me. I don't think you can afford both of us!"

"You drive a hard bargain, Mr. E. Okay, I have to disappear before she gets here. See you at 4."

Mr. E. went into the dispatcher's office and told her to call Flathead Harris in bus #6 to the office. He would have to double up on his and Mr. E.'s passengers to make up for the loss of one driver. Mr. E. said there was some family issue he had to take care of, which wasn't too far from the truth. Making an extra $10 would more than help his family out. The truth of the matter was that blacks were paid far less than they deserved in Oak Ridge. Working for Dale Hargrowe was a good part-time job, Mr. E. thought, and worth the effort.

Flathead knew he was on standby, waiting for the call. He was in promptly, ready to take Mr. E.'s line. Mr. E. didn't have to have an exchange with Flathead. He just left his bus in the lanes for departing buses and Flathead picked it up. Mr. E. got to his 1934 Ford Pickup and sat while the Clinton bus left with the quarry in hand.

The girl from Dale's picture was dressed in her starched food company uniform. She sat behind the driver, placing her small valise in her lap. Mr. E. knew the driver well. He and Freddie Joe Williams went way back, even playing on the same high school baseball team in nearby Crossville. It was during their many long trips to play other black teams that both Mr. E. and Freddie Joe learned to drive the bus, as they all got the chance to drive.

He followed behind at a safe distance. The sight of a worn-down pickup rumbling down the road in eastern Tennessee was a common sight. Other than the military-industrial complex of Oak Ridge, this was rural country; pickups do not attract attention.

The bus finally came to rest at the stop on Main Street in Clinton, across from the courthouse. Trudy Mac exited and walked the few blocks to the farmer's market on the corner of East Broad Street and Seivers Boulevard. This gathering of local farmers happened every week.

Mr. E. parked his truck and watched Trudy Mac. She went from seller to seller, paperwork out of her valise, in an apparent attempt to swing deals. She seemed successful on some, not on others. From what Mr. E. could see, some of the conversations between Trudy Mac and the farmers were quite animated. They seemed resistant to Trudy Mac's overtures for a sale, as they were feeling the squeeze from the Clinton natives who wanted to buy the food for themselves.

Wrapping up her business at the market, Trudy Mac went into the nearby Clinton Drug Company. Mr. E. could easily see her at the counter through the main glass window. She ordered a drink from the soda fountain attendant while looking over her paperwork.

Mr. E. noticed all the people moving about on the sidewalks of Clinton. Most wore very modest clothing. The men wore ill-fitting, faded dungarees and overalls with broad brim hats. Most of their shirts showed signs of multiple repairs. The women did their best to be presentable, but it was clear that the effects of the Depression were still very much felt here. Their dresses were simple and plain. Even the best dressed person on the streets of Clinton, who seem to have office jobs and not out-in-the-sun jobs, displayed a humbleness that betrayed the fact that their lives were hard in the rural South. Having the war effort place its many demands on products like rubber and steel didn't help their standings in life.

When the well-dressed man strode along the sidewalk, Mr. E. perked up. He could not be missed, as he stood out from all the others. His suit was fancy; it must have cost $40. His wingtip shoes were shined; the leather not worn like other men's. His hat was placed on his head so as to give his appearance a jaunt and not to protect a beaten, leathered face from the sun.

The man stood out from the native Clintonians.

"Well, well, well..." he muttered to himself when he saw the sharply-dressed man arrive on the scene. "What do we have here now?"

Mr. E. saw the man enter the drug store and sit down next to Trudy Mac at the counter. When they talked to each other, they didn't look like two strangers. A pretty young girl wouldn't engage an unknown man in such a setting.

Their conversation looked heated at times, with Trudy Mac making gestures and showing signs of stress of anxiety. The man held up his hands as if to tell Trudy Mac to calm down. But then he would point to her in a directive manner, with Trudy Mac listening in silence. The conversation didn't take long, just a few minutes.

Mr. Fancy Pants got up to leave. As he did so, he produced an envelope from his pocket and slid it on the counter to Trudy Mac. He pointed at her one last time, then turned and left the drug store.

Trudy Mac looked at her watch. Taking the last gulp of her drink, she placed the envelope in her valise and strode out of the Clinton Drug Company and walked a block back over to Main Street to The Union Peoples Bank. Mr. E. exited his pickup and ambled toward that direction, pretending to look at various store fronts as if trying to find something, but keeping a wary eye on his quarry.

When Trudy Mac entered the bank, Mr. E. took up residence across the street so he could see into the big glass panel in front of it. She went to a window at the counter, handed the teller the envelope, filled out a piece of paper, then left. It became clear that the dapper man had handed Trudy Mac some money in the envelope, which she was now depositing in this bank.

Mr. E. once again muttered, "Well, well, well..."

Leaving the bank, Trudy Mac looked at her watch again, then walked confidently to the bus stop to await transportation to her next stop. Her work in Clinton was done.

Mr. E. decided that he didn't need to follow the young woman. He had seen enough that looked suspicious to warrant a report back to Dale Hargrowe.

He had earned his $10, sure enough.

Chapter 36-Resistance

After the recap with Mr. E. at 4 p.m., back at the bus terminal, Dale went as fast as his still-sore ribs let him to Colonel Hutchinson's security building. The sergeant once again let the colonel know that Dr. Hargrowe wanted to see him.

Colonel Hutchinson didn't look pleased to see Dale.

"You still here? General Groves ordered you gone."

"I know," Dale said, "but there's been a glitch with my paperwork, or so I'm told. Mr. Lohorn in Personnel told me he was short-manned, but he'd have every available body working on my stuff."

"Well, what do you want this time?" the colonel growled, looking down at the mound of paperwork on his desk.

"Look, sir, I have a pretty good idea of who is behind all this stuff."

"I know too, Hargrowe," Colonel Hutchinson retorted through clenched teeth and a cigarette. "It was Ted Hildebrandt and that girl, Abby Felton."

"I disagree," Dale said. On his last visit, Dale had been more polite and conscious of Colonel Hutchinson's rank and position. Now, he was more direct and less concerning of protocol. He was already fired and kicked out of Oak Ridge; being blunt with the colonel wouldn't hurt his career. The urgency of the situation dictated directness.

Colonel Hutchinson eyed Dale.

"Those two were smaller fish in a bigger pond," Dale said. "Yes, they did some of the dirty work, but I have very good reason to believe it's not over yet and I know the identity of someone who's involved on a higher level."

Colonel Hutchinson fairly erupted. "Preposterous! We caught those two - even though you well screwed up - and this affair is over."

"Colonel, you're wrong," Dale replied. Dale could see the O-6 stiffen up. He wasn't used to anyone challenging him.

"And how do you know this?" he said, his face reddening.

"A couple of things. First, did you notice the firearm Ted Hildebrandt used to shoot at me and Bob O'Neil? It was an M1911, a pistol only used by the military. Where would he have gotten a gun like that, especially here in Oak Ridge? This means that he was working with or for someone else in the Army.

"Second, I have good reason to suspect a young woman whom I've known since I got here isn't all that she appears to be."

"This is getting ridiculous, Hargrowe! You had better have more than some suspicion."

Dale continued. "My friend Brenda Andrews was the only person I ever told about what I was doing in terms of poking into this affair. No one else knew, at the first. Even when I was threatened with a brick through my window, I never told O'Neil what was going on until later when I enlisted his aid.

"Brenda inadvertently told her roommate, Trudy McIntyre, about it one time, what I was doing. Not long after that, Brenda was assaulted and threatened and told to tell me to back down. That person was probably Ted Hildebrandt. Someone knew where she would be and was waiting for her to scare her like he did.

"Then today, I had someone follow Miss McIntyre into town to observe her. My contact said she met up with a man who gave her some money. We know it was money because she made a deposit at a bank right after they met. Colonel, please listen to me - this thing isn't over yet. I believe that somehow this girl Trudy McIntyre is very much involved. Abby Felton and Ted Hildebrandt were only doing what they were told to do. They weren't the whole gang behind this attempt to sabotage what we're working on here in Oak Ridge."

Colonel Hutchinson sprang up out of his chair. "This is utter nonsense, Hargrowe! We caught the two people responsible for tampering with the calutrons. This incident is over and case closed! Now I suggest you exit this office of your own volition before I have you thrown out of here in handcuffs. Further, I suggest you tell Mr. Lohorn to expedite your paperwork, because you have way overstayed your welcome. Is there any part of this that is not clear, Dr. Hargrowe?" Colonel Hutchinson's collar was threatening to explode due to the bulging veins on his neck.

"You're making a big mistake, colonel," Dale warned. "I guarantee you, this isn't over. I just hope it doesn't cost someone their life."

"The only life it has cost someone is due to your meddling in business that isn't yours, doctor," Colonel Hutchinson said with a "checkmate" smugness.

"Good one, colonel," Dale retorted, standing up. "At least I have the satisfaction of knowing that I tried. That's more than I can say for you."

Dale turned and walked out. Since he wasn't in the Army, he didn't have to wait to be dismissed by a superior officer.

Dale was disheartened his evidence and plea for action had fallen on deaf ears. Of all people, Colonel Hutchinson, the head of security, and a life-long cop in the Army, should be receptive to what he had to say. His resistance was hard to fathom.

Chapter 37-Confirmation

At Kaye's Kafé later that night, Brenda met Dale to discuss the day's events. He needed Brenda's presence to provide something encouraging into his life.

"So, you really think Trudy Mac is involved?" Brenda asked, pouring cream into her coffee.

"I do. According to my source, the guy who met up with her was so out of place in Clinton that it's obvious something's rotten in Denmark. The way I figure, if Abby Felton was doing dirty business for $10 a week, what could Trudy Mac be doing? For the right price, most anyone will do anything, including sell out their country."

"That's a terrible thing to say!"

"I know. But I'll never forget seeing Ted Hildebrandt when he came to pay off Abby. I knew I had seen him somewhere. Then it hit me: I saw him when we went to The Chapel on the Hill. He was one of the ushers, taking up the collection. Talk about a punch to the gut." Dale was looking down at his sandwich, but not very interested in eating it.

"What should we do now?" Brenda asked. "This puts me in a tough position. I'm Trudy Mac's roommate and I thought good friend. We've been together ever since Day 1 when we arrived in this dust bowl."

"I know. The main thing is to not ever let her know what we know, or suspect..." Dale's words trailed off.

"You're thinking again. I'm not sure if that's a good thing," Brenda said, ribbing Dale.

"You're probably right there. But I was just wondering if there was any way I could confirm my suspicion of Trudy Mac making some illicit money on the side. Knowing that would really help my case."

"Now you're talking!" Brenda said, lighting up. "Why don't you let me go and try to find out?

"How would you do that?"

"Well, I could go to the bank and pretend I was from Personnel or Payroll here, and then make up some story that I needed to see her bank account. I know what she makes here, and this will tell us if Trudy Mac has a side job. What do you think?"

Dale tapped his fingers on the table.

"That sounds crazy enough that it might work. How will you pretend to be in another department?"

"I know!" Brenda exclaimed. "I'll ask to borrow Sally Hardaway's badge. She looks close enough like me that they might not check it out too closely. An official-looking badge from Oak Ridge should get their attention."

"I normally wouldn't let you get any more involved, but I don't see much choice. I'm going to make Colonel Hutchinson see my point even if I have to break ribs on the other side. Just promise me that at the first sign of a problem, you'll get out of Clinton and back here, okay?"

"It's a deal, Dr.," Brenda reached over to shake his hand. Dale shook his head at the never-ending vivaciousness of this girl from Cincinnati. *She is one in a million,* he thought.

When she got back to her dorm, Brenda went up to the third floor and contacted Sally Hardaway from payroll, who did resemble her. Brenda convinced her to call in sick, then slipped her a $5 bill for her troubles.

"I think I might get sick more often!" Sally said with a laugh. "I need to buy a birthday present for my niece, and you just paid for it! I'm going to Miller's today. Just bring the badge back when you get done."

"Thanks, Sal," Brenda said. "Oh, and if I - you - get any good offers from any nice-looking men from Clinton, I'll accept on your behalf."

"Just make sure he's rich!" Sally said, laughing again. "Have fun. *I* will!" Sally twirled out of her room and headed to Miller's Department Store at Jackson Square with her new $5 bill.

The next day Brenda fixed her hair and makeup to more resemble Sally in the photo ID.

Brenda wanted to vindicate Dale in front of Colonel Hutchinson and, by extension, General Groves. She didn't like the man she cared for looking like a fool and getting humiliated by being fired when he was a very good physicist, not to mention the only one who was doing anything about what was going on. Even more than that was the matter of national security and the war effort. She and Dale had to get to the bottom of what was going on. What they were working on in Oak Ridge had to be of the highest importance, and everything pointed to an effort to prevent this project from succeeding.

The February morning was overcast and gray. The mud was broken up by a few scattered patches of snow. The bus ride was routine, with the appropriate stops and pick-ups and drop-offs along the way that Freddie Joe Williams had done hundreds of times since Oak Ridge's inception. This bus system had become a model in terms of efficiency. It was large and very well-run, providing Oak Ridgers with every opportunity for local travel, for either work or pleasure.

However far-fetched a gamble that Brenda's little excursion was, it was worth it. To mess with the "gadget" was to mess with Oak Ridge, and Brenda felt like this town was becoming hers. She had left her life in Cincinnati, Ohio, and Covington, Kentucky, far behind.

Freddie Joe brought his bus to rest at the main stop on Depot Street in Clinton. The posted schedule said he would be leaving for Oliver Springs in 20 minutes. After all his passengers got off his bus, Freddie Joe did as well to stretch his legs and have a smoke.

Brenda walked over to The Peoples National Bank on Seivers Boulevard. She clipped on Sally Hardaway's badge and put a scarf over her head, a normal thing for a woman to do in this weather, but also with the intent to further obscure the differences between her and Sally.

Brenda took a deep breath and entered the bank, walking confidently to a very young teller.

"Good morning, miss!" she said, cheerfully, with a little hint of a Southern accent.

"My name is Sally Hardaway, and I'm from the Payroll Department for the Clinton Engineering Works - " she lowered her voice, " - in Oak Ridge." Brenda held up the badge off her collar for just a second before lowering it, letting the teller see it but not inspect it. "We're conducting an audit of our employees and making sure their pay is being properly accounted for. It's my understanding that one of our employees, a..." she leafed through some papers, as if to hunt for the person's name, "...Trudy McIntyre banks here. I need to verify her account information. Would you be so kind as to produce it for me?"

Brenda smiled politely but put on an air of authority that the very young teller found hard to resist. Like most locals, she knew that Oak Ridge carried a mystique and aura about it that set it above the rest of what they knew. If this lady said she was conducting business from Oak Ridge, it must be legitimate and of high importance.

At least that's what Brenda wanted her to think.

"Yes, ma'am," she said, wide-eyed. She went over to a filing cabinet and pulled open the drawer that had the M through Z accounts. She was so flustered that she didn't think to get authorization from her supervisor before handing a stranger another person's banking information.

She returned to her station and produced Trudy McIntyre's folder.

Brenda continued with her authoritarian air.

"Uh huh. Yes. Very good," she said to herself, perusing the information. "Perfect."

Brenda closed the folder and slid it back to the teller. "Very good," she repeated. "This is all in order. It's obvious this bank is run very well. You should be proud to work in such a fine institution. You'd be amazed at how much inefficiency I see when I conduct my audits. Terrible."

The wide-eyed teller perked up at being complimented.

Brenda smiled at her. "I appreciate your cooperation, miss. You have yourself a very nice day, now, hear?"

The young teller smiled back, glad to have met this official person's approval. "Thank you, ma'am."

Brenda exited the bank and headed back to the bus stop. She was hoping that the bus was ready to take off again before the teller reported to anyone in authority what had just happened.

Freddie Joe Williams was stamping out his second cigarette when Brenda strode up. She mingled with the other boarding passengers. As the bus was backing up from its station, Brenda looked back in time to see the young bank teller and an older man cross over from Seivers to Depot, looking for the official lady from Oak Ridge. The man didn't look pleased. She slunk down in her seat as the bus moved forward. Brenda smiled to herself, proud of her ruse but a little bit sorry for taking advantage of such a trusting person. She would learn a painful lesson from this, Brenda thought, but experience is the best teacher.

Brenda was satisfied with her ruse in getting this valuable information, but at the same time chagrined to learn definitive proof that her roommate, with whom she had bonded, was being paid to play for the bad guys. Brenda was torn between getting this data and realizing what it meant.

When Freddie Joe's bus finally pulled up at Oak Ridge's terminal, Brenda could see Dale pacing back and forth, looking at his watch. His eyes lit up when he glanced up and saw the bus.

He fairly ripped the bus door open by himself so Brenda could get off first. Pulling her off to one side, away from the other passengers, Dale interrogated her.

"What did you find? Anything important?"

"Calm down before you give yourself a heart attack. Yes, I hit pay dirt."

"What is it? Was I right?"

"Unfortunately, you are. Our little Miss Trudy Mac is not the innocent farm girl I thought her to be. You won't believe this!" Showing the data to Dale, Brenda went over it.

"Look at these deposits. The total amount is $20,050. All the deposits were made in cash. She gets paid by check here, and not this much, trust me. And notice the dates of the deposits. They were made at times when we don't get paid, give or take. And I know she cashes her checks at the bank here in Oak Ridge like everyone else, not

Clinton. Dale, you were right - Trudy Mac is getting money from this fellow that Mr. E. saw and this doesn't look good at all!"

Dale digested this news. He felt glad to be finally finding the missing piece of the jigsaw puzzle. This was like Abby Felton's situation - a small-town girl getting money from some man. But what it didn't answer was why Trudy Mac was doing this or from whom she was getting the money. And why would she turn traitor to Oak Ridge's war effort?

"Dale!" Brenda snapped him back to reality. "Here is the proof we need that Trudy Mac is up to no good. So, what are we going to do about this now? Are you going to take this back to Colonel Hutchinson?"

"No," Dale said through tight lips. "I'm hitting too much of a brick wall with him. Besides, I can't prove what this money is for or whom it's from. He wouldn't listen to me."

"So, what next?"

"I have to go over Colonel Hutchinson's head and go straight to the top," Dale replied. "I've got to alert General Groves so he'll put men other than Hutchinson to look into this."

Brenda was shocked "You're going to talk to the general? I seem to recall he doesn't like you very much. What are you going to do - just call him up and invite him down here for tea?"

"More or less. I have to!" Dale was resolute. "And, I even wonder if our good friend Colonel Hutchinson isn't part of the problem as well."

"Dale Hargrowe! Are you sure you weren't sniffing too many bus fumes waiting for me?"

"Maybe. But what choice do I have? Look, I've already been fired. What else is the general going to do to me? Throw me out of here? He's already done that too."

"What about me?" Brenda asked.

"Go back to doing everything normal," Dale replied, tapping the paper on which Brenda had written the bank information, "but keep an eye on Trudy Mac. With the work on the gadget looking like it's nearing completion, she and her handlers may be getting ready to do something. But above all, Brenda, be careful."

"*You* be careful, you big lug," Brenda said. She reached up and kissed him on the cheek. "I almost lost you when you got shot, and you're running out of good ribs, not to mention time."

Brenda twirled and went to the bus stop that would take her back to her dorm. As much as it pained her, all the evidence led to the conclusion that her best friend and roommate since their Day 1 in Oak Ridge was a traitor for hire. Dale was right: there was no way her assailant in the alleyway would have known she would be out in the townsite all alone, except that Trudy Mac had set her up with the fake story of being ill. And, that story of wanting to break up her and Dale just because she was jealous smelled phony as well. What was more likely was that she and Dale were getting too hot on the chase and were finding things out, like the calutrons being tampered with in order to mess up the progress on the gadget. By telling Brenda the made-up story of Dale making a pass at the secretary, that would break them up and disrupt their two-man investigation into the sabotage effort Trudy Mac seemed to be involved in.

Pretending she didn't know anything around Trudy Mac was something that Brenda Andrews would have to work on.

Chapter 38-Arrest

Dale lost no time going to Administration #1, the main headquarters in Oak Ridge. He entered and proceeded to the guarded stairwell that went up to the second floor. Even if General Groves was not there at the time, the high-ranking officials up there still ran the day-to-day operations and had to be guarded.

The Army MP snapped to alert when Dale approached him.

"Private, this is very important," Dale said. "It's imperative that I get upstairs and talk to the leadership of this place. I need to get in contact with General Groves."

"Negative, sir," the MP said. "No one gets upstairs without the proper clearance, and you don't."

"I know I don't have the clearance, but can you escort me?"

"Negative, sir," he repeated. "No one gets upstairs." As he said this, he glanced over Dale's shoulder to get the attention of the MP at the other end of the first floor, on that stair's entrance.

Dale's voice rose.

"I know you have your orders, soldier, but the success of this whole operation is at stake. I've got to get in contact with General Groves. He needs to come down to Oak Ridge immediately!"

"Sir, I'm going to ask you to leave this area," the MP said in an authoritative tone. People were beginning to file outside their offices to see what the commotion was. Dale heard one woman whisper, "That's the guy who got shot and in all that trouble!"

Even though the other MP wasn't supposed to leave his post, he did so in order to assist the first one with this breach.

"Sir, we're not going to say this again," he said, "but you have to leave this area immediately."

Dale was getting further agitated. "No! I have to get in touch with General Groves so he can come here so I can tell him what's going on. There's a big problem here and it might get worse. They think they caught all the people, but they haven't. There's more!"

The second MP placed his hands on Dale's left arm to physically usher him out of the building, but Dale resisted. The first, lower-ranking MP did the same to Dale's right arm. Dale could feel his right side ache. His ribs weren't healed yet.

A voice from the second floor hollered down.

"What's going on down there?" it bellowed.

"Just a slight disturbance, sir!" the senior MP hollered back up. "We have it under control."

The owner of the voice stomped down the stairs. He was an Army captain.

"Corporal, explain!" he ordered. "Who is this man?"

"My name is Dr. Dale Hargrowe, sir," Dale responded. "I used to work in Y-12. Listen to me - you've got to get word to General Groves. This operation is in danger. They didn't catch everyone. But the colonel won't listen to me and - "

"Arrest this man!" the captain ordered again. "Get him out of here and take him to security and have him locked up."

"No!" Dale pleaded. "The colonel didn't arrest the right people. I mean, they were involved, but that's not all of them. There are more than even I know about. The general has to know because the gadget is in danger."

"Take him out of here right now!" the captain roared. The two MPs jostled Dale to the door. The corporal MP had one hand on Dale's collar. His other hand had pulled out his night stick, then he placed it between Dale's legs, lifting him up as he guided him in a riot-control maneuver. The private was on Dale's side, his hand firmly on Dale's elbow. Dale's right side was throbbing due to the exertion of his breathing hard and his rib cavity expanding.

The entire first floor personnel had come out of their offices to gawk at the scene. This did not happen in controlled Oak Ridge - a man causing a scene and getting arrested and hauled out of the main headquarters. They were wide-eyed with amazement.

The two MPs hustled Dale to their military staff car parked outside. They threw him into the back seat. Dale grimaced when his right side smashed on the passenger door's arm rest. The private moved next to him, pinning him to the door. The corporal hopped behind the wheel.

They staff car spewed up loose rocks as the corporal stomped on the gas.

Moments later, they screeched to a halt in front of Oak Ridge's main security building. A young MP who was idly standing outside having a cigarette had to dodge out of the car's way. When he saw there was a person in custody in the back seat, he threw his smoke down, and yanked the back door open, securing Dale when the private pushed him out.

"Inside with him!" the private ordered. The corporal got out, barely turning the car off as his feet hit the parking lot.

"Go! Go!" the corporal yelled to the MP who had been having the cigarette. Even though the young soldier did not know what the situation was, his training caused him to react automatically. He grabbed Dale roughly and moved him to the front door of the building. The private from the back seat joined him and the driver flung open the door.

The personnel in the building jumped to their feet in unison. While there had been the occasional arrest in town, like a drunk on a Saturday night or two guys in a fight, this scene spoke of a higher sense of urgency.

Hearing the commotion outside his office, Colonel Hutchinson sprang from his chair and stepped into the main reception area.

"What in the blue blazes is going on?" he roared.

"Bringing this guy in, sir, per Captain Connelly," the corporal reported. "He came to Admin 1 demanding we call General Groves. He said this project is in danger. He said he knew who was behind it."

"Hargrowe!" the colonel hollered when he got a look at the cause of the uproar. "You again? It wasn't enough for you to get shot and tossed out of here by the general himself? Now you went and got yourself arrested for causing more trouble? Lock him up, boys!"

As Dale was being pushed into a holding cell, Colonel Hutchinson approached him.

"Son, you've really done it this time," he said through gritted teeth. "I thought you were smarter than this, that you learned your lesson about poking your nose where it didn't belong. You're never going to see the light of day now."

"Look, colonel," Dale said back, "I don't think you know what you're doing at all! You don't seem to care about what's going on."

"I didn't get to be head of security because I'm an amateur, Hargrowe," the colonel snarled. "If I were in the mood to debate with you - which I am not - I would ask *you* where you got your police training from. But no - you're just some fancy pants scientist who thinks he knows everything. Well, boy, I guess you don't know as much as you think you do. You're staying here until your paperwork is done, and I'm personally going to see to it that it's done immediately."

Colonel Hutchinson clanged the cell door shut himself and stormed back to his office.

Brenda was in her room reading the newest *Life* when Trudy Mac came back from her trip into the three towns she had on her itinerary that day: Gatlinburg, Kingston and Wartburg. Brenda realized she would have to make an extra effort to play along as if she didn't discover what she did at the bank, that her relationship with Trudy Mac was as it always had been.

Trudy Mac looked beat when she entered the room.

"And how's Miss A&P doing today?" Brenda asked, not looking up from her magazine.

"Ugh!" Trudy Mac replied. "Whipped. Those farmers sure won't let go of their goods. I would say it's like pulling teeth, but I don't think

Daniel S. Zulli

any dentist every had to pull teeth this hard." She flopped down on her bed.

"Well, if you don't do anything else, just make sure Kaye has plenty of fresh beef so I can get my cheeseburger quota once a week," Brenda ribbed.

"I'll get right on it - first thing in the morning," Trudy Mac moaned. "I'm going to bed."

The pounding on the door startled them both. Trudy Mac sat up in bed and Brenda shot out of her chair to the door.

Another girl from the first floor was outside the door, still knocking when Brenda opened it up.

"Gracie!" Brenda said. "What on earth is going on?"

"I just heard the news! Dale just got arrested for trying to barge into General Groves's headquarters!" Gracie's eyes were wide and she was panting from running up the stairs. "Oh, Brenda, I'm so sorry! Dale's in a lot of trouble now!"

"Where's he at?" Brenda asked.

"He's locked up in the security building," Gracie said, trying to catch her breath. "From what I heard, Colonel Hutchinson is going to flay him alive for causing so much trouble!"

Gracie turned and ran away, leaving Brenda stunned and momentarily speechless over hearing this new bad news about Dale. She couldn't believe that for all his efforts in trying to save the gadget, Dale was just getting into more trouble. This time it looked like even Mr. Lohorn couldn't help him out.

Without looking at Brenda, Trudy Mac said, "Gee, that's too bad for Dale." She didn't sound convincing.

"Yes, isn't it?" Brenda replied with ice in her voice. "I guess he doesn't think that Abby Felton and Ted Hildebrandt were the only people involved in all this monkey business here in Oak Ridge."

"I guess we'll never know, will we?" Trudy Mac casually responded.

"Oh, I don't know about that," Brenda answered, her eyes narrowing as she looked at her roommate. "Anyway, it's been a long day, for *both* of us. Let's get some sleep."

Chapter 39-Deception

On her way to work the next morning, Brenda swung by the security building. Colonel Hutchinson was at his morning staff meeting in Administration #1.

She approached the sergeant at the main desk.

"May I see Dr. Hargrowe, please" she asked.

The sergeant looked up at Brenda. The look on his face suggested he didn't seem pleased to have this intrusion first thing in the morning.

"I'll just be a few minutes, promise," Brenda said.

"Five minutes," he said.

The sergeant motioned for a private to escort Brenda back in the holding area. She waited until the MP closed the door and left them alone before she spoke.

"Oh, Dale! Look at you!" Brenda said. "This is terrible! What happened?" When she saw Dale, it reminded her of when she first saw him in Kaye's Kafé. He was rumpled, unkempt, with blood-shot eyes. He looked like he had slept in a gutter after spending the previous night in a bar.

Dale winced as he sat up. His ribs were still sore.

"When I told the guards I wanted to get a call through to General Groves, they apparently did not think that was a good idea," Dale said with a forlorn look on his face. "I can't believe this is happening to me, especially since all I want to do is catch the bad guys and save this project."

"It does feel like it's us against the world," Brenda agreed.

"How did it go with Trudy Mac? Did you see her?"

"Yes. She was in our room when a girl from the first floor came up and told us. She sure didn't look upset at what happened to you. In fact, I'd say she looked pretty darn-near like the cat who ate the canary."

"Just don't get in a tiff with her. I don't think they want to turn this place into a coed jail."

"So, what do we do now, just sit back and watch Oak Ridge go to pieces and let these bums have their way?" Brenda asked.

"Funny you should say, 'bums,'" Dale replied. "That's what Bob used to call them."

"Well, do we?" Brenda repeated. "I'm about ready to take on Patton's Third Army, I'm so upset."

"I have an idea. Since my mobility is what you call 'limited,' I want you to snoop on someone else besides Trudy Mac."

Brenda's eyes lit up. "Now you're talking! Who is it?"

Dale motioned Brenda to come closer with a nod of his head. He didn't want an MP looking through the window in the door and read his lips. Brenda turned her head so he could whisper in her ear. Her mouth opened in her surprise.

"Really?" she said. "That's who you think is also involved?"

"It's just a hunch, but I've had plenty of time in here to think."

The MP opened the door.

"Time's up, miss." he directed.

"Okay, soldier. I'm done."

"Can she get me some fresh clothes?" Dale asked the MP.

He paused and thought. "Yeah, sure, I guess. No one told me you can't."

"Thanks." To Brenda, he said, "Go and tell Mr. Lohorn to hold off on my discharge papers for a bit longer, and to also review the file of the person I told you about. Maybe there's something in there. Tell him to dig deep."

"Aye, aye, captain." Brenda replied. "I'll be back later today with some clothes for you. And a comb. Your hair's a mess!"

After dropping off Dale's clothes, during her lunch break, Brenda swung by Mr. Lohorn's office to inform him of Dale's request to investigate a person's history and personnel files.

Work still had to be done. Brenda went to her shift at X-10, plotting her strategy on shadowing the individual Dale told her to watch. There was not anything more she could do regarding Trudy Mac. Their close friendship had cooled off, both sensing there was a reason for it but not discussing it. Brenda never let on that she had discovered Trudy Mac's banking irregularities, while Trudy Mac never let on that she knew that Brenda suspected something.

Brenda decided on her plan.

After work, she took the bus up to Colonel and Valerie Hutchinson's residence on Pine Ridge. Her plot involved the ruse of talking to her former supervisor in Administration #2, seeking relationship counsel from an older woman. Even though Val's husband was the chief of security and in whose jail Dale was locked, Benda and Val stayed on good terms. A visit to their house wouldn't arouse suspicion.

With winter ebbing, it was just getting dark when Brenda arrived around 7:30. Val came to the door when Brenda knocked.

"Brenda!" Val exclaimed. "I haven't seen much of you since you left us paper-pushers to become Oak Ridge's version of Rosie the Riveter."

"Hi, Val. Say, if you have a minute, can I bend your ear? I need to talk to someone."

"Sure thing. The rest of my bridge foursome won't be over here until 8 o'clock. Come on in."

"I'm not bothering you or the colonel, am I?" Brenda asked. "I don't want to intrude."

"You're not bothering me at all," Val said. "And the colonel is resting in the back before he goes back to work. That's why I have a bridge club coming over. He works so much that I took up bridge and am now one of the best in Oak Ridge. Have a seat. Would you like some coffee?"

"Coffee sounds great. Thanks."

After brewing a fresh pot and pouring the coffee, Val started. "How's work in the salt mines, now that you left all your friends in Admin 1?"

"Oh, I'm enjoying the work, sure enough, Val. But that's not why I'm here." Brenda looked downcast, as if something were weighing heavily on her mind.

"Look, I'm sure you've heard about what's happened to Dale," Brenda eventually said.

"Yes, I have. Very unfortunate. First the general - what? - fired him. Then while he was waiting to be processed out, he gets thrown in jail. That I most definitely heard about. So sorry."

"Me too. This is what I want to talk about - Dale and our possible future together."

"What do you mean?" Val inquired.

"Well, here's my dilemma. I really like Dale, and like any normal girl, I've often thought about a possible future with him. But now, I don't know. He started out okay, but he sure has gotten himself into a passel of trouble, and I don't know if he'll ever dig his way out of it. And the way he's been acting lately, I don't know even if he's stable or not."

"Makes sense. Even though you like Dale, you don't want to be involved with someone with no future, or else not a good future. Is that right?"

"Exactly. For all I know, Dale might end up in a real jail. Or out on the street, if he can't hold a job. I don't want to be involved with some yard bird or loony bin, but, the problem is I really like the guy. What if he were to propose to me? What should I do then?"

"That's a tough one," Val admitted. "If Dale really gets in hot water and does time, that would affect everything in his life from then on. Would he ever be able to find employment and support you? If you had to be the main breadwinner in the household, that would put a huge strain on your relationship. While I can't make that call for you, Brenda, I just think you ought to proceed slowly. If he were to propose - and what girl doesn't want a sharp guy to do that? - you'd have to see where he was in life. If he's about to go up the river due to what happened here in Oak Ridge, then I don't see much of a life for you two after that."

"Gee, isn't this just terrible?" Brenda asked. "I finally find a decent guy, and he may be wearing stripes before all this is done with!"

"I'm so sorry, Brenda. You're a good girl and deserve someone decent. If, by chance, your relationship with Dale doesn't work out, I'm positive you'll find someone, maybe even here. Lord knows there are a ton of eligible, single men in Oak Ridge."

"Yeah, I'll just have to play it easy. Maybe I'm just imagining the worst when I don't have to. I don't know if he'll ever even propose to me. So, there's no need of getting myself all worked up over nothing, right?"

"That sounds smart. I'm sure everything will work out for the best," Val soothed.

Colonel Hutchinson came out from the back bedroom, looking weary, but ready to head back to work.

"I thought I heard you talking to someone, Val. Good evening, Miss Andrews," he said politely but not too pleased to see Dale's close friend in his living room.

"Good evening, sir," Brenda replied. "Okay, Val, I must be going, before I get roped into your bridge tournament. Thanks for your time and the coffee. I'll go wait for the bus."

"Oh, don't take the bus, Brenda," Val said. "You can get a ride back with Wes." She turned to her husband. "Are you ready to leave? Would you mind giving Miss Andrews a lift back to her dorm?"

"Not at all, Valerie," Colonel Hutchinson said. "I'm ready whenever you are, Miss Andrews."

Brenda stood up and handed her coffee cup to Val. "Thank you, sir. And thank you, Val, for your time. Keep my desk warm in Admin 1 in case the factory doesn't work out. I may be back there."

"Have a good night, Brenda. And remember there's always a place for you at my bridge table. I'm always looking for new blood to conquer."

Colonel Hutchinson held the passenger door for Brenda Andrews as she got in his staff car, the same car in which she had taken Dale to Norris Dam for their picnic. It seemed like such a long time ago, Brenda thought to herself as she peered into the darkening night so typical of eastern Tennessee. It was getting warmer out than it had been recently, and a myriad of insects made every chirping noise, giving the night air a distinct hum to it.

"Back to your dorm, Miss Andrews?" the colonel asked as he slid behind the wheel.

"Actually, sir, could you take me to the bowling alley? It's very close to your security building, so it's not out of your way. I'll catch the bus home after I meet up with some friends and maybe bowl a game or two."

The drive was awkward. Neither one spoke. Brenda was riding with the officer in whose jail the man she cared for was locked up.

The colonel pulled up into the bowling alley's parking spaces. "Here we are, Miss Andrews. Have a good night."

"You too, sir," Brenda replied. "Thank you for the lift."

After Brenda shut the car door, she turned to enter the bowling alley. But as she heard the vehicle pull away, she stopped.

Instead of going into the bowling alley, Brenda stepped into the street and watched the staff car. When it had put enough distance between them, she proceeded to follow it on foot. It wasn't but 150 yards at best to the security administration building. It was one of the first buildings built in the Oak Ridge townsite, as security was paramount. The rest of the buildings had been built up around it.

Brenda could easily see the car. It did not stop at the security building. Instead, it made a left turn and went a few blocks before parking in a near-vacant lot.

The senior-ranking MP exited his staff car, then walked in the shadows the streets lights cast. Brenda stayed well behind him, but close enough to keep him in view.

Finally, he ended up at a small, nondescript building on a side street. A sign atop the front door read, "Roane-Anderson." *That's the company that runs this place,* Brenda thought. She knew that Roane-Anderson had acquired the contract to sustain the everyday workings of Oak Ridge, from laundry services to the various cafeterias to the hotel and diverse lodgings. Trudy Mac worked for them. Brenda imagined that this small building was one of many Roane-Anderson used for storage or other logistical needs.

The colonel went to a side door, then rapped one sharp knock.

The door opened silently. He entered and eased the door shut. Brenda could hear the *click!* of the door locking from the inside.

Intrigued, Brenda stealthily circled the building. There was enough glow from street lamps to where she could see the ground clearly enough. She didn't want to trip into a pile of scrap or industrial material and cause a commotion.

Looking for a window, Brenda finally found one on the opposite side from where she started her trek. It was covered with the dust from hundreds of passing automobiles.

Brenda pulled out a handkerchief from her purse and gently massaged the window, not wanting to give it a vigorous rub in case her movements drew attention from inside.

The opening she wiped away was small, just large enough to place an eye against the glass and peer inside. Fortunately, since this was the back side of the building, there wasn't any light directly behind her head, giving her a visible outline to anyone inside. Brenda had to stand on an old tire, but she could see through the opening inside the little building's main room. There was an inner room and from it came a soft light; the door was slightly ajar. While she couldn't see Colonel Hutchinson inside the little room Brenda could see the dim light of the room shift and fade in and out, caused by movement in the room. Brenda continued to look, wracking her brain to comprehend why the colonel would end up in this nothing building, especially when he said he was going back to work. This didn't make sense.

Brenda continued to spy into the building for a while. Sometimes, the faint glow from the light would remain constant, as if there were no movement coming from the inner room. She couldn't hear any sounds coming from inside the shack as exterior noise drowned any interior noise out.

Finally, Colonel Hutchinson came from the back room. He was adjusting his Army uniform shirt, putting it back into regulation position. As he stood in the doorway, firming up his tie, a form came up behind him and placed its arms around the colonel's midsection. They were a woman's arms. *This is not good,* Brenda thought. Brenda couldn't see whose arms they were at first, but then their owner moved her head to one side of the colonel.

Trudy Mac!

Brenda almost fell over backwards. This new revelation about her roommate hit her like a hammer to the temple.

Gaping at this surreal scene, Brenda almost went airborne when a stray cat meowed behind her. Worried that she might make a noticeable sound, Brenda inhaled deeply, gathered her wits, then slunk away. Her adrenaline forced the blood in her heart to be pumped at double speed.

She needed to be far enough away and out of sight when the two occupants exited the building. Brenda forced herself to not run. Staying in the shadows, she stealthily moved from building to building. Finally, she managed to get back to the bowling alley. Her nerves were as frayed as when she was assaulted in the alleyway previously.

"Give me your thickest and most potent soda!" she said to the soda jerk at the snack counter. Her eyes were wide and breathing shallow. The "flight or fight" part of her nervous system had kicked in.

Sitting down on a stool at the counter, Brenda mumbled to herself, "Man, oh, man!"

"You okay, miss?" the soda jerk asked.

"Yes. No! Yes. I think. I'm not sure," Brenda stumbled for her answer. "Man, oh, man!"

Daniel S. Zulli

Chapter 40-Clarity

The next morning, Brenda came to the security building to see Dale. Colonel Hutchinson's olive drab staff car was parked in his spot. Brenda couldn't help but wonder what had happened when he finally got back home. She imagined Val saying, "How was work, dear?" and the colonel replying, "Just fine, Valerie. Good night." Brenda's feelings alternated between revulsion at both the colonel and Trudy Mac and heart-wrenching sympathy for Val, who appeared to be oblivious.

When Brenda came in, she asked the sergeant if she could see Dr. Hargrowe.

"This must be his day for visitors," the sergeant grinned. Brenda didn't see the humor in Dale being locked up and his career tossed away. She glared at the MP, who lowered his gaze from hers and slunk away, closing the door behind him.

Mr. Lohorn was sitting on a chair opposite Dale's cell. He had a stack of papers on his lap.

Dale sprang from his bed. "Brenda! Boy, are you a sight for sore eyes. Come on in. Mr. Lohorn was just having me sign my release papers."

Mr. Lohorn stood up.

"Good morning, Miss Andrews," he said without much emotion.

"Hello, Mr. Lohorn. Do you know anything regarding Dale's status? Will he be prosecuted or merely released from Oak Ridge?"

"From what I can gather, Miss Andrews, Dr. Hargrowe won't be tried for any crime. Causing a commotion in General Groves's building isn't an offense. He will be simply discharged from all duties and responsibilities from the Clinton Engineering Works project."

Dale added, "I have to sign all kinds of non-disclosure forms, saying I won't write a book or give any interviews or even star in my own movie about my time here, which suits me just fine. The sooner I can get back home, the better."

"Oh?" Brenda asked with a hint of a dare in her voice. "So, you want to be like the rat leaving the sinking ship? What about your - our - little project, the one that got you in this place?" she nodded at the cell area.

"I don't think you or I can do any more than what we've done. It's probably best for me to leave and try and get my life back in order while I can."

Mr. Lohorn chimed in. "Dr. Hargrowe, I'll have the rest of the paperwork for you once you are released. I'll...ah...let you two discuss your plans on your own. Have a good day, Miss Andrews."

"Have a good day, Mr. Lohorn," Brenda replied with a bow of her head. She took his chair when he exited the holding area.

"Look, I've had plenty of time to think in here," Dale said. "I really think I've done the most I can accomplish. It's time for me to get out of here with what's left of my hide."

"You might change your mind once you hear this. You won't believe what I found out last night," Brenda challenged.

Dale perked up. "Oh? Enlighten me."

"Remember you told me to follow a certain someone?"

"Sure. Did you do it?"

"Brother, did I," Brenda answered. "I went up to their house with the phony excuse of my wanting to talk to Val about our relationship. You know, like how's it going to work out with you in Sing-Sing?"

"Gee, thanks," Dale said in mock politeness.

"The colonel gave me a lift to the bowling alley because he was going back to work after dinner and a rest. Only he didn't go right back to work. He ducked into a small storage shack. I followed him there. I had to peek in through the window. He was in a back room of this place. He was there, all right, and you'll never guess with whom."

"All right: With whom was the colonel in this building?"

"Just my one and only roommate."

"Trudy Mac? I can't believe that!"

"I can barely believe it myself. She is turning into quite the busy bee," Brenda said, almost sadly.

"Trudy Mac and the colonel," Dale mumbled to himself. "Now this really complicates things."

"Right," agreed Brenda. "Like, how does this figure into all this hanky-panky with the calutrons and Ted Hildebrandt and Trudy Mac getting lots of money from some well-dressed schmuck in Clinton? What's the common denominator?"

"Bingo." Dale concurred. "And, what is the next step for us? For you? I'm not sure when I'll be tossed from Oak Ridge, but it won't be long." He paused, then snapped his fingers. "Now I get it!"

"Get what?"

"Why nothing was being done when I approached Colonel Hutchinson about all I - we - had discovered. He said nabbing Ted Hildebrandt and Abby Felton closed the case. He could say that as the head of the ones doing the investigation. But it really didn't. Now this deal with him and Trudy Mac, and her getting funny money from this guy in Clinton, well, that part I don't get yet."

"Which means we still have work to do, right? What were you saying about leaving Oak Ridge for New England?"

"I stand corrected. Say, I think I'll be released today. Meet me in Mr. Lohorn's office at 5, when you get off. There may be more we can learn."

"Are you and Mr. Warmth getting on good terms these days?" Brenda laughed.

"Actually, yes. He's really a swell guy, and he's on our side, if you can believe that. He's been sitting on my discharge papers ever since the general fired me. I would have been out of here as soon as I got out of the hospital if it weren't for him. He wants me to find these creeps and get to the bottom of it all."

"In other words, you have Mr. Lohorn to thank for delaying your dismissal from Oak Ridge? That means he's responsible for you being tossed in the slammer because you normally shouldn't have been here." Brenda had to find humor amid an ever-increasing troublesome situation.

"You better be thankful there are some bars between us right about now!" Dale warned with a mock threat.

"Hey, it's not my fault they finally caught up with you for stealing Kaye's glass!" Brenda was merciless in her teasing. "Goodness! Will you look at the time?" she said, glancing at her watch. "At least *one* of us has to make an honest living, so if you'll please excuse me."

"See you at Mr. Lohorn's office at 5, unless, of course, President Roosevelt is giving you a medal for saving the world at that time!" Dale hollered as Brenda closed the door behind her.

Dale smiled as he flopped down on his bunk.

Shortly after lunch that day, Army MP Sergeant Rodney Ferguson came into the holding area. Keys jangled in his hand.

"Okay, hot rod," he said. "Time to go. I know you've enjoyed your stay, but you have to leave now."

"And I was just getting ready to do some remodeling, too," Dale replied. "Oh, well; I'll leave if you insist."

When the sergeant opened the cell door, Dale gathered up his few items - toiletries, some spare clothes - and walked out into freedom.

"Any paperwork to sign?" he asked the sergeant.

"None. Just report to Administration #2 for your final release."

"I have an appointment up there at 5 o'clock. Mind if I go into town and relax a bit? I'd like to get something different to eat instead of your wonderful hot dogs."

"Suit yourself. Just keep your nose clean, will you?"

"Promise," Dale declared, knowing that he would only promise to do his best at it, but not guarantee the results.

Daniel S. Zulli

Chapter 41-Musings

Dale stepped out into the sunshine, enjoying being out of his cell. All those MPs and security personnel are only doing what they are told to do, he thought. They were not responsible for the lack of investigation into the real cause of the monkey business in Oak Ridge, with its possible serious impact on the war effort. No, the river was blocked at its source - at the top. With Colonel Hutchinson. Dale truly didn't care if he - a married man and career officer who had risen to the top - was having a fling with a much-younger girl. The problem was whom the girl was and the possible implications of the fling. There had to be a connection between Trudy Mac, her mysterious financial benefactor, and the dead end on the investigation on Ted Hildebrandt and Abby Felton.

Dale found himself walking around the Oak Ridge townsite too deep in thought to realize his surroundings, other than the great feeling of being able to walk around again. The air smelled extra fresh, and the sunshine felt extra warm.

When he looked up, Dale saw one of the many drug stores that were in Oak Ridge. He decided to continue his thinking at the soda counter with a slice of pecan pie and some better coffee than what he got in his cell. He could have sworn that the MPs liked to brew and re-brew the same coffee grounds over and over again. They liked their coffee the-stiffer-the-better, apparently.

But Dale's treat tasted especially good. The pecan pie was sweet and the coffee from a fresh pot. With his stomach appeased, a thousand thoughts swirled about in his head.

Primarily was this unsolved mystery in the Clinton Engineering Works. It wasn't going away. Dale couldn't figure out what was next. What was the end goal of all this wicked activity? What was the connection between Trudy Mac, the colonel, and this mystery man from Clinton? As it stood, maybe Trudy Mac was earning legitimate money from a part time job. That was possible. And, she and the colonel having an affair wasn't a crime in and of itself, just repugnant.

But with all roads leading to these two, Dale couldn't help but smell a rat. Or, rats.

Then, Dale's mind wandered to his own status.

His once-promising career at the Massachusetts Institute of Technology got derailed when he was thrust down to eastern Tennessee. Even if he had stayed in Oak Ridge until the very end of this project, he didn't know if he would ever be able to return home. Surely there would be another up-and-coming young buck who would take his place. MIT ran well before him and would continue, even if he never came back. Everyone there retires, quits, moves on, gets fired, or dies. He was as expendable as anyone else.

Still, Dale certainly hadn't ever expected his time in Oak Ridge to be such a disaster. He had been shot, fired by the general, then thrown into jail by the colonel, only because he was trying to save this operation from something bad. This portion of his career would not look good on a résumé or go well on a potential job interview.

He thought of that conversation. "And how did your time at the Clinton Engineering Works go?" the interviewer would ask.

"Not too good. I got shot by a guy I went to church with, got fired by the commanding officer when I was in the hospital after being shot, got my friend killed, then arrested when I wanted to speak to the general when I wanted to warn him about possible sabotage at his top-secret operation. Do I have the job here?"

"Afraid not, son," the interviewer would say. "We don't hire ex-convicts who engage in gun battles."

Dale shook his head. It was too hard to comprehend. The pie and coffee sure tasted good, though.

If that were not enough, Dale thought of Miss Brenda Andrews, that wonderful, adorable, charming, beautiful, infuriating, wonderful, adorable, beautiful young lady he had met. What would be their future, if any? If he got tossed from Oak Ridge, he would surely go back up to Massachusetts and try and reclaim his life. Would Brenda go with him? Would she stay in Oak Ridge until the duration? Would she find someone else if he went back up north? Would she return to her native Cincinnati once she was done? That was her home; going back made sense. He could not blame her if she did not want someone with his track record.

Dale couldn't help but think about that verse in Proverbs that Pastor Mike Miller told him to read. He had memorized it: "Trust in the Lord with all thine heart; and lean not unto thine own understanding. In all thy ways acknowledge Him, and He shall direct thy paths."

Dale wondered if he had been trusting and acknowledging God through all this turmoil. More than likely not, was his conclusion. He had been trusting in his own wits and wherewithal. And the only place that got him was shot, fired and in the slammer.

He mentally prayed a silent prayer: "God, I don't know too much about You or Your ways, but if You could maybe help me out here with all that I've just been thinking about, I sure would be grateful. And if You do, I promise to do better at acknowledging You more. Sorry for all the times I haven't been. Amen. Oh, and thanks for getting me out of that crummy jail. The coffee was awful."

Chapter 42-Information

Brenda met Dale at Mr. Lohorn's office in Administration #2 promptly at 5 p.m. The day had grown quite warm. Mr. Lohorn had his lights dimmed, as usual, only the desk lamp was lit, and his shades were closed to keep the afternoon sun from assaulting his office. His desk fan was always on.

Brenda started the conversation.

"Dale tells me you're on our side. I guess I should thank you for playing along with his discharge paperwork and keeping him here longer."

"I'm only trying to help in some small way, Miss Andrews," Mr. Lohorn said in his quiet tone. "I try to avoid excitement as much as possible, and prefer to merely do my job and keep to myself. But I have my reasons for wanting to assist you two in what you are trying to accomplish."

"We appreciate it, Mr. Lohorn," Dale chimed in. "Were you able to find anything out about Colonel Hutchinson?"

"*I* sure did," Brenda said.

Not getting her inside remark, Mr. Lohorn pulled out a thick folder from his desk.

"I had to do some convincing for my military counterpart to release this to me," he said. "I promised it would go nowhere. He took a big risk."

Mr. Lohorn inhaled and exhaled deeply. "As you can imagine, Colonel Hutchinson has had a sterling career. One does not get placed in a position like this for being an amateur. However - " he paused.

"Find something?" Dale asked.

"I had to make some phone calls," Mr. Lohorn continued. "I found some items deep within his files that suggested that Colonel Hutchinson has been the recipient of some very good top cover. These remarks in his record were very subtle, but I was seeing tidbits of clues. Therefore, I made the calls. One of the nice things about working in CEW is we get 100% priority on anything we want, including information. And I've been around long enough in the personnel business to have made lots of contacts."

"So, what was it?" Brenda questioned.

"It seems that our good Colonel Hutchinson has had two things repeat themselves throughout his career, things that would normally have derailed any officer's career. But, like I said, he has enjoyed some robust support from friends in high places. These two things are: gambling and women."

Silence followed that announcement. So, Trudy Mac was not Colonel Hutchinson's first dalliance, apparently. And, if gambling were in the colonel's history and profile, that might explain him not doing a thorough investigation. Knowledge of financial impropriety by a less-than scrupulous person could easily force the colonel's hand to compromise his position.

"What form was the gambling?" Dale asked.

"Mostly horses, but he's done pretty much everything: baseball, boxing. The colonel had a bookie in New York place his bets through a system of code they used between them. He would call him up and the bookie would place the wager for him."

"How did he do?" Dale asked.

"Won some, but lost more than he won, from what I can gather. I found out that he had to apply for loans several times to cover his gambling losses."

"Wow," Brenda said in a hushed voice. "Poor Valerie. She's too sweet to deserve this."

"I know," Dale echoed. "I guess what the preacher said about sins and how mankind will never solve all our problems is right. We are all sinners, even the ones with high ranks and positions."

"Even sweet and innocent-looking farm girls," Brenda added.

After some moments of silence and reflection, Dale asked Mr. Lohorn, "So, what now? When do I have to be out of here?"

Mr. Lohorn shook his head. "I can only give you two more days. I cannot delay any longer than that."

"Understood. Sir, we deeply appreciate your time and effort. Brenda and I don't know what's next or what to do next, but I think *I'm* going to trust in the Lord and acknowledge Him. There doesn't seem to be anything else we can do. We'll take off now. It's been a long day."

Chapter 43-Deliberations

Dale and Brenda stepped out into early spring evening. Neither spoke.

"I'll walk you back to your dorm," Dale said eventually.

Brenda slipped her arm into Dale's. She huddled close to him as they journeyed from Administration #2 up the gentle slope to the female's dorm where Brenda roomed with Trudy Mac.

The evening was peaceful and quiet. The nighttime bugs were coming out, serenading the couple as they strolled. They could hear the sounds of activity down in the townsite as the day-shift workers were gathering to socialize.

"So, what do we do now, Dr.?" Brenda asked in a quiet tone.

"Don't know. I would love for a bolt of lightning or a voice from heaven to tell me what to do next. I'm supposed to trust in the Lord, but Mike never told me how to do that."

"Suppose we never catch Trudy Mac or Colonel Hutchinson red-handed, other than with each other. What do we do then?"

"I only have two more days here. That's pretty much all I know for certain," Dale replied.

"When you get unceremoniously bounced out of this bar, what are you going to do? Are you going back to MIT? If so, what about us?"

"Don't know that, either," Dale did not look at Brenda as he replied, rather straight ahead. "It would be only natural if I did go back. Let me ask this: How much longer do you have here in Oak Ridge? Are you committed to seeing this project through to the end, or would you quit all this excitement to perhaps join me in Massachusetts?"

Brenda looked up to the sky. "Hmmm. Say, if you ever get that bolt of lightning, could you send it my way too? I see what you mean about needing to trust God for answers and direction. I'm stumped. I wanted to stay here until the very end, whenever we win the war, or finish whatever we're working on. *But,* I *suppose* I could leave here before it's done if I were to get a better job offer somewhere." Dale heard the emphasis on her words.

"What kind of job?"

"Not sure on that, either. Maybe one with better pay, *or* a different title," she said, chuckling.

"What kind of title? 'Queen of the Earth,' or something like that?"

Brenda laughed. "Something like that. I'll let God direct your path on that one!"

Leave it to Brenda to bring levity to a bleak situation. Dale had two days in which to do some serious thinking and inquiring of the

Lord for the answers to all these questions. Going back up to Cambridge sure seemed like the most logical thing to do when he left Oak Ridge. Even if his old job had been given to an up-and-comer at MIT, Dale felt sure he could find another position there, or another place like Harvard, Yale, or Boston College.

But Dale could not imagine being 1,500 miles away from Brenda if she wanted to stay in Oak Ridge until the end of either the war or this project. As they walked, Dale wracked his brains for the solution to this dilemma. He had always been in control of his life, other than hurting his knee his freshman year of college and not being able to continue playing football. Even still, Dale knew he had no future in sports, as he was going to be a scientist, so hurting his knee didn't derail his life's plan.

College, graduate school, then full-time employment had come on his terms, right on schedule without any hiccups. Life had been on track.

Not now. He never planned on being forced to work on the Clinton Engineering Works project. He certainly was not planning to get fired from it, either. This was his first time ever being fired, from any job. Nor did he ever plan on ending up in jail, then having two days in which to map out the rest of his life.

Finally, he never thought he'd meet someone like Brenda. He was not even thinking about a relationship. Not here. Not now. Not this way. Not with only two days possibly together.

Dale said a silent prayer for something - anything - to show him the way. As they walked, arm in arm, Dale thanked God for Brenda, but desperately asked for a sign - a ray of light, a celestial vision - anything that could help him put all these pieces together and make things clear.

Dale stopped thinking and enjoyed the moment with Brenda. He felt so good next to her. He was glad their relationship had been restored, even if it took getting shot to do it. He did not want the night to end.

"We're almost at your dorm," he said.

"So, we are," Brenda agreed, matter of factly.

Chapter 44-Meltdown

The mournful wail of the fire engine siren down in the townsite suddenly shattered the quiet evening. Turning their heads to the right, looking south, Dale and Brenda heard more sirens, coming on one by one, until they formed a chorus of urgent response to some situation. They could see the MP's vehicle lights illuminate the evening sky.

Forgetting their destination, Dale and Brenda turned and began heading down the slope to the townsite. The lights and sirens were heading in the direction of X-10, in the southwest section of Oak Ridge.

People were exiting buildings to inspect this intrusion into their night. Before Dale and Brenda knew it, they had briskly walked down to where people were congregating.

They reached an off-duty MP just as he was bolting from a malt shop, surveying the situation.

"Hey, soldier," Dale tugged at the MP's arm. "Do you know what's going on?"

"Not sure, mister, but it looks like something happened by X-10!"

He shook off Dale's hand and took off in a sprint.

"Dale, we have to go there!" Brenda exclaimed.

A civilian was getting into his vehicle. Dale asked him, "Say, are you heading to X-10?"

"Yes!" he answered. "There's been a problem!"

"Give us a lift!" Dale shouted over the din. "This girl works over there."

"Get in!" The man hollered.

Dale jumped in the front passenger seat and Brenda did the same behind him. They barely got both feet into the car when the man threw it into reverse, then squealed forward, jerking his occupants wildly. Rancid, bluish smoke arose from where his car had been parked. He meshed gears, winding his car to the limit of each gear before shifting upward.

The car flew west on Bethel Valley Road, then turned left toward Brenda's plant at a speed that caused Dale to blanche, hoping the driver would keep at least three tires on the pavement simultaneously.

Among the major plants in Oak Ridge, the X-10 graphite reactor was the smallest, but it was only the second nuclear reactor in the world, and the first designed for continuous operation. If there had been a design flaw, it could prove to have fatal consequences. Those who worked there did not have to know the end result to know they were working with forces and materials and procedures previously unknown in history.

The plant was surrounded with emergency vehicles. Scores of lights were swirling, blending together, casting an unearthly hue on vehicles and bodies. Everyone on that swing shift had been evacuated and assembled in the main parking lot on the south side of the building. Some workers were visibly shaken at the prospects of a catastrophe.

Soldiers were barking orders at anyone who would listen, adding to the chaos of not knowing what to do. While the plant workers had practiced evacuations in case of emergency, the unspoken wish was that this type of incident involving nuclear materials would never happen. Everything had run smoothly up until this point. This was new, the first of its kind anywhere, and people were stunned.

Dale and Brenda stood and took this scene in, not knowing what to do except stay clear of the responders.

Brenda saw a man in the crowd whom she knew, Joey Hamilton. He had been on the day shift with her when she started and they had met in the break room one day. Joey had moved to the swing shift and Brenda had not seen him until now.

Brenda waved and called. "Joey! What's going on?"

Brenda could see Joey look around at the source of his name. Dale and Brenda ran up to him to get his attention.

"Joey! It's me, Brenda. What on earth happened here?"

Joey was frantic. "Something happened to one of the slugs! We can't figure it out. It was supposed to be cooling off before it fell back into its chute and into the water. It was still hot and glowing like a hot coal. Somehow it hit the ground and all heck broke loose at that point. The floor super hit the alarm and we all bolted."

"How did that happen?" Brenda asked.

"Not sure. Everyone was all suited up like they should have been. I don't know everyone on that detail, so I don't know any more than that. All I know is it's bad and we don't know how long it's going to slow us down!"

Joey took off running. It was clear he was spooked. This world of radioactive materials was too new for anyone to know what to do or what was next. People's imaginations were free to play out any and all scenarios, the worst case being the one people thought of the most. It was too soon to know if anyone's scenarios had any merit, of if there was nothing to be concerned about. People were not sticking around to find out. They were all running away from X-10.

Just then, Dale saw his old supervisor from Y-12, Hal Rainey, running away from the contaminated plant. He was carrying what look like a sack or bag.

"What's he doing here?" he asked Brenda. "Did he get transferred to X-10?"

"He might have, but I haven't heard his name come up or seen him," Brenda responded.

Dale saw Hal racing to a car, which he thought was strange. Everyone on Hal Rainey's level took the bus to work. Only the highest levels of management had their own vehicles as there were far too many workers in Oak Ridge for everyone to have a car. Hal Rainey was simply a supervisor on the first level of work in his department.

"If he did get transferred here, he still wouldn't have a car," Dale concluded. "Something's wrong here."

"Let's go after him and find out," Brenda suggested.

Dale shrugged. While it was a great idea and seemed like the best thing to do, they had gotten a ride there from a man and he was gone. And Hal Rainey was leaving in a hurry.

Dale spotted Sergeant Ferguson, the MP who had released him from his cell. He had responded to the plant, as had every available cop.

Dale grabbed Brenda's hand and ran toward him.

"Sergeant Ferguson! Say, we need a ride right now. See that guy?" - Dale pointed to his former boss - "he may be up to no good. Do you have a vehicle?"

"I have one of our jeeps," the MP said. "Why do you think I should chase him?"

"I used to work for him in Y-12 and he doesn't belong here. You have to trust me. I've been right on several screwy things here, like your own Colonel Hutchinson. Can you take us?"

The sergeant looked at Dale and Brenda steadily. "I may be crazy, but I've felt like something hasn't been right with Colonel Hutchinson for a while. Call it an insider's opinion." He looked around and thought about the implications of what he was about to do, then said, "Okay, let's go!"

Daniel S. Zulli

Chapter 45-Chase

Even though Hal Rainey had a decent head start on the trio, there were limits to where he could go inside the reservation. The only true way of escape was to exit through one of the several gates to the outside world. Hal left X-10 on Bethel Valley Road, then went north on White Wing Road. When he hit the Oak Ridge Turnpike, he turned east, paralleling the Black Oak Ridge series of hills on the reservation's north border. With emergency vehicles and others escaping the X-10 meltdown, a rapidly-moving vehicle would not attract attention.

Sergeant Ferguson kept pursuit in his jeep. Following Hal's vehicle was easy as it was the only one taking this route away from the affected area. He was taking the long way back to Y-12 instead of the direct route on Bear Creek Road.

Despite the roads being new and smooth, the Army-issued jeep bounced and jerked as it sped along, provoked by the slightest bump or defect in the pavement. Dale threatened to catapult out of the vehicle several times. He glanced behind him to see Brenda bobbing up and down like a rag doll. Despite this, she would occasionally holler, "Faster! There he is! Don't let him get away!" as she pounded on the

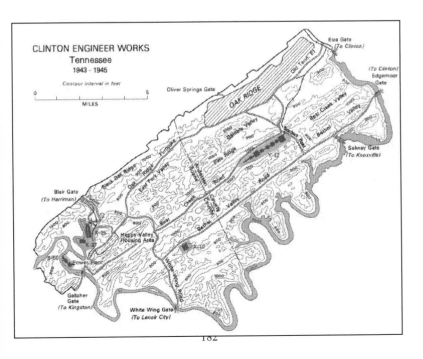

back of Dale's seat. Dale could only marvel at her being charged with level of excitement. He would have preferred to be sitting in an easy chair, reading a good book, but Brenda seemed to be thrilled that she had finally found what she craved out of life.

She was loving this.

Dale, however, found that each jostle of the jeep reminded him of the fact that his ribs still were not 100% healed. He was hoping not to re-break them in this frantic ride.

With Gamble Valley to the right, Hal Rainey went right on Scarboro Road, which bordered Y-12 on the east side. Since it was not a full 90-degree turn, he took it at a high speed, fortunate there was not another car in the other lane as he swerved into it to make the turn.

By the time Sergeant Ferguson was at that intersection, a laundry truck came from the other direction. He had to hit the brakes and downshift furiously to not have a head-on collision with the truck. Dale and Brenda had to hang on to anything in the jeep for support as the sergeant was both slowing down rapidly and turning right at the same time. Dale was trying not to end up in Sergeant Ferguson's lap. They momentarily lost Hal Rainey's car.

Dale hollered in the rushing wind, "I bet he's going back to Y-12 where he works. Go there!"

Sergeant Ferguson found the parking lot on Y-12's east side. With another slam of the brakes and thrusting downward on the gears, he pulled in, tires screeching. There were many cars in the parking lot as the swing shift was working. Hal Rainey's black Dodge blended in with the other cars. The MP slowly drove around as they scouted the lot for his car.

Dale stood up in the jeep and pointed to a car. "That's it! I saw his plates as we chased him. He's here!"

Running to the plant, Dale said in a mournful tone, "I can't go in there anymore."

"Me neither," Brenda echoed. "I turned in my badge to work at X-10."

"Don't worry!" Sergeant Ferguson hollered.

As the trio approached the gate, they saw the security guard from the firm that worked the plants. He was looking in the direction of the glowing responder lights in the distance at X-10.

The guard was startled when he saw three people run up to his gate shack, led by an Army MP.

He stepped out of his shack and challenged them before they got to him. "Hey, you guys! You can't come here like that."

Sergeant Ferguson pulled out his badge, which technically did not allow him to enter Y-12 either. But he did place his other hand on his service revolver and said, "The colonel sent us here. They're with me!"

grabbing Dale and Brenda and hustling them past the startled guard. He stood there, slack-jawed as the trio hustled past him and toward the plant.

The MP asked Dale as they were making their way into the main hallway, "Where does this guy work at?"

"Down here!" They turned into another corridor, past some bays of calutrons, and into an office area.

Regina Rivera was getting up from her desk, wrapping up another long day of work. She jumped when Dale led the other two into her area.

"Where's Hal Rainey?" Dale challenged.

"He just came by here, running like you are! He was white as a ghost. He got some stuff out of his office and took off again." Miss Rivera said. "Say, what's going on here? I heard something happened at X-10. Are you in trouble again, Dr. Hargrowe?"

"Hopefully after tonight I won't be! Which way did he go?"

Miss Rivera pointed to another corridor. The three of them turned and ran off, leaving the receptionist looking stunned and speechless.

They took off running. People

were coming out of their work spaces to catch a glimpse of this odd track team, running through their top-secret facility. Having an armed Military Police as one of the team stopped anyone from halting or challenging them. His revolver was out of its holster and in his right hand.

Turning a corner, they caught a glimpse of a shadowed figure running down a darkened hallway leading to one of rooms that housed the huge electromagnets that processed the radioactive isotopes. These were the oval-shaped "racetracks." The figure was heading toward the Alpha racetracks.

The figure was Hal Rainey.

Sergeant Ferguson led Dale and Brenda in the pursuit.

"Halt!" he ordered over the hum of the machinery. His shout startled the workers on the racetrack floor, who, apparently, did not hear or notice them coming in.

Dale's former supervisor led the chase on the level above the oval of electromagnets. He looked behind him and saw the three pursuers gaining on him. He flew down the metal steps leading down to the main floor, while carrying a burlap sack. Rainey's black hair was a shock of unkempt ebony wires, pointing everywhere.

"Halt!" the MP ordered again. Dale could feel his ribs throb from the exertion. His breathing came from deep within his lungs, not shallow. The expanding of his rib cage was more than his injured bones could handle.

"Stay here!" Dale shouted to the soldier and Brenda. They stopped. As Dale continued forward, he smoothly stripped off his belt, drew off his wristwatch, and tossed them far from him. He reached into his pockets and pulled out his loose change, flinging it away. Brenda saw the coins zip across the plant floor without stopping. With a *ching!* the money landed on a far Alpha racetrack in the direction of Dale's throw, firmly stuck to a side panel.

Dale had disposed of anything metal on him as he ran after Hal Rainey, who ran toward a racetrack.

That was his undoing.

He was wearing a lot of metal.

Hal's glasses with its metal screws were the first thing affected by being too close to the electromagnetic machine. They flew off his head and crunched onto an exposed panel.

Dale then saw his former boss suddenly slam against the racetrack, banging his head on the metal. Dale saw Hal's old Navy dog tags, which he still wore, pull out of the top of his shirt. His left arm was pinned due to the large wristwatch he wore. He must have been carrying a hefty amount of change from the way his left pants pocket was glued to the machine.

The magnetic pull of these machines was the reason all the floor workers wore special clothing with no metal in them, with rubber boots. Hal Rainey, in his haste to escape his pursuers, had gotten too close, and it caught him. Even the metal eyelets on his shoes were affected by the irresistible magnetic attraction.

When he banged against the magnet, his head smacked hard, stunning him.

Brenda and Sergeant Ferguson were coming up on the racetrack.

"Stay back!" Dale warned. The MP alone had enough metal on him to render him helpless if he got within 10 feet of the magnets.

Working through the ache in his head, Hal tried to free himself from the massive Alpha electromagnet. It was too late. Dale reached him with a flying leap and crunched into him like a linebacker on a halfback. A plume of air blew out of Hal's mouth. Hal garnered enough energy to force a wild swing at Dale with his right hand, which was not secured to the machine. Dale easily avoided the swing and countered with his own right hand that would have dropped Hal Rainey entirely to the floor had he not been held in the electromagnetic grip of the racetrack.

Dale gave him another right for good measure.

Dale pulled his groggy former supervisor off the racetrack and drug him over to where Sergeant Ferguson and Brenda had stopped. The MP twisted Hal's hands behind his back and banged his handcuffs on him. Dale went back and picked up the sack Hal had been carrying.

"Look what we have here!" Dale announced. Pulling his hand out of the bag, he had a hand full of bills.

"Hoo-wee!" exclaimed the sergeant. "Looks like you got yourself one good-paying part-time job here!"

"And I bet if you inspect his getaway car, you'll find the overalls of the workers in X-10 that he was wearing when he snuck in and 'accidentally' dropped that hot rod on the floor," Dale proclaimed.

"What made you suspect your old boss?" Brenda asked.

"It was the same as with Colonel Hutchinson, and it bugged me just the same. I kept telling both about all this monkey business we had uncovered, and both said they were on it, but nothing was ever done. And I know we have specialized security people all over this place, watching for leaks and stopping information from getting out. There's no way that the suspicions we had would not be checked out if Hal had really told someone about it. But you never did, did you?" Dale challenged Hal. "And I bet someone paid you this money to keep it quiet and get you to do what you did in X-10, right?

Hal Rainey snarled at Dale. "You never should have poked your nose where it didn't belong. I guess you didn't want to heed all those warnings we tossed your way. If you had played your cards right, you could have walked out of here a rich man, smart boy. At least you wouldn't have gotten shot!"

"You're not going to be able to spend any of this money where you're going, pal!" Sergeant Ferguson declared. "Let's go!"

Grabbing him by the back of his collar and his shackled wrists, the MP pushed Hal Rainey toward the closest exit. Dale and Brenda followed behind him.

"So, when do you learn to punch like that, Dr. Hargrowe?" Brenda asked.

"That? Oh, when I hurt my knee my freshman year of college playing football, I joined the boxing team so I could get some exercise without having to run and get tackled."

"Not bad!" Brenda said, with a proud tone in her voice.

"Actually, my knee feels pretty good not having run like that in years. Wish I could say the same for my ribs!" He winced as he ran his hand up and down his right side.

When the trio exited the plant with their prisoner and stepped out into the early spring night, they were met with a half-dozen MP vehicles, led by Colonel Hutchinson. The ruckus they had caused must have been called in by the guard at the gate shack, bringing the cops from X-10 to Y-12.

"Dr. Hargrowe! Sergeant Ferguson! Miss Andrews!" the colonel shouted. "Halt where you are! You are all under arrest. This time, Hargrowe, we are going to throw away the key. And, Sergeant Ferguson, I don't know what got into you, but the only thing you'll have to do in this man's Army is scrub toilets in Ft. Leavenworth!"

Brenda brazenly walked in front of them and toward the colonel.

"Oh, I don't think so, Colonel Hutchinson!" she countered. "When I get done singing, you just might be peeling potatoes in the prison's Kafé yourself. You see, I just happen to know that you and my lovely roommate, Miss Trudy McIntyre, are very close friends. I mean, *very* close friends. Why, just the other night, when you gave me that ride from your house to the bowling alley, I followed you to that little shed, because you didn't go back to work like you told your wife, now did you? When I looked inside, guess what I saw? I saw you and Trudy Mac leaving the back room, and with you fixing up your nice Army uniform. It doesn't take a genius to know what you two were up to.

"And since we know that Trudy Mac is getting money from some fellow in town, I bet that if we try hard enough, I think we can add up 2 plus 2 plus 1 and come up with five skunks - you, her, this guy," pointing to Hal Rainey, "and Ted Hildebrandt and Abby Felton. And, I bet there's a whole lot more, too. So, now, Colonel, what's that you were saying about arresting us?"

Colonel Hutchinson's face blanched. Even though the MPs had their weapons drawn on Dale, Brenda and Sergeant Ferguson, they all looked at their commander. Brenda's pronouncement had thrown a twist into their simple task of arresting the three.

Sergeant Ferguson broke the pause.

"*Now* I get it!" he exclaimed. "I remember seeing a young girl come around to our building sometimes, even at night. She always told us she had to inspect our snack area and inventory everything. I never did think that was a legit answer, but I couldn't prove her wrong. She wasn't coming to inspect our food, but to see you, colonel! And all those long hours you worked at night, you weren't just working, were you?"

As a full-bird, Colonel Hutchinson was not used to an E-4 addressing him in that tone of voice.

"Sergeant Ferguson!" he roared. "I order you to release that man!" indicating Hal Rainey. "Men, arrest all three of them!"

Three of the MPs with the colonel hesitated, then slowly stepped toward them.

Sergeant Ferguson had relaxed his grip on Hal Rainey, during this tense exchange. Seeing an opportunity, Rainey bolted forward.

"Shoot them!" he screamed. "Shoot them all!"

Daniel S. Zulli

Chapter 46-Capture

No one moved. Soldiers do not take direct orders from civilians, especially hand-cuffed ones ordering them to shoot another soldier and two other unarmed civilians.

Sergeant Ferguson lifted his voice and all eyes turned on him.

"St. Paul wrote in 1 Corinthians, Chapter 5," he proclaimed: 'I wrote unto you in an epistle not to company with fornicators: Yet not altogether with the fornicators of this world, or with the covetous, or extortioners, or with idolaters; for then must ye needs go out of the world. But now I have written unto you not to keep company, if any man that is called a brother be a fornicator, or covetous, or an idolater, or a railer, or a drunkard, or an extortioner; with such a one no not to eat. For what have I to do to judge them also that are without? Do not ye judge them that are within? But them that are without God judgeth. Therefore, put away from among yourselves that wicked person.'"

He drew his service revolver and pointed it directly at Colonel Hutchinson, his commanding officer.

"Sir, I am placing *you* under arrest for conduct unbecoming an officer and a gentleman, for you have sinned against God and man!"

Colonel Hutchinson just had the tables turned on him. In an instant, he had gone from the one in charge, to the scoundrel. He broke the formation of MPs and charged for his staff car.

The MPs stood frozen. They had never seen their commanding officer placed under arrest before, especially by an enlisted man.

Colonel Hutchinson started his car and rammed it into motion. The screech of his tires assaulted their ears. What should have been a pleasant March night in Tennessee had turned into a raging torrent of insanity. First, a top-secret facility had been breached with a first-ever-of-its-kind nuclear accident, sending Oak Ridge into an emergency response frenzy.

Then, men of differing Army ranks were arresting each other in full view of their peers and subordinates. Finally, a hand-cuffed civilian was ordering to have other civilians shot by the Army.

This was not in any military manual on procedures.

Sergeant Ferguson took charge of the situation, bringing some order to this chaos.

"You two take this prisoner back to HQ and place him in a cell!" He was an NCO who out-ranked the other MPs. His experience and savvy gave him the authority the men trusted. "You two go back to X-10 and help secure that scene. You two," he said to the remaining soldiers, "follow me. We've got to get the colonel!"

Dale and Brenda joined the sergeant as he ran for his jeep. The other MPs raced for theirs and they all joined in on the chase for the colonel.

Colonel Hutchinson disappeared into the night. He had gotten a good jump on his pursuers.

The senior-ranking MP did not return to his security building. He went instead to the women's dorm.

He screeched his staff car to a halt, causing multiple room lights to snap on at the disturbing sound in the dorm parking lot. Blinds and curtains pulled aside as the ladies attempted to discover the source of the disturbance.

Colonel Hutchinson stormed inside the building and passed the dorm mom, sitting at her station in the day room.

"Sir!" she ordered. "You can't come in here!"

The colonel ignored her and bounded up the stairs to the second floor. When he reached room 212, he tried to open it, only to find it locked.

He pounded on the door. "Trudy Mac! Open up!"

Young women were peeping out their room doors at this scene, eyes wide. Many were in pajamas and hair curlers, frightened by this older man's intrusion into their living space.

Trudy Mac flung the door open.

"Colonel! What are you doing here?"

"Let's go!" Colonel Hutchinson repeated. "Get your shoes on and grab your coat. Don't worry about packing anything else. Now!" he commanded.

Once Trudy Mac slipped her shoes on and picked up her jacket, the colonel grabbed her by the wrist and dragged her out of the room and down the stairs. The other women slammed their doors shut, frightened at seeing one of their dorm-mates forced to leave in this unseemly manner.

Trudy Mac protested. "Ow! Stop! You can't do this!"

"They're on to us! We have to get out of here!"

He flung open the door to his staff car and threw Trudy Mac in. All reason had left the colonel. He was acting like a wild man. His career and marriage were over, both caused by the vices that had been covered up so well in his past, but now have caused his world to come crashing down.

Throwing the car into gear, the colonel's acceleration caused gravel to shoot out from the pavement.

"Where are we going?" Trudy Mac had to yell.

"Out of here. Anywhere! Maybe I can lose them in these hills!"

The soldier turned left on Bethel Valley Road and headed for the Edgemoor Gate, which would lead out toward Clinton and, more importantly, in the direction of the rugged Smoky Mountain terrain, where a car could not be found.

Sergeant Ferguson had been methodically driving his jeep around Oak Ridge to locate the colonel's staff car, having lost him when he was parked behind the women's dorm. He had just pulled onto Bethel Valley Road after checking out behind some stores when they saw a car swerving at a high speed onto the main northeast-southwest artery in the distance in front of them.

Brenda, standing up in the back seat of the jeep, recognized the staff car. "That's him! Get him!" she hollered, pounding on Dale's shoulders in front of her.

Sergeant Ferguson hit the accelerator on his jeep, shifting up to the highest gear. Dale and Brenda were thrown back into their seats. The colonel's staff car was a big sedan with a bigger engine, and it out-paced the jeep. But, the renegade O-6 had to slow down considerably as he approached the gate leading out of Oak Ridge.

This gave Sergeant Ferguson opportunity to get closer. His headlights shone into the colonel's car, illuminating both passengers.

"Trudy Mac's with him!" Brenda shouted. "They're trying to escape!"

As the racing motorcade approached the gate, Dale could see the swing shift MP jump to his feet at the sound of the colonel's V-8 staff car approaching at a speed faster than exiting cars normally did.

The startled gate shack guard looked back into Oak Ridge, seeing the Army sedan and the MP jeep behind it, also heading toward his quiet evening post at a high rate of speed.

He took his place in the center of the exit lane, frantically waving his arms to get the cars to slow down. His eyes grew wide and frightened as it became clear neither driver was going to do as he was ordered.

The sentry blew his whistle in one last attempt to restore order, but had to jump out of the way to avoid being run over. As he lay on the pavement, he could see the driver of the staff car - his own commander!

The staff car accelerated once it passed through the gate area onto the open road that led off the Oak Ridge reservation. Staggering to his feet, the private turned in time to see the jeep driven by Sergeant Ferguson rush toward his post. In vain he waved his arms again and hollered, "Hey! Stop!" He blew his MP whistle again, but the NCO ignored him and went through the gate shack's exit.

The colonel's car disappeared from the sentry's view. But then he heard a screech of brakes and tires and the awful sound of a car wreck.

Sergeant Ferguson revved the engine and shifted to a higher gear when he, too, heard the noise.

When the occupants in the jeep came upon the accident scene, they saw the staff car on its back, tires spinning futilely in the air.

"They flipped!" Dale shouted.

Both Colonel Hutchinson and Trudy Mac had been ejected from the sedan. Neither looked to be seriously injured, although they were dazed, with blood visible.

Colonel Hutchinson tried to walk but promptly fell to his knees. The headlights from the approaching jeep illuminated blood trickling down the side of his head, showing it originated in his scalp.

Trudy Mac also staggered to her feet, but could make her legs move enough to get her running from the scene.

Brenda hollered, "You two get the colonel! I got her!"

As soon as the jeep came to a jarring rest, Brenda hopped over the side and began to sprint after her roommate.

Trudy Mac looked back and gave a yell. Adrenalin and fear enabled her legs to produce a good speed.

But adrenalin was not enough to give Trudy Mac the distance she needed. Brenda was fueled by anger and her desire to capture this *femme fatale* who seemed to be at the heart of all the trouble she and Dale had experienced.

Trudy Mac stumbled in some tall grass, allowing Brenda to leap like a diver off a board when she was a few yards from her prey. Brenda wrapped her arms around Trudy Mac's knees and brought her to the ground with a groaning escape of air from her lungs.

The two women rolled on the ground, embraced in a ferocious wrestling match. Arms, knees and elbows flew. Feet kicked. Hair flew. Finally, Brenda had her roommate beneath her for just long enough for her to throw a right cross haymaker, landing in on the left side of Trudy Mac's chin, snapping her head to her right. Her eyes rolled and she let out a load moan. Her body went limp. Brenda had delivered the knockout blow.

Dale ran up to the scene. Brenda was sitting on Trudy Mac's back, who was face down in the sod.

"Wow! Did I just see that? That was incredible!"

"Not bad for a math major!" Brenda laughed.

"Where did you learn to do that?" Dale asked.

"Hey, you're not the only one able to box. My younger brother used to get on my nerves enough to force me to take action."

"Well, I'm sure glad you're not my big sister!"

Dale and Brenda rousted Trudy Mac to her feet, who had begun to stir. Dale clasped her wrists together behind her back, while Brenda grabbed a handful of hair. They returned to the gate shack where

Sergeant Ferguson and the colonel were. Trudy Mac's chin was turning color from Brenda's punch.

Colonel Hutchinson's hands were cuffed behind his back. The colonel was slumped over on a stool, caught and defeated.

Brenda spoke up and cheerfully declared, "Well, here are two fine peas in a pod!" She shoved Trudy Mac into the private's gate shack chair. "Sit!"

Sirens and headlights signaled that reinforcements were arriving.

Soldiers with MP armbands poured out of the vehicles, flashing weapons. A youthful-looking lieutenant took charge of the scene.

"Sergeant! Explain!"

"At ease, lieutenant," the sergeant calmly replied with a raised hand. "I can explain everything."

"Sir," the NCO continued, "you need to place the colonel and his accomplice here under arrest and take them to the cell area. I can't go into everything here, but these two, as well as that Hal Rainey fellow who was brought in earlier, are involved in a conspiracy to commit sabotage here in Oak Ridge. We need to question them to get the whole story."

The young lieutenant was incredulous. "You want me to arrest a colonel?"

"Trust me, lieutenant," the sergeant grinned, "once this is over with, you'll be outranking him by a mile!"

Daniel S. Zulli

Chapter 47-Interrogation

The procession of military police vehicles made its way back to their headquarters building. The soldiers on duty in the building watched in wide-eyed horror as their own O-6 was led, in handcuffs, to an empty cell. Dale noted the irony of the colonel being secured in the very cell in which he had placed him several days ago when he was arrested.

Trudy McIntyre was placed in her cell and Hal Rainey was already in his.

Once the doors clanged shut to the two cells, the young lieutenant, who was the officer in charge of the swing shift, sat at his desk in the front office area. Sergeant Ferguson, Dale and Brenda surrounded. The blank look on his face betrayed his uncertainty as to what would or should happen next. He was young, newly commissioned, just out of college not long ago.

The sound of several cars braking furiously in front of their building interrupted his contemplation. Sergeant Ferguson went to the front door, only to see another Army staff car with two stars on the front license plate. It led two other cars in churning up dust in the front of the HQ.

"It's General Groves, LT," Sergeant Ferguson announced.

The lieutenant groaned. "Oh, no!"

His worst nightmare just became a reality, as Clinton Engineering Works' commanding officer bounded out of the back seat of his vehicle, looking like he might rip the door off its hinges.

The rest of the cars unloaded with other Army brass and civilians. The general stomped into the building as Sergeant Ferguson snapped to attention and held the door.

Spying the lieutenant, General Groves motioned to the conference room. "Inside!" he bellowed.

"This had better be good!" the two-star warned. "I was heading to Alamogordo when my plane got diverted, and now I have to explain this to President Roosevelt in the morning, so this had better be good!" he repeated. It seemed doubtful that any amount of chocolate was going to appease him.

"Sir, my name is Sergeant Rodney Ferguson, First Charlie Company, and this is Second Lieutenant Bradley Riley. And I can explain, along with Dr. Hargrowe and Miss Andrews."

General Groves noticed Dale. "You again!" he growled. The veins in his neck were noticeably growing. "I thought I threw you out of here!"

Daniel S. Zulli

"Yes, sir, you did," Dale answered in a calm tone. "But I think when you hear our story, you'll be glad I stuck around for a while."

General Groves took his seat at the head of the conference table. "Okay, everyone," he said more calmly, "let's sit down and hear what they have to say. But it had better be *very* good." His request sounded more like a threat.

Dale began.

"General, I was working at Y-12 since I got here last August. Miss Andrews joined me at the Y-12 plant when it opened, working on the calutrons as a supervisor.

"It wasn't too long when I started to notice some anomalies in my work. They were not just corrections, but intentional alterations that would have either slowed our work down, or totally compromised the result.

"Then, Miss Andrews was made aware that some of the calutrons were being tampered with. Dials and numbers were intentionally messed with to hamper our work. All these things, added up, could not have been a coincidence.

"Someone warned, then threatened me. Miss Andrews was accosted one night with another warning for me to not raise any concerns.

"I voiced my findings and concerns repeatedly to my supervisor - Hal Rainey in cell #2 - as well as Colonel Hutchinson. While I was assured that the situation was being taken care of, I wasn't convinced. So, I enlisted the aid of my former housemate and took a night to spy on the calutrons. That is when I discovered the girl, Abby Felton, tampering with the numbers on them. You know this part: she was getting paid to do this by Ted Hildebrandt. I did my best to try to catch them in the act of him paying her off, but my plan didn't work out well, and unfortunately, Bob O'Neil got killed and I got wounded. That's when you fired me, when I was in the hospital recovering."

General Groves and the rest of the room sat silently, absorbing all Dale's recap of these strange doings in Oak Ridge.

"But, it still wasn't clear. Because of how some things went, I suspected Miss Andrews's roommate, Trudy McIntyre. I had someone trail her one day as she went into town, and he saw a man in Clinton give her what turned out to be a nice bit of cash. Then Brenda - Miss Andrews - discovered that Miss McIntyre had an account at a bank there with a substantial amount of money in it, money that she couldn't have earned in Oak Ridge in the job she had."

Brenda interjected. "Dr. Hargrowe also suspected that Colonel Hutchinson was somehow involved when nothing was being done to investigate this mystery. So, he asked me to trail him. I did, and I

197

happened to find him in a very compromising situation with Trudy McIntyre. They were having a late-night rendezvous. The rat."

"So, now we have a woman making a lot of funny money, having a fling with the head of security who isn't investigating like he should be. And you have a supervisor at Y-12 - Dale's former boss - mixed up in something awful in X-10, which could have been terrible. After the accident, your married colonel and his very young sweetie are caught trying to go on the lam together and leave happy Oak Ridge. General, all this adds up to one big mess here in Dodge City, with Ted Hildebrandt and Abby Felton being the first two caught. Now we have these three low-lives."

No one spoke in the crowded conference room.

Finally, the general asked, "What about this mystery man you say was giving the girl money?"

"We're developing a plan to catch him, general," the lieutenant spoke up.

"Well, lieutenant," General Groves said, standing up. "I'm going to go and prepare my report for the president. I want you to interrogate these three and bring me your findings within the hour."

He and his entourage stormed out of the conference room leaving the lieutenant, Sergeant Ferguson, Dale and Brenda looking like they just had their death sentence commuted.

Lieutenant Riley led everyone into the cell area. Brenda took charge.

"Let's start with Mata Hari. I think it all revolves around her. Okay, Miss Priss - spill it," she demanded.

Trudy Mac glared at her captors. Looking beaten, she inhaled deeply and began.

"I was on one of my runs into Clinton shortly after I got here. This one time a man came up to me. He had seen me before and knew I came from Oak Ridge because of the bus I was on. He was dressed all fancy-like and started talking to me. He bought me lunch and was real nice to me. He gave me $5 just so I could buy myself a new dress.

"I told him I was from a farm in a small town. He knew I wasn't making too much money here. Then one day, he showed me a whole bunch of money and said it could be mine if I helped him out."

Brenda interrupted her narrative. "Why did you do it, Trudy Mac? Why'd you sell us out?"

"Why did I do it?" Trudy Mac replied, her voice rising. "Because I'm just a farm girl who hated everything about the farm. Everything. It was a miserable life. We never had money for nothin'! When I was growing up, Daddy would send me and my three worthless brothers out to do chores. It wasn't bad until I got a little older. Then those three monsters would do terrible things to me. They took their turns hurting

Daniel S. Zulli

me. One would hold me down while the others did what they wanted to. Momma knew what was going on because she saw my clothes. But she never said anything because if she did, Daddy would beat her just as bad as he beat the rest of us. When he got all liquored up, he was even worse. My brothers hurt me so bad the doctor said I could never have kids. That went on for years.

"So, when this man offered me some money, I took it. I wanted to get as far away from the farm and here as I could. I was saving up to go to Paris after the war. I was going to have champagne and caviar for breakfast and stay in fancy hotels and wear fancy dresses and pretty shoes and sleep in a nice, soft bed."

"What did this man want you to do?" Dale asked.

"All I had to do was to help him mess this place up. I didn't care - I don't care -about Oak Ridge or anyone in it! He told me he had that fella Ted Hildebrandt running the operation that got all those calutron numbers changed and slowing the progress down. My job was to make sure no one knew about it. That's when I roped in the colonel and your old boss here. They would stop anything from happening to Ted's people, who were doing the dirty work."

"How did you involve the colonel?" Lieutenant Riley inquired.

"Are you kidding me?" Trudy Mac sneered. "It was easy. Men are bigger pigs than any of the hogs I ever had to slop on the farm. All I had to do was pretend to come here to check on the food supplies, and then flirt with him a little bit, and while his wife was busy at her job or at home, I had him wrapped around my little finger so fast your head would spin. Then when I had him where I wanted him, it was a cinch to keep him quiet while everything was going on. If I ever spilled the beans, his career was cooked."

They looked over at Colonel Hutchinson. He sat on the chair in his cell with his hands in his head, bent low, a pathetic figure. He had traded everything good in his life for this deceitful excuse for a woman. They all felt rotten for Valerie.

"And what about Hal Rainey?" Dale asked, jerking a thumb in his direction.

"Same with him. All I had to do is find a few key men and they'd do whatever I wanted them to do, if they got what they wanted. I wasn't just ordering food. With Ted Hildebrandt away in the slammer, I got him to drop that radioactive rod in X-10. My contact was on my case to get busy with more bad stuff, so I got Hal Rainey to move faster making a mess. So not only did he keep your information quiet, but he also did some of the dirty work. He had to 'cause I made him."

Dale addressed his former boss. "How did you know I was looking into these irregularities?"

"Lou Cunningham told me you had found something. Don't worry, Lou's not part of it. He just can't keep a secret, like when you first told him about it."

Dale looked relieved. He was glad Big Lou was innocent and not part of this treacherous conspiracy.

He glared at Hal. "And it was you who was fudging all my calculations, weren't you?"

"Yeah," Hal mumbled in a defeated tone. "I didn't think you'd catch them."

Lieutenant Riley chimed in to Trudy Mac. "So now that we're getting to the bottom of this, tell us who this mystery, well-dressed man in Clinton is who paid you to turn on your country's war effort?"

"He goes by Harry Ginter but his real name is 'Hans' Ginter. He's American but German. I don't know who he works for. All I know he was my ticket to a better life somewhere other than on a stupid farm or this cow patch."

"Can you arrange another meeting with him?"

Before Trudy Mac could answer, there was a commotion outside the door leading into the cell area. They heard a soldier outside, saying, "Ma'am! You can't go in there!"

The door to the cell area opened and Valerie Hutchinson stepped into the room, leaving the protesting soldier behind her. Her eyes were rimmed red and mouth was drawn tightly. Her normal pleasantness was not with her tonight.

Lieutenant Riley and Sergeant Ferguson were expecting to restrain her if she were to come unhinged and cause a scene. Word had obviously gotten to her about her husband. Dale did not move. Brenda did not greet her former supervisor from Administration #1.

Valerie walked to the front of Colonel Hutchinson's cell. She glared at her husband, absorbing the revelation that not only had her husband been cheating on her with a much younger woman, but had also endangered the work being done in Oak Ridge by his refusal to allow an investigation. He had violated everything an Army officer of high rank stood for.

Without speaking but staring at her husband, Valerie clasped her wedding ring with her right hand, twisting and turning it on a warm night. She removed it. Without turning her gaze to Trudy Mac, Valerie tossed the ring into the young woman's cell.

"She can wear this when you're both rotting in Leavenworth." Valerie Hutchinson then turned and walked out, slamming the door behind her. It was as if all the oxygen had been sucked out of the room at her departure. The only sound was the ringing in their own ears that people notice when everything else is dead silent.

Daniel S. Zulli

Chapter 48-Plans

Finally, Lieutenant Riley spoke up.

"Miss McIntyre," he said, returning to the subject, "can you arrange a meeting with this Ginter, without him knowing we're on to him?

"What will it get me?" she snarled.

"Probably nothing, to be honest. This is war time, and any act against a country during war won't go favorably, even if you help us out."

Trudy Mac was thoughtful. "Yeah, I can do it. Might as well. He won't be giving me anymore money, so I don't care if he gets caught and hangs too."

"Did you meet him at a scheduled time?"

"Yeah. It's always on a Friday when I come into Clinton in the morning. If I don't show up, he knows I'm in another town or here doing my job."

"Good," the young officer said. "Today is Saturday. That gives us six days to get things in order. We will arrange for you to go into town next Friday as normal so we can catch your benefactor. We're done here for now, Dr. Hargrowe and Miss Andrews. Sergeant Ferguson and I have a long night before us. We'll contact you if we need anything, but now, you're free to go home and get some rest. We appreciate all you've done to help us solve this mystery."

"When you give your report to the general," Brenda said, "can you please put a good word in for Dr. Hargrowe? If it were not for him, this thing never would have been figured out and everything we've been trying to do here would have been in jeopardy."

"I'll do my best to make him look good before the general," the MP agreed.

"It might help to bring him some chocolate when you do," Brenda joked. "I heard that works wonders!"

Lieutenant Riley and Sergeant Ferguson gave their back-brief to General Groves and his executive officer. The general's secretary furiously typed his report to be ready for President Roosevelt first thing the next morning. An incident like the one they had this dramatic evening would send shockwaves through those who knew about the Clinton Engineering Works.

"So, you see, sir," the lieutenant said, concluding his report, "if it were not for Dr. Hargrowe's perseverance and diligence in following his hunches that something was wrong, we'd be so far behind in this project that the damage would be incalculable."

"General, I agree," echoed the sergeant. "Both he and Miss Andrews are the ones really responsible for the capture of the perpetrators. We owe them a lot."

General Groves sat quietly, digesting all he had been told. He tapped his pencil against the edge of his desk.

"As much as I hate to admit it, I was wrong when I fired that young man," he said. "It's clear he and the girl salvaged this operation. He can stay."

"Thank you, sir," the lieutenant said. "He'll be relieved to hear that. Oh, and we have a plan to capture the German man who was paying Miss McIntyre to betray her country. That will happen next Friday."

"Very good," the general said. "Press on and keep me informed. I have to go to Alamogordo tomorrow but my exec can reach me."

"10-4, sir."

Lieutenant Riley and Sergeant Ferguson were dismissed. Just as the sergeant was exiting General Groves's office, he turned to him and said, "Oh, and you should have seen the right cross Miss Andrews gave Miss McIntyre. Pow! Right in the kisser!"

Chapter 49-Kiss

Dale and Brenda walked slowly back to the women's dorm. Brenda's right arm was tucked into Dale's left.

"Well, Dr. Hargrowe, I think we've had enough fun for one night. What do you think?"

"I think I've had enough for the rest of my life!" Dale said. "You can't imagine how relieved I feel with those three rats behind bars."

"Agreed. It really bothers me that Trudy Mac - who was such a sweet girl when we got here - would turn into such a Benedict Arnold. She lied to me about you flirting with that secretary. She deliberately sent me to get her medicine, knowing I would be attacked. And she sure didn't seem to care that you had gotten shot. And all the while she was smiling and pretending to be our friend. That hurts so bad."

"I know how you feel," Dale replied. "I was working for a guy whom I thought was on the side of the good guys. I was telling him everything and he was in on it too. That's a crummy feeling."

"And," Brenda continued, "how about Val Hutchinson? That is so awful that the man she married turned out to be such a schmuck, in every terrible way. She didn't ask for this. But, I must say, sir, that you did a great job in getting this case rolling to being solved. I'm so proud of you!"

"Thanks," Dale grinned, "but when I was in the slammer, it was you that really got some answers. You are quite the detective, not to mention you pack one heck of a wallop. Remind me to never get on your bad side."

"You should see my uppercut, buster!" Brenda gave a fake punch with her left hand to Dale's midsection, causing a reactive flinch. They both had a hearty laugh, just what the mood needed.

"It's going to be strange going back to our room all by myself now," Brenda continued when they straightened up. "I guess they'll come pack her stuff up. But good riddance, I say."

"Here we are. This is where this whole night started. Strange. I guess God has a lot more in control than I ever thought He did. There seems to be divine touch on what we have been through."

"Well, if you ever give up the engineering, you can always take up preaching," Brenda chuckled.

"I think I just might knock *you* out!" Dale laughed.

"I'm ready any time you are if you want to go a few rounds!" Brenda one-upped him again.

"I think I'm more on the mood to wrestle," Dale replied. "Just watch this move."

Dale spun and faced Brenda. He wrapped both arms around her and pulled her close. He bent down, found her sweet lips, and landed a tender, lingering kiss on her. Brenda responded by placing her hands behind his head and holding him firmly, kissing him back. *About time!* Brenda thought.

When they separated, Brenda looked up dreamily to Dale and said, "I think I want to join the wrestling team."

"Tell you what: you just be outside your dorm and ready to go at 0900, soldier. We have to see someone. 0900."

Chapter 50-Proposal

Sunday, March 18, 1945, at nine o'clock in the morning, was like it should be in Tennessee at now: an inviting spring day. The sun was bright, even though it occasionally hid behind big, bilious clouds, making the air alternating between warm and chilly but warming up nicely.

Brenda Andrews was standing in front of her dorm at the appointed time. She wore a floral print dress and white sweater with matching hat that made her look like she had stepped out of a Sears catalog. She was the picture of femininity.

She was not expecting Dale Hargrowe to pull up in Sergeant Ferguson's Army jeep.

"Okay, you nut," she said, placing her hands on her hips, "what is going on?"

"Hey, you're not the only who can steal a military vehicle!" Dale called out, proud of himself. "Get in. That's an order!" Brenda could see Dale was enjoying whatever it was he was planning.

"This had better be good, Dr. Hargrowe. I could still be in bed getting my beauty rest," Brenda complained.

"I think you'll approve. There are a couple of things I need to do and they involve you."

Once they passed through the Solway Gate, Dale sped up. The jeep bounced and jostled on the roads, paved though they were. It had been a long time since Dale had driven a vehicle, and he was enjoying this, shifting up and down with vigor. He was in a great mood. The country miles flew by.

"Where to, if I may ask?" Brenda had to half-holler in the open jeep, holding her hat on.

"We're going to see an old friend in Maryville," Dale shouted back.

Brenda thought for a moment. "You mean Pastor Miller?"

"Yep!" Dale revved the engine into the next gear. "He's not scheduled to preach at The Chapel on the Hill today, so I thought we'd go out to his place."

Brenda did not know what to say. She knew it was Dale's idea to visit Pastor Miller's service when he came to The Chapel on the Hill, and she knew he visited him at his church during the period of their separation when he needed counsel, but this was unexpected. She wondered why Dale could not just wait for the next time when the preacher came onto Oak Ridge to visit one of his services.

But she just sat back and followed Dale's lead. Brenda discovered it was refreshing to leave the drama of Oak Ridge behind on a cheery Sunday morning. So many surreal events had happened, she had to remind herself that there was such a thing as "normal" outside the gates of Oak Ridge. The regular world did not have nuclear meltdowns.

When they finally pulled up to Pastor Miller's humble country church, they could see the service had already begun. The windows were open to allow fresh, spring air inside.

"I think we're late for the start," Brenda stated.

"Sorry. I think I made a wrong turn in town. I don't know these roads as well as Mr. E. or Freddie Joe, that's for sure. Come on, let's get inside."

They could only find a seat on the second-to-the-last pew on the far-right side, closest to the window. The church was full, and the air felt good.

They came in during the sermon. Mike Miller spotted them as he preached.

"...and the Apostle Paul reminds us that what the Prophet Jeremiah said in chapter 17, verse 9: 'The heart is deceitful above all things, and desperately wicked: who can know it?' is true. Paul said in the book of Romans that we all have sinned, even the nicest one of us. No one has met God's standards of perfection except His only-begotten Son, Jesus."

Of all the things for Dale and Brenda to come in on, this was too much of a coincidence to actually be one. Pastor Miller's words reminded them of how innocent and upstanding everyone involved in their drama had been, from Trudy Mac and Colonel Hutchinson and Hal Rainey, not to mention Ted Hildebrandt - who ushered in Pastor Miller's own chapel service in Oak Ridge - to Abby Felton. The heart *is* deceitful and corrupt, and all of them were Exhibit A's.

But the pastor's words did not just apply to those who committed crimes, Dale thought. He felt his own heart being stirred. While considering himself a nice person, he had to admit to himself that he also had fallen short of God's standards.

"Yes, beloved," the pastor continued, "as much as we hate to admit it, all of us are sinners needing the sweet grace of Jesus' blood applied to our own personal accounts for us to be forgiven of all our trespasses against a holy God. The Apostle Paul said in Romans 5:1 that 'Therefore being justified by faith, we have peace with God through our Lord Jesus Christ: By whom also we have access by faith into this grace wherein we stand, and rejoice in hope of the glory of God.' In a simple act of faith, we can place our trust in Jesus' sacrifice on the cross for us and our accounts are wiped clean and we stand before God declared innocent of all our sins. What a tremendous feeling!

"As Mrs. Shipley plays hymn number 372, would you please stand and sing, *What can wash away my sins; nothing but the blood of Jesus?* The altar is open if you would like to come down and let me pray for you."

Dale could not put his finger on what he felt, but he knew he felt something. Through watery eyes he looked over to Brenda and saw her dabbing away her own tears. Dale knew that his meager overtures toward church and religion in his earlier life were for naught. This, however, was too strong to deny. God was calling him. God had called him to this top-secret outpost in Tennessee for this reason, and not just to foil a plot to subvert the war effort, but to call him to Himself. Dale knew he was spiritually bankrupt, but at this moment, in a small country church, Dale knew the opportunity to be made whole had presented itself.

A few people left their pews and had come forward to pray with Pastor Miller. Fighting back tears, but not doing a very good job at it, Dale clutched Brenda's hand and he led her up to the altar area. They knelt as Pastor Mike Miller prayed for them to receive Christ as their personal sin-bearer. They had gone from Jesus from being *the* Savior to *their* Savior.

Dale did not remember the service ending; he was just aware that he and Brenda were standing in the back with the regular parishioners. Some were filing out to their cars, others were going to the small fellowship hall to grab some coffee and mingle for a while.

Mike Miller approached Dale and Brenda.

"Say!" he said. "This is a most welcome surprise, first in coming here and then coming forward. How are you two doing, besides being new creatures in Christ?"

"Well," Dale had to admit, "a little shell-shocked. I wasn't expecting this, but then, I wasn't expecting any of what has just happened to us recently."

"What's been going on?" the pastor asked.

Brenda tugged at Dale's elbow. "Oh, that's right - I can't talk about it. Trust me, I would love to but not now. Just believe me when I say things have been a real doozy for both of us."

Pastor Miller eyed them both. "Looks like things are better with the both of you. If I remember correctly, the last time I saw you, Dale, you were in a real pickle over this young lady."

"We're doing fine now, pastor," Brenda said. "Let's just say we had some crossed signals that someone had tossed us."

"Actually, that's one of the reasons why I came here today, Mike," Dale said. "Can we go to your office?"

"Sure thing," he answered. "Let me grab some coffee and shake some hands and I'll be right in."

In his office, Brenda questioned Dale. "So, you said you had a couple of things you wanted to do today. Have you done them?"

"One of them was coming to church to hear from God. Boy, did I! I wanted some answers for what we've gone through. I sure couldn't figure it all out. I wasn't expecting to have God talk to me personally like He did, though. But I feel a lot different, like a huge weight has been lifted off me. How do you feel?"

"Same here," Brenda replied. "I thought I was ready for some excitement, but it's gotten a little out of hand lately. I could use some order in my life."

Pastor Miller came into the office, coffee in hand.

"So, you two, what can I do for you?" he asked, taking his seat behind his desk.

"I guess the first thing is to help us along now," Dale spoke for them both. "What comes next now that we accepted Jesus?"

"Don't worry about that," Mike said. "I'll help you get established in a Bible study with others in Oak Ridge. I find it's best to take things slow and easy. I never like to rush the work of the Holy Spirit in new believers' lives."

"Thanks," Dale looked relieved.

"Okay, what else?" Mike asked.

"Now that you mentioned something else," Dale drawled. "I came here with two agendas. The first was to attend your service and get some spiritual direction. That I did. The second thing I wanted to do was to ask you if in maybe a couple of months from now, say, maybe June or July…"

Brenda was looking intently at Dale as if he had gone off his rocker. She had no idea what he was talking about.

"…you'd be willing to perform the wedding for Brenda and me at The Chapel On the Hill."

Brenda was shocked. "What? Dale Hargrowe! What are you saying?" Turning to Pastor Miller, she demanded, "What's this all about?"

"Don't look at me!" he said, holding up his hands, declaring his innocence.

When Brenda turned back to Dale, he had slid out of his seat and gotten down on one knee, next to Brenda's chair.

"Brenda Leah Andrews," he solemnly said, using her middle name, "from the moment I met you, even if I was half dead from the trip down here, I've been crazy nuts about you. As the months wore on, I realized that every second I've been with you made my heart complete. And, I discovered that we really made a good team together and that I can't imagine ever living without you, even if I have no clue as to where that might be. But would you do the honor of marrying me?"

Brenda was struck speechless.

Dale pulled a small ring out of his coat pocket.

"This ring isn't much. I'll get you a bigger one, I promise." He took Brenda's left hand in his left hand and slid the ring onto her finger.

"Will you marry me? You're not going to say no in front of the pastor, are you?" he warned.

"Oh, you big dope!" Brenda said. "I fell for you the moment I first saw you too, even if you did look like you had just come out of the dryer. Of course, I'll marry you!"

Dale stood up and lifted Brenda out of her chair for a sealing embrace. Forgetting that there was another person in the room with them, Dale said, "I love you so much it hurts, especially right around this area." He motioned with his hand his right side where the bullet had struck him.

Brenda whacked him in his shoulder.

Pastor Miller cleared his throat to get their attention.

"To answer your question, I'd be delighted to marry you two. But only if you don't kill each other first."

"You don't have to worry until she gives you a right cross straight in the kisser!" Dale laughed.

"I'm going to knock both of you out!" Brenda laughed back.

Both items on Dale's agenda had been successfully completed.

The trip back to Oak Ridge was joyous. They were on Cloud 9, not only for becoming Christians, but getting engaged.

Brenda kept holding her left hand out in front of her, repeating, "'Brenda Hargrowe.' 'Dr. and Mrs. Dale Hargrowe.' 'Dale and Brenda Hargrowe.'"

Dale laughed at her. "So, being married to an ex-con like me won't put a crimp in your style?"

"Well..." Brenda hesitated, "I was sort of holding out for my old boss, Mr. Sweeney, but since he never took the bait, I guess you'll do!"

Dale made the jeep fly back to Oak Ridge.

Daniel S. Zulli

Chapter 51-Clinton

The resiliency and resolve of Oak Ridge's workers made them quickly get things cleaned up and back to normal after the hubbub of the incident in X-10 and the high-profile arrests. There was too much to do toward the goal of producing a finished product - the unnamed "gadget" they were creating. With the war pressing on, Oak Ridgers pressed on.

Art Rossi, one of Dale's fellow Y-12 engineers, was moved to assume the position vacated by Hal Rainey. He quickly took charge and kept everyone focused to not let recent events distract them. If anything, they ramped up their energy level with renewed dedication. They plunged headlong into their work with a robust sense of purpose, not wanting for anything or anyone to deter them from seeing their work through to a successful completion.

Early Friday morning, Dale and Brenda reported to the security building to look up Lieutenant Riley and Sergeant Ferguson. They found the two in the conference room with two other MPs. They were all dressed in civilian clothes, purchased from Samuels Men's Store.

"Dr. Hargrowe. Miss Andrews," the lieutenant said, nodding. "What brings you here?"

"Lieutenant Riley, Miss Andrews and I would like to accompany you into Clinton to catch Hans Ginter. I know it's irregular, but Miss Andrews and I have been involved with this since the beginning and we'd like to see it through to the end."

The lieutenant began to speak in objection, but when Brenda folded her arms and stared at the young officer, it conveyed the message that she and Dale would not be denied.

"All right," he finally acquiesced. "But you two will sit in back of the bus and stay on it while we do our jobs. Got it?"

Dale looked at Brenda, who nodded. "Deal," he said.

Lieutenant Riley re-capped the meeting. "All eight, everyone, let's go over it one more time. I will be in the front seat behind the driver. Sergeant Ferguson will be behind me, with Miss McIntyre next to him. Privates Armbruster and Lopez will be on the other side of the bus. I want you two," he looked at Dale and Brenda, "to sit in the back. When we stop in Clinton, Armbruster and Lopez will get off the bus first and take your positions on the sidewalk, close to the drug store. Then Miss McIntyre will get off and go into the drug store and wait for Ginter. I'll be on the other side of the street and Sergeant Ferguson will stay close to the bus. When Ginter comes up, we grab him. Keep your

Daniel S. Zulli

weapons stowed unless we have to use them, and be careful about any stray civilians who may walk into the scene. As soon as the bus gets here, we board. Private Lopez, bring Miss McIntyre out here."

Trudy Mac looked terrible. It didn't appear she had gotten much sleep in the past week. Her eyes were bloodshot and hair unkempt. She looked older than her 20 years.

All of Trudy Mac's belonging had been emptied from her old room. A female clerk had assisted in getting all the clothing and accessories she needed when she went into town on a food run.

Sergeant Ferguson announced, "The bus is here." They had arranged for Freddie Joe Williams to pull his bus out of its normal bus route to be used just for this purpose.

They boarded silently and took their positions. No one else would be on this bus for their covert mission.

When the lieutenant took his place behind him, Freddie Joe asked, "Anything special you want me to do, sir?"

"Negative, driver. Just drive to your normal stop and stay inside the bus."

"Yes, sir." Freddie Joe swung the handle and closed the door.

Since this wasn't a typical bus route with regular occupants, there wasn't any idle or friendly banter. Not this time. No one spoke.

The March morning was still. A wave of fog and humidity had crept in during the night, making the barely budded trees look ominous along the way. The wild grass which hugged the roads outside the reservation's gates was damp with dew. The entrance into the civilian countryside was normally a refreshing thing. But this time each passing mile caused the tension in the bus to rise.

Trudy Mac hung her head down, not looking up to gaze out on this new morning.

Finally, the bus entered Clinton. Freddie Joe Williams had made this route hundreds of times since being hired by the company that ran Oak Ridge's transit needs. The humid air caused beads of sweat to tickle down the back of his neck onto his collar.

"Here y'all go, folks," he announced when he reached Main Street. "We're at my stop."

Lieutenant Riley turned to Trudy Mac, "You know what to do, Miss McIntyre. Do not display any signs of our presence or of this being a set-up. You clear?"

"Yes, sir," Trudy Mac replied in a weak voice.

The young officer gave the order. "Let's go, people."

The two young privates, barely out of their teens themselves but looking older than their years due to being in the Army during a war, discharged from the bus and nonchalantly walked over to the Clinton Drug Company. Private Lopez went in and came out with the morning

213

newspaper. Private Armbruster went over to a bench on the sidewalk about 20 yards from the drug store and sat down. Private Lopez walked by him and handed him part of the newspaper, then he leaned against the brick wall of the business which was next to the drug store and across from the bench.

Trudy Mac exited the bus next and went inside the drug store, taking her usual spot at the counter. She could be easily seen through the big plate glass window ordering a coffee and a sandwich. She placed her valise on the seat next to her.

Sergeant Ferguson got off next, staying by the bus at its stop. Lieutenant Riley got off last, according to plan. He strode across the street and took up a spot in front of the Courthouse. People were filing in and out of it, doing the business they came to do. There was a directory on the outside, and the MP was pretending to be perusing it in order to find the office he looked like he wanted.

Dale and Brenda stayed on the bus per the lieutenant's instruction. They slumped down in their seat in the rear of the bus as much as they could in order to be inconspicuous, while at the same time not wanting to miss any of the fireworks which might happen.

Brenda said in a hushed voice, "I sure hope he shows up." Without thinking, she reached over and grasped Dale's hand for moral support, inadvertently digging her nails into his palm. Dale placed his other hand on her arm in return.

"I hope so too. I'd like to see the guy who's been causing all of this trouble. I have a good mind to kick him in ribs just so he can be sore like I was. Or, maybe you should just clobber him with another right cross."

"One more crack out of you, buster, and I just might clobber you," Brenda whispered, in a mock warning.

Daniel S. Zulli

Chapter 52-Betrayal

Time stood still.

Trudy Mac requested a second cup of coffee. She pulled papers out of her valise and thumbed through them, making notes on some. She gave the impression of being thoughtful and busy and this being a normal day in town.

To the local townsfolk who passed by the scene at the bus stop and drug store, this was a routine day in Clinton. But the four MPs were on a high-tension stakeout, and their senses were on full alert. They scanned every civilian when they entered the area, looking for the one to whom they could trace all the sabotage efforts in Oak Ridge.

Privates Lopez and Armbruster traded sections of the paper. Then they read the previous sections over again as they went through the entire morning edition.

Sergeant Ferguson lit up his third cigarette, leaning on the bus. Freddie Joe Williams stood in the opening of the door and joined him in a smoke.

Dale happened to peer out the big window on the back door of the bus. He was the first to see the smartly-dressed man coming down the street toward the drug store.

"It's him!" he hissed. Both he and Brenda jumped in their seats.

"He is a fancy pants," Brenda noticed. "Someone's paying him some good dough to afford those duds."

Dale and Brenda called on every bit of self-control they could muster to not wave or holler to the men stationed on the sidewalks.

Passing the bus stop, Hans Ginter continued on the sidewalk until he arrived at the drug store.

When he walked up to Trudy Mac and tapped her on the shoulder, they could see her startle.

They talked. The others assumed she was giving a progress report of Hal Rainey's attempt at sabotage at X-10. She had to be telling a whopper of a success story. Ginter looked pleased. He patted her on shoulder, as if giving her his approval.

Trudy Mac held out her hand. Ginter dipped his into his suit pocket and produced an envelope. If this was more money for her bank account, Trudy must have realized that she would never spend it in Paris. At this point, she didn't care anymore. Her dream was over; it didn't concern her if Hans Ginter went down in flames like she was going to.

Trudy Mac gathered up her papers, placing them all in her bag. She paid the soda jerk for her food and drink, then the young lady from the farm and her benefactor left the drug store together.

The soldiers tensed.

When they got to the sidewalk, Lieutenant Riley started to slowly cross the street. Private Armbruster tossed his newspaper section in the trash can by the bench. Private Lopez sat his down on the bench seat. They began to amble toward the two traitors. Sergeant Ferguson tossed his cigarette down and likewise started to walk in that direction.

Ginter noticed the movement of the four men. He stopped. Their movements seemed different than the casual person on the street. Trudy Mac had been on his side, but he tugged on her arm until she was in front of him, creating a human shield.

This was too much for Trudy Mac to stand. She was too tired and her nerves too frayed to calmly continue her ruse.

"Look out!" she yelled.

Panicking, Ginter held Trudy Mac with his left hand in front of him, and with his right hand, reached under his jacket at his left armpit and came out with a .38 Special revolver. Ginter was alternating pointing it at everyone, including to the rear of Trudy Mac's head.

"Stop!" Lieutenant Riley shouted. "Put your weapon down!"

With this instant burst of commotion with visible firearms, people in the crowd screamed and began running in all directions. A mother with two young daughters grabbed each girl by their hair and drug them behind a car in front of the Courthouse. The girls screeched loudly.

Another man yelled at anyone and everyone, "Get down!" People ducked behind any available object, including thin lamp posts in an attempt to be shielded.

The lieutenant was in the middle of the street. Tires screeched as cars came to a halt. Some thrust their cars into reverse and generated noxious smoke from burning tires.

When Dale and Brenda heard Trudy Mac scream and the subsequent movement, they bolted from their seat in the rear of the bus and rushed to the front and out the door, pushing past Freddie Joe, who had hunkered down by his driver's seat.

When Ginter turned to his left to keep an eye on Sergeant Ferguson, he saw Dale and Brenda hit the pavement behind him.

"Hold it," Ginter ordered, "or the kid gets blasted!" He was twisting with Trudy Mac held securely in front of him in an attempt to keep visuals on all his assailants. The MPs had halted in their rushing of Ginter, but had their weapons drawn and pointed at him.

Trudy Mac screamed.

"Don't shoot!" she begged.

From behind Sergeant Ferguson, Brenda yelled, "Trudy Mac!"

When Ginter turned to his left to the source of that yell, Private Armbruster, from Ginter's right, fired off a round, hitting Ginter in the back of his right thigh.

Yelling in pain, Ginter swung back to face the two privates and began shooting back at them. His shots went wild, spitting up bits of concrete. One shot produced a metallic *twang* as it hit a parked car. Armbruster and Lopez hit the pavement and rolled away from each other, trying to make themselves harder targets.

The second after Ginter fired his rounds, Lieutenant Riley opened fire on Ginter. But with Ginter's contortions, now exaggerated from being wounded, the soldier's shot missed its intended mark and instead struck Trudy Mac in her upper right chest area, near the collar bone. Crimson exploded from her and a spray of blood hit Ginter in the face.

Trudy Mac slumped, exposing Ginter and giving Sergeant Ferguson a clear shot. His one shot hit Ginter square in the torso. He dropped the wounded girl, who fell limply to the ground. Ginter staggered. Lieutenant Riley fired. The bullet found its mark and Ginter thudded to the pavement.

Everyone converged on the shot pair. Private Armbruster kicked Ginter's revolver from his limp hand, lest he managed one last burst of energy.

Dale and Brenda came up to Trudy Mac. They rolled her over on her back. The round had penetrated deep. Blood spurted from a severed artery, covering her pale blue food services dress with red.

"Trudy Mac!" Brenda yelled, grabbing her. "Hang on! We'll get a doctor here soon!" Despite her being the focal point of the sabotage efforts, Brenda still had good memories of their time as roommates together since the first day they arrived in Oak Ridge. Going to jail was one thing; bleeding to death from a bullet not meant for her on a damp sidewalk was another.

Trudy Mac coughed and gurgled, blood spewing out of her mouth.

"You and Dale - " she sputtered, " - good - "

"Don't try and talk, Trudy Mac," Brenda said. "We'll get you some help in a second!" Brenda was holding her. Trudy Mac's blood soaked her clothes as well.

"Looks like...I got off the farm after all..." With a slight grin on her face, Trudy Mac grew limp in Brenda's arms as her spirit left her body back to the One who gave it.

Brenda clutched her former roommate and friend close and sobbed deeply. Kneeling beside her, Dale placed his hand on Brenda's shoulder is some effort to provide comfort.

The four MPs were with Ginter. "He's gone," Private Lopez said, taking his fingers off Ginter's neck when he could no longer detect a pulse.

Sirens wailed in Clinton. The four soldiers covered Harry Ginter with his own suit jacket. Dale took off his and covered Trudy Mac. Private Lopez collected up her valise. The contents had spilled out on the sidewalk during the confrontation. The two $20 bills Ginter had given Trudy Mac had come out of the envelope in which they had been placed.

Lieutenant Riley showed his identification to the first Clinton policeman who arrived on scene and said they would need an ambulance to bring the bodies back to Oak Ridge.

The few minutes of terror had given way to dumbfounded silence. Instead of two healthy people standing upright, in an instant they had turned into two lifeless bodies lying on a bloodied sidewalk on an overcast spring morning.

Onlookers gathered around but maintained a respectable distance.

For Brenda, this tragic turn of events hit her the hard. Trudy Mac may have betrayed everything and everyone, but Brenda was reminded of the good times before she did so. They met Dale in Kaye's Kafé the first day he rode into Oak Ridge. They had lived and laughed together. And she was too young to end up this way.

But in this final act, Trudy Mac betrayed Hans "Harry" Ginter from continuing with his nefarious designs on Oak Ridge's war effort. Who was behind him would forever remain a mystery, but at least his evil deeds had been stopped.

Brenda was reminded about what Pastor Miller had said about how everyone being a sinner. No one was exempt except Jesus. This was the only explanation for Trudy Mac turning her back on her country and friends—her sins led her astray, just so she could have a better life away from the farm and her torturous upbringing. Unfortunately, Trudy Mac's sins had cost her the ultimate.

Dale assisted Brenda to her feet and put a comforting arm around her shoulder.

Lieutenant Riley gave the game plan. "Dr. Hargrowe and Miss Andrews, it would be best if you two went back to Oak Ridge now on the bus. Us four will stay here and ride with the ambulance with the bodies. We'll escort them to the hospital."

Freddie Joe Williams was standing outside his bus a few yards away. Hearing this decision, he strode up to the scene.

"I'll take y'all back now," he said softly.

"Come on, hon," Dale said. "Let's go. Lieutenant Riley has everything under control here."

He gently guided Brenda to the bus and up into a seat. Freddie Joe fired up the ignition. Clinton police held back the crowd and traffic as the bus took the whole of Main Street to turn around to begin its trek back to Oak Ridge. Brenda looked back at Trudy Mac one last time. The finality of death, especially for one still so young, was hard for her to understand or accept.

The ride back to Oak Ridge was silent. Dale wrapped his arm around Brenda as she nestled into his side. His other hand held both of hers.

When Dale finally got Brenda back to her dorm, he asked, "Will you be all right?"

"Yeah," Brenda murmured. "I just need a bath and a nap." She didn't sound convincing.

"Tell you what," Dale said, "get your things for a weekend and I'll take you to the guest house. You don't need to be back in this room right now."

"Good idea, Dr.," Brenda smiled. "Now I know what you must have gone through when Bob O'Neil got killed and you had your house all to yourself."

"It wasn't fun," Dale agreed.

Dale got permission from the dorm mom to escort Brenda up to the second floor while she got her clothes and items from her room. He told her briefly what had happened. Even though the dorm mom knew Trudy Mac had turned traitor, hearing she was now tragically dead saddened her too. All the residents of the dorm had bonded by sharing in their common experiences on this project.

Dale brought Brenda to the guest house, Oak Ridge's quarters for transients and DVs, and got her a room for the weekend.

"Get some rest," Dale whispered and gently kissed her.

Daniel S. Zulli

Chapter 53-Summation

Dale was reinstated into the good graces of Oak Ridge, per the order of General Groves. He went back to work at Y-12 the following Monday morning. Brenda, after spending the weekend at the guest house, returned to her old room and resumed her duties in X-10.

The news of the war showed that the Allied forces were making strong headway in defeating the Axis powers.

By April the Soviet army was pushing into Berlin, while General Eisenhower's troops entered Nuremberg. Dale and Brenda sat aghast, with the other movie theater patrons, when they saw the footage of the liberation of Buchenwald. Pastor Miller had talked about how all people are sinful, but to see the depths of the Nazi depravity made them wince in horror.

By the end of April, Mussolini had been captured and hanged, his body displayed upside down in the public square.

Then, on April 30th, the impossible happened. Hitler himself, who had boasted of a 1,000-year Reich, shot himself in his hidden bunker, along with his new wife, Eva Braun.

When the Nazi dream perished with their Führer, they surrendered on May 7th. The war in Europe was over. The collective shout from the Allies reached to the heavens. All that was left of the war were the Japanese in the Pacific. The Clinton Engineering Works Project pressed on. With the Allies now taking island after island, as well as conducting bombing raids on Japan, surely, they would soon realize the fruits of their labors.

In June, however, Japan declared that it would never surrender, but rather fight to the very last man. This news provoked 1,000 bombing raids on mainland Japan in July in the attempt to get them to reconsider. They did not.

On Tuesday, August 6th, 1945, the three main plants announced over their loud speakers for work to temporarily cease and for everyone to pay attention to the radio broadcast that would come momentarily from new President Harry Truman.

The hush was almost deafening. Dale could feel his pulse beat in his temples as the PA system crackled with the broadcast which originated from the USS *Augusta,* while the president was en route back to the United States.

"Sixteen hours ago," President Truman stated, "an American airplane dropped one bomb on Hiroshima, an important Japanese Army base. That bomb had more power than 20,000 tons of T.N.T. It had more than two thousand times the blast power of the British

"Grand Slam," which is the largest bomb ever used in the history of warfare. It is an atomic bomb. It is a harnessing of the basic power of the universe. The force from which the sun draws its power has been loosed against those who brought war to the Far East.

Immediately, Dale bolted his plant. He found a soldier outside with a vehicle, listening to the broadcast on the jeep's radio.

"Get me over to X-10 ASAP!" he hollered to the MP, jumping into his jeep. The stunned soldier cranked up his vehicle and head down Bear Creek Road. Dale could see people streaming outside whatever type of building they were in - house, store, restaurant - on the one hand excited, on the other hand confused, trying to make sense of what they had just heard.

The MP turned left on Bear Creek Road, left again on White Wing Road, finally the last left on Bethel Valley Road. X-10 was near that intersection.

As he approached the plant's parking lot, Dale could see the same thing: people outside, moving back and forth without thinking but shouting, yelling, crying, celebrating.

Dale spotted his fiancé outside in the crowd.

"Stop here. Thanks!" Dale jumped out of the soldier's jeep and ran up to Brenda when he spotted her.

"It was a bomb! Can you believe it?" Dale shouted, half laughing. "This is what we've been working on - an atomic bomb! Can you believe it?"

"Does this mean the war is finally over?" Brenda asked.

Dale paused. "I don't know. I haven't heard any news of Japan surrendering." Despite not knowing this, Dale hugged Brenda close, trying to absorb her essence in this world-altering event. He didn't know what else to do.

They got their answer in short manner. A second atomic bomb was dropped on Nagasaki, Japan, on August 7th, 1945. Oak Ridge had been stunned with news of the first bombing, but this second one drained everyone to the core. A week later, on August 14th, Japan finally surrendered.

With the second world war finally over, Oak Ridgers wondered about their fate. What was to happen to this new town and operation? General Groves made the pronouncement the next day in an open-air message to the workers who had worked so hard to produce a weapon which ended the war.

"I thank you for all your hard work and dedication, sometimes under very difficult circumstances, in producing a product that has never in the history of mankind been made. Here in Oak Ridge, you made the enriched uranium-235 which was the fuel for the first bomb that fell on Hiroshima. Without any precedence, you accomplished what no one else ever did. And your nation is grateful. Now, we don't have to risk hundreds of thousands of military lives in an invasion of Japan.

"We have entered into the atomic age. We had to do it, otherwise the forces of evil would have beaten us to it and used it to destroy and enslave millions. We have entered into a realm that before now was reserved only for the Divine. This is a new era, and this work must continue."

As the general was speaking, Dale and Brenda instinctively clutched each other's hands, uniting their hearts and spirits as they heard and tried to fully comprehend this news by the general.

"I don't know," Dale murmured to his fiancé, "whether to say, 'Praise the Lord' for ending this war, or, 'God help us' because of what we have just done."

Brenda squeezed his hand and summed it up: "Maybe it's a little bit of both."

About the Author

Dan Zulli was born in the atomic city of Oak Ridge, Tennessee. His father worked for the Atomic Energy Commission before teaching music in local high schools. Dan also lived in the neighboring towns of Norris, Oliver Springs and Coalfield.

When Dan was 11, the family moved to the Springfield, Massachusetts, area. After graduating from high school, Dan attending Springfield College, birthplace of basketball. But after three years of college, Dan enlisted in the United States Air Force, becoming a security policeman and spending the next six years stationed in California.

During his last year of his enlistment, Dan was called to the ministry, but also to come back in the Air Force as a chaplain. With new wife Cindy, Dan left California for Dallas Theological Seminary in Dallas, Texas. After graduating in 1988, Dan spent three years pastoring a tiny country church in southwest Oklahoma, while being a reserve chaplain at Altus Air Force Base.

In 1993, the goal was coming back on active duty as a chaplain happened, as Dan was selected by the new chaplain ascensions board. Dan, Cindy and their three kids spent the next 23 ½ criss-crossing the globe serving as a chaplain. Dan finally retired after 30 years, nine months and 29 days on 1 July 2017 in the rank of lieutenant colonel. He was deployed six times. They finally stopped moving where the Air Force all began in 1977, in San Antonio, Texas.

77208488R00136

Made in the USA
Columbia, SC
30 September 2019